ASCENDING
POWER

ASCENDING
POWER

Malcolm Gibson

STOREHOUSE
MEDIA GROUP

This book is dedicated to the memory of Jack and Barbara Gibson.

LCCN: 2019908497

Paperback ISBN: 978-1-63337-290-0
E-book ISBN: 978-1-63337-291-7

Printed in the United States of America
1 3 5 7 9 10 8 6 4 2

1

BILLY STRIKELEATHER STARED OUT THE PASSENGER WINDOW of the ancient pickup as it lurched down the highway. In this part of Texas, there was nothing but a few cacti, and fewer people. A hot desert wind sent auburn dust billowing. In the distance, the Chisos Mountains, framed by a summer sunrise, stood guard over the emptiness.

His uncle, Sam Longbird, drove them through the Lost Pines Reservation, home of the Chinati Indians. Three hundred square miles of hardscrabble so desolate the government had been glad to unload it on them a century before.

Sam was old school. His white ponytail was thick and his jaw set. It took a tough Indian to survive in the West Texas desert. Sam had done it for eighty years.

Billy's jet-black hair, high cheek bones, and copper complexion affirmed his mother's tribal background, but his softer eyes, her Caucasian lover—the one she'd never seen again. His six-foot-three, two-hundred-pound frame gave Billy the look of a hero. The sadness in his eyes, less so.

Billy took a deep breath and looked at the skyline ahead. He was raised on these plains. Just another Chinati half-breed, but he could throw a football farther than any schoolboy in the state. There'd been little else to do. He was good enough to earn an athletic scholarship at the University of Texas and, having grown up exploring the caves and cliffs of the Big Bend country, bright enough to leave with a geology degree.

After five years with the New Orleans Saints, one with the Houston Texans, a torn ACL, and a half dozen DWIs, he was now 'pursuing other opportunities.'

"So, you want to tell me why you called?" he asked Sam.

"I'll explain when we get there."

"Where?"

"You'll see."

Sam had picked up Billy at the airport in Alpine, the county seat forty miles north. Billy refueled his old Piper airplane there after making deliveries of equipment from Houston to West Texas oil rigs. The plane, once a classic, was now a relic and all that was left of his high-flying days in the NFL.

In thirty minutes, they reached Chinati Flats, the only village on the reservation. Rows of terracotta shanties just shy of squalor dotted the road.

Billy scanned the mesquite fences blanketed by drifts of red sand the texture of talc, and a junked school bus knee-high in tumbleweeds. Little had changed since he'd been away.

The shotgun house where he was born crept by.

Ahead was a dirt playing field flanked by listing goal posts and low stands. Billy took in the scene where he had debuted as a football phenom. He swiveled his shoulders as they passed, until his right knee flashed a painful reminder of the night that dream had died with the hit of an NFL linebacker.

When the truck rolled through town without stopping, Billy frowned at Sam with head cocked. On the outskirts, swirls of dust shrouded the road. From the haze, a crumbling limestone sign emerged reading *Chinati Flats. Birthplace of Billy Strikeleather.* He remembered the dedication ceremony a decade ago.

The truck drifted across the center line. Billy glanced at Sam, who was fumbling under the seat, then reached over and straightened the steering wheel.

Glaring at Billy, Sam sputtered, "I've got it."

"Sorry," Billy said. "You got started early this morning. Want me to drive?"

His eyes back on the road, Sam replied, "I'll let you know if I need your help."

"You already did, remember?"

"Don't flatter yourself."

Sam lifted a thermos from the floorboard and pushed it across the seat. "You handle the coffee."

Billy found two Styrofoam cups in the glovebox, poured, then closed the jug. He handed one cup to Sam.

Billy sat back to take a sip and thought about the day Sam had called. At first, Billy had turned him down. Chinati Flats was the last place he wanted to visit. He'd been a hero there. To come crawling back, even as a favor, after being drummed out of the NFL would have been another blow to his ego.

But oil prices had dipped due to an oversupply from fracking. Drilling equipment, and Billy's plane, sat idle. He realized he had nowhere else to go.

They rode in silence until there were no more road signs.

Billy reached into his shirt pocket for a cigarette. A book of matches fell to the seat—*Joe Bob's Ice House. Wives and Dogs Welcome*. He winced. It was an embarrassing reminder of the depths to which he'd sunk in Houston society. He hid it from Sam behind cupped hands as he sparked a flame.

"You know, those things will kill you," said Sam from the side of his mouth.

"That problem's not too high on my list."

"A man who doesn't care whether he lives is either a hero or a fool," Sam said. "I can't decide which you are."

"That's a tough one," Billy replied with a tinge of sarcasm. "I'm worth more dead than alive."

The truck labored up and down two low water spillways, both dry as Billy's throat. Sam glanced at his nephew, then touched him on his knee.

"So, is it the loss of all that football money that's got your dauber down? Did you think it would solve your problems?"

Billy resented his tone. "Well, you can't exactly live off the land in Houston."

"Money is never the answer," Sam said, shaking his head.

"Is that so? I suppose next you'll tell me our people are better off without it," Billy said.

"Oh. So, it's *our* people now."

"You know what I mean."

"No, I don't," Sam snapped, throwing back his ponytail. "Suppose you explain it to me. Explain how all that white man cash worked out for you. If you are still one of *us*, explain to me why that kind of easy money would be better for our tribe than being self-sufficient."

Billy scratched his head and gave Sam a puzzled look. *This isn't about my troubles anymore*, he thought. *It's about the tribe. Something's got Sam worried.*

Billy took a drag from his cigarette and blew smoke through bal-looned cheeks. "Okay, you've got a point, Sam. But just because I didn't handle my money well doesn't mean every Chinati would be better off without it. From what I've seen this morning, the tribe damn well needs something or it'll dry up and blow away. Money, leadership, something. You've been out here what, eighty years? Maybe it's time you took a little ownership in the situation. You've got to admit, a few more bucks in cir-culation would help."

Sam stared straight ahead. His knuckles turned white on the wheel. "At what price? There are always trade-offs."

A moment passed—Billy stole another look at his uncle. *What the hell is up?* he thought.

Throwing his cigarette out, Billy changed the subject. "How's your family, Sam?"

"Getting by. How's your wife handling all this rough water?"

Billy flinched. With a sigh he said, "No damn good, Sam. Leslie Jean had to trade her tennis league for a job with a big investment outfit. We're too broke to be clients."

Sam nodded. "You came out of the chute pretty fast, son. Now that things have changed, it could take her a while to settle in."

"If ever."

The hum of the engine dwindled to a growl. They were climbing. Billy remembered his college training. Sheep Mountain, and others in this range, were born of lava explosions and uplifts. Magma had surged up-ward through volcanic rock leaving pyroclastic chokers, greenish in the morning sun. He'd studied the ash deposits and layers of gravel and clay from erosion between eruptions.

Sam wheeled left onto a dirt road leading to a small arroyo. A grove of mesquite trees signaled water and a wooden sign read *Hot Springs Parking Only*. There'd never been a violator.

"Anyone come here anymore?" Billy asked.

"A few tourists hoping for a miracle cure. Haven't seen anyone since last fall."

Gravel popped under the floorboard as Sam pulled to a stop. The shocks groaned as they stepped out. Sam motioned Billy to follow.

A stone path led down to the spring, a natural pool the size of a basketball court carved into the bank of a ravine. From boulders around the perimeter, you could wade into warm mineral water bubbling up from the bedrock. The overflow snaked through pampas grass to the Rio Grande below.

When they reached the bottom step, Sam nodded toward the water, wiping his brow with his sleeve. "So, what do you think?"

"About what?"

"God, man, have you gone loco in Houston? Look at the plants. This water's had minerals, but never enough to kill grass and trees. Something ain't right."

Squinting into the sun, Billy studied the ravine bed. The trunk of each mesquite was a deep gray, the branches withered. A dark powder etched the shoreline. He squatted and put a pinch of the powder on his tongue, then grimaced and spit hard. "It's brine, but stronger than any I've tasted. Has there been any oil drilling around here lately?"

"Only shallow stuff. Trans-National sent their fracking crews not long ago. Their drill site is about a half-mile west of here, across the creek bed. Just off the reservation."

"Where'd you hear about fracking, old man?"

"Well, when your windows start rattling from underground explosives, you learn fast."

Billy let the brackish water sluice through his fingers, then reached into his back pocket for a silver flask. He took a swig of vodka and emptied the remainder onto the ground. He filled it with spring water and put it away. Over his shoulder he asked, "Does anyone else know about this?"

"Well, since I noticed it two weeks ago, the only one I told was—"

A shot rang out. Billy turned just in time to see the old Indian fall backward head first onto the rocks, a bullet hole under his chin. A second shot ricocheted off the heel of Billy's boot, spinning him into the shallows.

He crawled behind a stump, scouring the horizon for the shooter. Sam lay motionless, his body spread-eagled across a field of stones along the shoreline. An apple-sized abrasion distorted the side of his head from the fall onto a jagged rock. Blood oozed from his ear. The bullet had shredded the collar of his shirt, leaving a wound that bled through like a gruesome bib. Billy crawled toward him, his eyes still darting around the perimeter of the springs. He grabbed Sam's pant leg and dragged him behind a boulder. The old man's pulse was faint but steady.

"Hang on, hang on," Billy whispered into his ear.

2

SAM WAS BLEEDING BADLY. Billy shrugged off his shirt and wrapped it around the wound. After scanning the rocks above, he hoisted Sam over his shoulder and started up the path. He half expected to be cut down, but the silence held.

With Sam in tow, opening the passenger door was a struggle. Finally inside, Billy laid his uncle across the seat, then stumbled to the driver's side on his damaged boot. Swinging in behind the wheel, he reached for the ignition. It was empty. "Shit," he muttered, going through the old man's pockets till he found the keys. The truck roared to life. He cradled Sam's head in his lap and dropped the gearshift into drive. Sam moaned and flicked open his eyes.

"You're okay, you're okay," Billy said. After struggling to navigate the rutted dirt road onto the highway, he floored the gas pedal.

When they careened into the village, necks craned. "That's not like Sam," a woman with a baby remarked to the grocer.

Holding Sam's head with one hand and the steering wheel in the other, Billy pulled into the caliche parking lot of the Chinati Flats Medical

Center, a converted strip mall with a flat roof and cracked stucco walls. He lay Sam's cheek gently on the seat and grasped his hand.

"Sam," Billy said into his uncle's ear. "Can you hear me?"

He felt Sam squeeze his hand then watched his eyes open, blue as the summer sky that loosed the bullets.

"Someone shot at us," Billy said. "Hit you pretty bad. We're at the clinic in town. I'm going for help."

The old Indian nodded, but held fast to his nephew. A crowd formed at the open truck door. Loosening his grip, Sam used his pointer finger to trace the letter "R" on Billy's palm. He looked into his nephew's eyes, then his weathered hand went limp.

Billy bolted from the truck, through the onlookers, and inside the building. He returned with two young orderlies who lifted Sam onto a gurney. They pushed him up a low ramp, pausing for a nurse to open the doors. Billy followed with his hand on Sam's foot.

"Stay here. We'll call you," one of the men barked over his shoulder. They rushed their patient down a hall toward a door with a hand-stenciled sign: *Emergency.*

Exhausted, Billy retreated to a tiny waiting area with peeling wallpaper. An assortment of worn furniture was stacked with last year's magazines. A ceiling fan turned too slowly to matter.

"Excuse me," he said to the young Indian girl at the desk. She was reading *Seventeen Magazine* and drumming her fingers to the song on her earbuds.

"Excuse me!" he repeated, lowering his face to her level. "Do you have a shirt I can borrow?"

"Can I help you?" she said, pulling out the ear pieces. She smiled and gazed appreciatively at his bare chest.

"Please. That was my uncle they just rolled in."

"When?" she said, throwing back her hair.

"Forget it. Where's the nurses' station?"

She motioned behind her to a yellow swinging door with a round window. "But you're not allowed in. Too bad for them."

Billy said with a weak grin, "Could you please just ask them for a shirt of some kind?"

"I'll try." The tall teenager slipped out from behind the desk, swinging her hips as she disappeared into the bowels of the clinic.

Billy collapsed into a red plastic chair and closed his eyes.

When she returned, her hair was pulled back and her lipstick fresh. "This is all we could find, Mr. Strikeleather," she said, handing him some pink scrubs.

"Thanks," he said, arching into the top.

She sauntered back to the desk with a smile.

Outside, a constable's car, siren blasting, skidded to a halt in a cloud of dust. Through the front window Billy saw a weasel of a man with a big Stetson exit the cruiser. His high school classmate, Deputy Martin Metcalf, clad in a brown uniform with a badge the size of a saucer, hitched his pants and strode toward the clinic. Belying a wispy physique, his waist was huge with a .38 in a black holster, a fat barreled mace gun, a notepad, and a yellow Taser circa Buck Rogers.

When he entered, Billy grimaced. *For barking dogs and fender benders*, he thought, *Marty Metcalf would be fine. Not for attempted murder.*

The officer strutted through the sliding doors, into the hall, and up to the front desk, hardware jangling. The receptionist's eyes were fixed on Billy.

"Ma'am . . . Ma'am!" he blurted.

She glanced up.

"One of your nurses called. Said there'd been a shooting."

Her gaze traveled to Billy then back again. *Hard to believe they're the same species*, she thought. "It was Billy Strikeleather's uncle, Sam Longbird," she said. Her hand waved regally as if making a presentation. "Mr. Strikeleather's over there."

She watched the little deputy glance across the room then step back and pluck a cell phone from his breast pocket.

After dialing, he said in a clipped tone, "Sheriff. Metcalf here. It was Sam Longbird." He listened. "Yes, sir. I will."

The girl peered over the top of her magazine and smirked as he snorted and cinched up his weapon belt. Striding past her toward the red chair, he gave her a wink. She cringed.

Billy's eyes were shut and remained so even when he heard Deputy Metcalf approach.

"So, Mr. Strikeleather . . ." Marty began.

"For Chrissake, Marty, cut it out," Billy sighed, running his hands through his hair.

"Okay, okay. So, Billy, who shot Sam?"

Billy's fingers traveled up the sides of his face, stopping at his temples to trace tiny circles. "Marty," he answered, blinking his eyes open, "if I knew, don't you think I'd have mentioned it by now?"

"Just procedure, Billy." The deputy took a seat and pulled out a pad and pencil. "Now tell me about it."

"We were standing by the Rio Hot Springs when shots came from behind us, up on the road I'd say. One hit Sam in the neck, the other hit my boot heel," he said, pointing to his foot.

Marty's eyes narrowed in contemplation. "There're a lot of hunters out there this time of year. Maybe a stray shot."

"Really, Marty? Two shots hit within three feet of us."

"Did Sam say anything to you?"

Billy drew the fingers of his right hand across his mouth and paused them over his lips. When he turned to answer, the deputy was staring at his compass-sized tactical field ops police watch. Billy was about to tell him of Sam's cryptic hand message when Metcalf blurted, "Gettin' late." He stood and pivoted toward the door.

"Let me know if you think of anything," the policeman tossed off. "Sheriff wants me to drive out to Paint Creek. A fence is down, cattle on the road." Putting his pad away, he tipped his hat and left.

As he watched the patrol car pull away, Billy squinted and shook his head. *Of the hundreds of NFL interviews I've given*, he reflected, *none has been so useless.* He dropped his head back into the chair and stared at the ceiling. His lips pursed together in a thin line as he replayed the conversation in his mind. *He's either incompetent or complicit.*

In the waiting room, time slowed to a crawl. Billy drifted in and out of a half-sleep. For an instant, he was back at the Rio Hot Springs. *Get down, Sam!* He tried to reach him, but the old man's legs buckled. He watched him go down. Suddenly the scene changed to a football field. The crowd was deafening. A lineman bore down on him. *Slide!* It was too late. He could only wait for the hit. It bent his knee in half, sideways. They were the kind of dreams you have when you long to regain control of your life, but feel powerless to do so.

He awoke in a panic, his eyes darting about the room. The receptionist looked up and cocked her head, as if to ask what demons could frighten a superstar. Billy shook his head and dragged himself up to the front desk. "Can you please find out how he's doing?"

The girl studied Billy's face. "Are you okay?"

Good question, he thought. "Sure."

"I'll ask." She slithered around the desk and disappeared through the ER doors. When she returned, she said, "They'll be out to talk to you."

The doors swung open, presenting a bespectacled woman in blue scrubs with black hair pinned back and a stethoscope dangling. "Mr. Strikeleather?"

"Here."

She took an adjoining seat. A plastic name tag identified her as Ms. Stone, Physician Assistant.

"Is he going to make it?" asked Billy.

"He's stable now, but it's been touch and go. Most men his age wouldn't have survived."

Billy's shoulders slumped as he gave out a sigh of relief.

"Can I see him?"

"Mr. Strikeleather," she said gently, "your uncle is in a coma." She waited for her words to register. "It's not the bullet wound. We stopped the bleeding in time. It was the fall."

Billy sat back, his hands grasping either side of the seat.

The PA put her hand on his arm. "We don't know how serious it is. He suffered a concussion for sure. I spoke to a neurologist in Midland. She also suspects a brain bleed and prescribed sedatives to put him into a coma. At his age, anything can happen."

They both sat in silence.

The moment was eclipsed by the clatter of the front door. Into the waiting room burst a slender Indian man in his early twenties, wearing a white shirt with sleeves rolled, designer jeans, and a black felt western hat.

Taking in the room, he locked eyes with Billy and hurried over. "I came as fast as I could," he panted.

"Oliver," said Billy. He turned to Ms. Stone. "This is Oliver Green-tree, Sam's grandson."

"Of course," she said looking up at the young man. He had a narrow jaw thrust out Mussolini style, with deep set eyes, and a shock of thick black hair protruding from under his hat.

"How is he?"

"He's got a chance," Billy said. "But there are problems."

"What kind?" The grandson frowned, looking closely at the PA.

She explained Sam's condition.

"Can we see him?" Oliver asked.

"For just a minute, no more," she said, rising. They followed her.

Inside the ER was the gurney surrounded by trees of mobile IVs sprouting tubes and wires, all tethered to Sam. A woven blanket covered him chin to toe, a gauze bandage wrapped around his head. From an EKG machine, his heart pinged a faint beat. A young doctor tracked it on a blue monitor. As the visitors approached, he looked up. "He's stable, starting to settle down a bit. We're going to move him to ICU. The neurologist from Midland will be down tomorrow to have a look."

"What are his odds?" Billy asked.

Oliver leaned in over his shoulder, interrupting, "Can he remember anything? Will he come out of it?"

With a steady gaze, the doctor turned to the young Indian. "He may not."

Billy stroked his uncle's cheek. With wrinkles smoothed by the swelling, Sam's face brought to mind a photo, cherished by Billy's mother, of Sam and her in their early teens. They had roamed the reservation, living off the land—like their ancestors. It was a time, she would tell her son later, when the Chinati still had ancient warrior chiefs and the soul of a nation.

Billy's mother, Nightingale, or Gale as she was called, had told Billy about moving to San Antonio and about the white soldier she fell for there. Burt Cole was the son of a rancher from La Mesa. He was introduced to Gale by Jimmy Littlebow, a Chinati boy in Burt's Army unit, awaiting assignment to Vietnam. Burt and Jimmy shipped out a week before she learned of her pregnancy. In letters, his father had promised to come back for them after the war. When he returned, however, it was in a coffin.

For years, Billy recalled a one-hundred-dollar bill arriving each month with no return address or postmark. She wasn't sure how he'd managed it, but each delivery reminded Gale of how much Billy's father cared. Her son blamed the soldier only for stealing his mother's heart.

Growing up, his Uncle Sam had been the closest thing to a father Billy had. He taught him to throw—not a football, but an *atlati* that consisted of a shaft with a grip on one end and a cup on the other used to fling projectiles, *jai alai* style. By age twelve, Billy could sling a rock the size of a baseball through a barn door from forty yards. Transition to a football had been easy.

It was at that time Sam's daughter and her husband were killed in a car crash. Their infant, Oliver Greentree, survived. Sam was heartbroken, but assuaged the pain by taking in his grandson. Twelve years younger, he grew up in Billy's shadow. Awkward and an average athlete at best, Sam could only ascribe Oliver's caustic nature to his cousin's shadow. The perfect anti-Billy.

The sound of the doctor's voice brought Billy back. "He needs rest."

"I'd like to sit with him for a while," Oliver said.

"Fine," the doctor replied. "But please, no talking. His brain has taken a blow and needs time to heal."

Oliver nodded and followed the gurney as the orderlies rolled Sam out of the ER toward the semi-private rooms.

"I'll call you tomorrow, Oliver," Billy said, as the procession passed. Oliver didn't reply.

3

BILLY LEFT OLIVER WITH SAM at the hospital and headed to a motel on the edge of town. The Petrified Forest was an old-fashioned motor lodge built from brown flagstone. A dirt parking lot fronted ten decrepit rooms with doors dappled by decades of blowing dust.

Sam's pickup wheezed to a stop at the office, under a sign flickering *Vacancy.* The *No* was rusted out. The only link to a forest was a front step of petrified wood.

Billy killed the engine and stepped out, stumbling on his damaged boot. He made his way to the entrance and turned the knob. A bell atop the door rang. The manager, a paunchy Chinati in his early thirties, glanced up from his newspaper. "Help you?"

"I need a room," Billy responded in a tired voice.

The clerk put down the paper. Screwing up his eyes behind thick glasses, he inspected his guest and said, "Billy Strikeleather, right?"

"Yeah, how you doin'?" the ex-star responded robotically, reaching for his wallet.

The manager took a key from the wall but paused to see if Billy would remember him. He didn't. The quiet was awkward—a wall clock ticked. Finally, he took mercy on Billy and handed it over to him. "Jimmy Quinta. Chinati Flats School, Class of '96."

Relieved, Billy nodded and shook his hand.

"Right. Good to see you, Johnny."

"Jimmy."

"Oh, right. Sorry."

"Haven't seen you around here in years."

"Yeah, it's been a while."

"Used to watch you play on TV. Too bad about the knee."

"Bad luck. Part of the game," Billy murmured, scuffing his heel on the wood floor.

Jimmy looked out the front window at Sam's truck, then back at Billy's pink medical shirt. "Seen Sam?"

"Yeah. He had a little accident."

The clerk's eyes narrowed. "Need any help?"

"No thanks. He'll be fine."

Quinta nodded his head tentatively.

"Cash or credit, Billy?"

I guess he thinks I don't have a good card, Billy thought. *News travels fast.*

He handed the clerk a fifty. "Will this cover it?"

"Sure," Jimmy said, smiling slightly with his fat lips. He put the bill in the drawer and handed back two twenties. Billy felt his face redden. It was charity and he knew it.

Jimmy watched him hobble to the door. "Billy," he called out. "You did good. You did good."

"Thanks," Billy replied softly.

The engine of the old truck coughed as Billy moved it ten yards down to Number Three. The room was sparse but clean, with a woven rug and Gideon Bible. He threw down his faded Nike grip, pulled off his boots, and fell onto the bed. With eyes closed, he tried to make sense of things.

Except for his DWIs, he'd never been around a police investigation. This one, however, seemed a quarter turn off. *Why didn't Deputy Metcalf ask more questions . . . or even go to the scene of the shooting to investigate?*

Billy needed a drink. Out of habit, he rolled over and reached into his jeans for the flask. He unscrewed the cap and lifted it to his mouth. The briny fluid made him flinch and sputter. *That's one way to kick the hooch.*

He sat up and shook two more drops onto his tongue. They were bitter and metallic, setting his teeth on edge. As he set the flask on the bed stand, something registered in his memory. *I know that taste. What the hell is it?*

A smile crossed his lips. *Of course. Clive Larsen. How could I forget?* His thoughts drifted back to an eccentric geology professor at the University of Texas who'd recruited Billy to help with a research project on some obscure mineral, a so-called "rare earth" mineral known as dysprosium. *It had a taste*, he recalled, *so unique you could never forget it. And it was easy to test for. One part citric acid (Coca Cola would do in a pinch), one part sodium hydrogen carbonate (baking soda), and one part dysprosium. The foulest tasting stuff in the world.*

He stood and walked into the bathroom to rinse his mouth. *Probably the less Leslie knows about this the better. That would only make her a target, too. But then I'd have to lie to her. Through all our ups and downs,* he thought, *that's one thing I've never done.*

He reached for the phone and dialed home.

In a McMansion on the west side of Houston, Leslie Jean Strike-leather stepped from the marble shower into a white terrycloth robe. With her left hand, she wiped a swath of fog from the mirror. She brushed back her dark hair, then bent forward to touch a wrinkle on her neck.

The slender brunette picked up the bourbon and branch water from its usual spot on the sink and took a sip, then padded across the hardwood floor of her bedroom through the hall and into a paneled office. Sitting down at a rolltop desk, she clicked on the computer and began studying a double screen of financial projections. Tomorrow at nine she was meeting a fat-cat prospect. *It's showtime*, she told herself.

At LaCour Financial they called Leslie the Velvet Closer. She had the gift of gab and a cum laude intellect. When a client of either gender needed a push, they brought in Leslie. She always came through.

She printed the financials and tucked them into a leather briefcase. Returning to the bedroom, she tossed the case on the poster bed and glanced at the picture on the dresser. In it, the King's float of the Krewe of Bacchus parade bore a grinning Billy, wearing a bejeweled crown, white toga, and gold chains, through the streets of the French Quarter. Krewes were the New Orleans equivalent of high society, and Billy was that year's royalty. Following atop the rear of an exotic convertible, Leslie—in a white ruffled gown—waved to their subjects. That was the happiest day of her life. Now, ten years later, the party was over.

After a gulp of whisky, she sauntered to the bed and placed the glass down on the nightstand. Arching her back, the Velvet Closer slipped out of her robe and into the sheets. Sleeping au natural was a luxury she allowed herself only when Billy was away. Leslie knew most of her girlfriends wouldn't turn down the chance to make love to her husband. She didn't blame them. They just didn't know the price.

She closed her eyes remembering the years when passion trumped reason in their marriage—how they'd followed their emotions, blind to each other's faults. When it began to unravel, passion was the first to go. Even now, however, Leslie couldn't block out those halcyon days. She drained the bourbon and snapped off the lamp.

Laying back, the sheets felt cool against her breasts. She recalled her first thrill of Billy's body. It would teach her pleasures she'd never imagined, then catapult them to stardom with the New Orleans Saints.

For five years Billy and Leslie had owned the Big Easy. Their lives, she remembered, had been a whirlwind of penthouses and wild parties. As the bourbon hit, she drifted back to the delicious impieties of life in the French Quarter. Beneath the sheets her fingers traced a delicate path.

Leslie's breath grew ragged and her pulse quickened. For a moment Billy again held her captive in his arms, savage as the Chisos but gentle as a desert breeze. At her core she still longed to feel his power, if only for a final taste of the man—the life—she'd lost. Her lips parted in a circle of passion. Her hips twitched. Then, with a sob, she surrendered to the memory of Billy Strikeleather—the Billy she'd married. Afterward she wept.

When her body had calmed, she rolled onto her side and checked the time. It was 11 p.m. She lit a cigarette, exhaled, and reflected for the hundredth time on the demise of her marriage. It had begun the day Billy was injured. She pictured the vicious tackle at the goal line that tore his ACL, sidelining him for the season. For Billy, it began a precipitous fall.

As his rehab foundered, so did his confidence. She glanced at the empty glass and remembered how he'd turned to booze to bridge the gap. In three months, her prince had melted into a mean drunk. The nightmare continued even when Billy returned to the team. He was a step slower and a stride closer to unemployment. Riding the bench, his drinking spiraled.

Finally, the Saints had enough and traded Billy to the Houston Texans for a fifteenth-round draft pick.

She crushed out her smoke and lay back on the bed, recalling the terrible quarrel the night she urged him to quit the game for broadcasting. He stormed out, got liquored up, and drove his SUV into Buffalo Bayou, destroying his chance at either career.

Rubbing her temples, she recalled how Billy's downfall began her own emancipation. She'd dusted off her finance degree and landed a job at LaCour, the biggest investment banking firm in town.

Leslie remembered how, like Newtonian opposites, she had prospered while Billy stumbled. Even in a wide-open oil town like Houston, his continuing brushes with the law cancelled the value of Billy's celebrity. With each new DWI, the Strikeleather brand, and those who bore it, had suffered. She knew the Billy she married was no more, and began planning her escape.

The former NFL wife knew she needed to maintain her lifestyle, even enhance it, to succeed in the high dollar world of LaCour. Her ticket to the big paydays was dependent on an upscale image. She needed money. For the last two years Billy had provided none. Their savings were depleted.

Leslie scanned the bedroom with its lavish wall coverings and appointments. *This*, she said to herself, *is what I've earned. He may be foolish enough to throw it away, but not me.* While her body still craved him, with each passing month, her lust for the largess of LaCour waxed, while her tolerance for marriage waned. Billy was the only one who couldn't see it. Something had to give.

When the phone rang, Leslie checked the ID and picked up the receiver. "Hi, Billy. It's late."

"I know. Did I wake you?"

"No. Couldn't sleep. Anything wrong?"

She listened expressionless as Billy reported the trip to the Rio Hot Springs with Sam and the rifle shot that took Sam down. When he went on to tell of the second shot intended for him, her eyes widened. A sick feeling welled in her stomach, but not from horror.

"Are you still there?" Billy said.

"Yes, yes," she answered, struggling for the right tone. She drew the sheet up under her chin as if to hide from the source of her anxiety. *My God. I'm sorry he missed.*

As Billy continued his description of the attack, Leslie tried to deny her feelings, to write them off as the kind of dark fantasy where you push an annoying stranger in front of a train. But the more he described how close the bullet had come to him, the more she thought what a perfect solution it would have been. She shook her head and blinked. *This has gone too far. I've got to get out.*

As Leslie considered this new reality, Billy continued his story of the day's events. "The taste of the water was familiar, but I couldn't place it," he said. "It wasn't until I got to the motel and tried it again that I remembered. I did a few simple tests and they held up. High-grade dysprosium."

He recounted Clive Larsen's experiments with that and other rare earth minerals. "Since we've got no money to go any further with development, I'm thinking I need to do two things, and fast. Find Larsen to get confirmation of the mineral, and line up someone to help us process it.

"If it checks out with Larsen," Billy said, "Luke Stasney might be interested. Stasney Energy is independent and has a history of taking risks. I'm afraid the big nationals will just steal it, or worse. So, what do you think?"

The wheels were turning in Leslie's head. Luke Stasney had been a fraternity brother of Billy's at UT. Luke and Leslie had dated for a year before she met Billy. Rich and handsome, Luke had all the credentials. She recalled the day she'd left him for Billy. It was ugly. First, he'd been angry, then sad, then pitiful—not a day a man likes to recall. Especially a man who'd always gotten what he wanted.

Leslie opened her briefcase, took out her iPhone, and entered the name Stasney Energy into her Dunn and Bradstreet account. "Well, I'm sure Luke would be happy to hear about the discovery," she said, buying time.

"You think he'd hold any grudges?"

Her pulse quickened as she read the company's report. "Annual Sales: $50,000,000. CEO: Luke Stasney." No spouse's name. The thought of another chance at one of the most eligible men in Houston was a powerful drug. She responded casually, "I'd give him a call."

"I'll do that. Looks like I'll have to be out here for a few days. Will you be okay?"

Now is the chance, she thought, *to solve all my problems at once.* She closed her briefcase. "Sure, Billy. Be careful."

She turned out the light and slept better than she had in months.

4

THE TELEPHONE JOLTED BILLY FROM A FITFUL SLEEP. He fumbled the receiver.

"Good morning, Mr. Strikeleather. It's 7:30 a.m."

"Uh huh," he rasped, falling back against the pillow. Squinting at the ceiling, he tried to recall whether this was the Crown Plaza in the French Quarter or the Motel 6 across from Joe Bob's. The fog lifted. *Jesus. I'm not even hung over. Damn concussions.* He swung his legs off the bed, hands anchored on either side, and struggled for a breath. His lungs crackled like a Frito bag. When he stood, his bad knee buckled. Pushing up on the nightstand, the NFL superstar hobbled toward the window.

He parted the drapes, revealing the emptiness of the West Texas desert. Moonscape rocks and army green sage brush shimmered in the morning heat. Gray formations of rock, polished smooth by the elements, protruded like humpback whales in a brown sea of sand. Dykes of hardened lava splayed out across the desert floor marking the path where ancient lava flows escaped through faults in the pyroclastic rock. In contrast, the snowcapped Chisos range loomed on the horizon.

To the west lay the most desolate land in North America. The Rio Grande knifed through it in a five-hundred-mile semicircle called the Big Bend. South of the river crouched the mountains of Mexico, a battleground between drug smugglers and fair-weather police whose allegiance was traded daily to the highest bidder.

If you had to rid yourself of an inconvenient population, this would be the place. On the fringe of the Texas frontier, unlike cultural mélanges in the east, Indians hadn't assimilated. They'd fought hit-and-run, then fallen back and waited for the winds to change.

Never was there a more perfect reflection of this process than Billy Strikeleather. Tough and independent, he was not just *from* the Big Bend, he was *of* it. He'd fought the Anglos on the gridiron, ten yards at a time, and won. Yet, here he was back in the desert in a third-rate flophouse on a fool's mission. It wasn't supposed to end this way.

Billy reached in his bag for jeans and a golf shirt. As he put them on, along with worn Nikes, he caught sight of himself in the mirror on the closet door. *It must be the faded glass that's making me look so old*, he told himself.

After packing, Billy pulled open the door and shuffled to Sam's pickup. Stones rattled under the floorboard as he pulled onto the highway. Two blocks later he was in what passed for downtown. He parked and stepped out. More than half of the storefronts were boarded up. Walking the main street, he shook his head at the sight. Groups of old women dressed in coarse blouses and long skirts shuffled toward a Quonset hut at the far end of town. A sign over the front door said *Tribal Hats*, and a smaller one in the window, *Not Hiring*.

Middle-aged men sat like mannequins on the boardwalk steps, whiling away the morning. Billy stopped to take it in and gave a low whistle. An Indian wearing wire-rimmed glasses and a green cap looked up and said, "That's right, Billy. Baseball caps. They're the biggest employer in town now. Minimum wage."

Billy did a double take. "Coach Baker?"

"In the flesh," the man answered with a smile.

Billy stooped and shook hands with his high school football coach. "I didn't recognize you."

"It's been a while," the coach replied.

"Sure has. Let's see. I graduated in '96."

There was a pause. "School's out for the summer, huh?"

"That's right."

"How is the team looking this year?" Billy asked.

The coach shook his head. "You haven't heard, have you?"

"Heard what?"

"The high school discontinued sports five years ago. No money for equipment. Funny how that happens when you stop winning."

Billy's jaw dropped. "Sorry, Coach. I didn't know."

"I figured you didn't. When you made a name for yourself at UT and in the NFL, families started moving in from around West Texas so their boys could play in the same program as the great Billy Strikeleather. I told them you'd promised to keep running those football camps. We got some damn good athletes that way. I guess you just got too busy with the NFL and all. Pretty soon the kids stopped coming and it was over."

Sensing defeat in the coach's bearing, Billy pressed his lips together and lowered his gaze.

"Coach, about the years when I was gone . . ." His voice trailed off.

The coach shrugged then turned back toward the street.

Billy walked away, torn between anger and guilt. Part of him chaffed at the coach's capitulation to the town's demise. *Damn it, I can't rescue you like I did when I was your star quarterback. Why don't you get up, fight back?*

But from a deeper place, he felt the ache of guilt. *There was a time when I had the power to keep this town on its feet. All it would have taken was a few investment dollars, some public appearances. I had the money and the contacts.*

As people nodded curtly, another feeling began to creep from his core like a winter chill—one that had become all too familiar. Fear. *Will I ever have the strength to reclaim my life? What if I screw up the mineral discovery, let these people down again?*

Then he remembered something Sam had once told him: *In the heart of all men lies a special power they spend a lifetime seeking to unleash. The irony is it's always within them, close at hand, but just out of reach. That is, until the moment one least expects it, when for an instant it is there for the taking.* Billy hoped that moment was here.

On the Lost Pines Reservation that summer, in the faces of the people who ground out each day of their squalid existence, no hint of such power could be found. Like Billy, the village people lived lives of desperation. Only now their destinies were inextricably intertwined with his by a secret force bubbling through miles of rock beneath their feet on a journey to the Rio Hot Springs. A million to one shot, just like Billy.

Billy headed off to find Chief Angus Whitecloud. Memories surfaced of visiting the chief's place outside of town with his uncle. Sam and the chief were close. The truck kicked up a trail of dust, drawing residents from their huts. At first, they waved. But when they realized the driver wasn't Sam, they only tracked him with suspicion into the sunrise, hands shading their eyes.

Billy knew that, although the implosion of his high-profile world was common knowledge among the tribe, the details were not. To regain their acceptance, he'd have to come clean about the demons that brought him down. Avarice, excess, ambition—the antitheses of Native culture. Seeing Chief Whitecloud would bring them into focus. His stomach churned at the thought.

In a moment, a stand of mesquite trees broke the horizon. They grew along a creek that paralleled the road, traversing it at low water crossings. Trickles of water snaked among white, fist-sized rocks fanning into shallow pools.

At the end of a small canyon, Billy spotted a spiral of smoke. When he cleared the hill, Chief Whitecloud's home came into view. Double tire paths laced with caliche led the pickup off the road, across the stream to a mesquite grove shading his house.

A chimney topped with a rusty cap was the source of the plume. The door was set back from the wall, guarded by a metal gate. It squeaked when he entered. When his knock went unanswered, Billy found the chief at a picnic table behind the house, mixing watercolors in plastic cups.

"Chief," the younger Indian called out. "Billy Strikeleather here."

Startled, the old man's head bobbed up from his work. Two gray ponytails swung forward from under his flat brimmed reservation hat and a white choker of bone hair pipes jingled against his neck. "Well, *a'shoma um loma*, Billy. It's good to see you. I heard you were in town."

"It's been a long time," Billy said as they shook hands.

The chief nodded. "Since we dedicated that sign, maybe ten years." He considered the younger man's face, the pensive smile. "Lots of water over the dam, eh?"

Billy broke the stare by looking down at the chief's project. "You could say that."

There was an awkward pause.

"So, what are you working on out here?" Billy asked, bending down, hands on knees. The chief had painted a picture of two red wolves with snouts pointed high toward a full moon.

"I come out here to blend colors," the chief said. "Light's better outdoors. Inside I can't see to get 'em right."

"This is very good. I didn't know you were a painter."

"There's a lot you don't know about me," the chief said.

He touched Billy's arm with his left hand and pointed with his right toward a small stand of poplars near the rear of the property. They walked together across the sandy soil sloping to the edge of the creek.

Near an old barbeque pit was a wooden table. The top was weathered and creased like the old man's face. The chief gazed past the trees to a clearing on the far side of the stream where the desert gave way to rust-colored cliffs of volcanic rock.

This is his whole world, his life, thought Billy as he watched the chief's almond-shaped eyes embrace the landscape. He wondered whether he would have thought of his life in the same way, but for the damn football.

"How is your family?" Billy asked.

"Edith passed last winter. A stroke."

"Sorry, Chief. I hadn't heard."

"Now it's just Maria and me. Have you seen her in Houston?"

"Only on TV."

The men sat in silence.

Finally, Billy spoke just above a whisper. "I read about the rape while she was covering the prison riot."

Another moment passed with no response. "I should have reached out to her," Billy said.

The chief looked up into Billy's face. "It might not have done any good," he said softly. "She withdrew like a wounded animal. I tried to get her to quit—to come home."

"And?"

"She'd have no part of it. But it changed her."

"I understand," replied Billy, lowering his eyes. "You know there was a time when she and I thought everything was possible, if only we could get away from here."

Billy's shoulders sagged as he exhaled, remembering how often he'd thought about Maria over the years. He admired her success on television, wondered if she shared his insecurities about fame. Being in Chinati Flats with her father brought back memories. Always calm and reflective, Maria was more grounded in the tribal ethos than he was. He wondered if she felt the same after the rape? *I should have offered to help her.*

A gust rustled the branches overhead, unloosing a flurry of brown leaves. The elder Indian followed them down till his eyes connected with Billy's.

"So, what's on your mind, son?"

"Sam called me a few days ago. Remembered my geology degree and asked me to come from Houston. Something about brine water. Yesterday we drove to the Rio Hot Springs. The water was different, full of minerals. I got a sample. Then someone put a bullet in him."

Whitecloud was studying a red-tailed hawk perched on a bolder. "You know they live their entire lives within ten miles."

"What?"

"A circle." The chief pointed to the bird. "They're born with all they need. They take what's required to live, and leave the rest as they found it. Only when the circle is broken does trouble come."

Billy rubbed the back of his neck. "Chief, I don't see what you're getting at. Sam's hurt bad. He may not make it."

"I heard about Sam."

Billy's eyebrows arched.

"Is that why you came to see me?" the chief said.

His visitor looked down. "Yes. A test I ran on the water showed dysprosium, an extremely rare substance, in high concentration. I know this mineral from college and how it can increase gasoline mileage tenfold." He paused, raising his gaze. "It's a golden opportunity for the tribe."

The chief spread the fingers of each hand and put the tips together mirror style under his chin. With eyes closed, he leaned forward over his elbows. "That may be. But because of your mineral, Sam broke the circle. Now he's in a coma." He opened his eyes and locked them with Billy's. "I made the same mistake. Something I thought was just as important."

Billy frowned and cocked his head.

"The casino," Whitecloud said. "You were just a kid." His shoulders slumped, like a boxer. "They told me it would revitalize the reservation. The money came to town, all right. So did drug dealers, prostitutes, and camp followers. One night, I burned it down."

Billy had heard stories of the degradation caused by the casino—the lives it had wrecked. He wished he could take away the chief's memory of it—absolve him of any blame. But all he could do was watch the old wound bleed.

Looking up at Billy, the chief said, "So you see, I have experience with these great opportunities."

It was not like the chief to show weakness or remorse. But the Rio Hot Springs discovery brought back bitter memories. Studying the old man, Billy was apprehensive. Not because of the chief's recollections of the casino nor the scars they had left. But because they both knew the mineral deposit was more, much more, and fate had again chosen him to guide the tribe.

Gathering himself, Billy said gently, "No matter what we think of our plight, Chief Whitecloud, we have to deal with it."

He was relieved to see the chief's braids dip.

"If we knew who opposes us, we could prepare," said Billy. "Who would be so desperate?"

The chief's lips pursed. Then, in a measured voice, he said, "When the Chinati were promised land in South Texas fertile enough to farm, we agreed. When more settlers came, they took it away and pushed us into the desert. This," he said, sweeping his hand across the horizon, "they told us would be ours forever."

Billy knew where the chief was headed.

"There's always a reason greater than the white man's promise for why he breaks it. He always wants more."

They sat in silence. A brown leaf blew across the wood surface landing near the chief's hand. He picked it up and rolled the stem gently between his thumb and forefinger. He looked at Billy. He didn't like the sadness. It was the sadness people get before they give up.

"So, you think someone from the outside knows about the minerals?" Billy said.

"Maybe."

"They can't take the Rio Hot Springs. They belong to *us* . . . well, to the Chinati."

Whitecloud studied Billy's face.

"So, the two are no longer the same for you?"

The young Indian reflected on the chief's words.

"No," Billy whispered. It had never been put to him so bluntly. He knew the chief's question was a fair one.

Whitecloud's expression softened. "You're not the first. I've seen it happen to many of our people who left the reservation. The white man's world is about quantity, not quality. Wealth equates to success. The millionaire is the hero. Our people have not fared well."

"But, there's so much the tribe needs," Billy said. "They can't live on dreams forever. The minerals could provide that."

"At what cost?" the chief said, steepling his hands.

With palms up, the young Indian made one last attempt. "If the wealth really is there, surely we're smart enough not to repeat the white man's mistakes."

Whitecloud leaned across the table. "You, of all people, should know the answer to that."

Billy sat back. He covered his face in his hands. For the first time it came to him. It wasn't just the minerals that had drawn him to the chief. "Can we walk a bit?" he said.

They strolled along the creek bed. The morning sun had crested the cliffs, sending shafts of light across the water. As the two men wove through the trees, each was occasionally highlighted by a sunbeam—like actors on a stage. A north breeze gave a hint of fall. *Seasons changing*, the older man thought.

"You know I came to speak to you about the dysprosium," Billy said, "but also to ask for another chance."

"To do what? Show the world you're more than another drunken Indian? Make the tribe proud of you again?"

"Some of each, I suppose."

"What makes you think I have that power?"

"I guess I just thought you would be a good place to start, again."

"You think I've judged you? That I hold you in low regard?"

"I could hardly blame you."

"I barely knew you when you were young, except when Sam brought you around. Then you got your fame and you were gone. I never knew you as a man."

Their feet snapped branches washed up and baked into kindling by the sun. The chief's steps were light in buckskin boots, disturbing little as he picked his way along the creek. Billy trailed stride for stride. Although the terrain was uneven, after a while he realized he had not noticed his damaged knee. Neither had he reached for a cigarette or a drink. This was a peace of mind he remembered as a boy roaming the reservation. Never as a man. *But*, he thought, *maybe I never really knew that man.*

They continued down the creek until it fell away into a deep ravine. Billy stopped and squatted in the shade of a boulder. He prodded into the sand with a stick. The old man knelt beside him.

Billy recounted his days at UT. "When I arrived in Austin, I was just an Indian kid. All I knew were hard times, hunting, and football, probably in that order. I'd never seen so many white people. But they either looked right through me like I wasn't there or laughed behind my back. That is until the first-string quarterback went down with a cracked collarbone and his backup was arrested for cocaine. I made the most of my chance and we started winning. Then, everyone was my friend."

The chief rolled from his knees to a sitting position back against the rock. "Let me guess. You figured you'd made the move from the boundary land to the white man's world."

"I didn't know any better." Billy shook his head. "It just got better, or worse, if you will, when I moved on to New Orleans. By then I was married to Leslie, a white girl from Houston society. Her parents didn't mind an Indian in the family as long as he was an NFL star."

With each chapter he became more an apologist than a reporter. As the story wound down, the ending was never in doubt. "When I blew out my knee, I was too proud to admit my career was over. I was angry."

For a moment, neither spoke.

The chief broke the silence. "You don't owe me any explanations, Billy. Your slate is clean with me. Whether a blessing or a curse, we both know there's something important going on in the Rio Hot Springs. If you've got a plan, I'll let you present it to the council. But I won't guarantee to go along with it."

Billy stood and offered his hand, helping the chief to his feet.

As they retraced their steps, Billy said, "What was it about the wolves that made you decide to paint a picture of them?"

"There are two red wolves that battle inside us. One is evil—anger and false pride. The other good—peace and compassion. The color red can mean either, depending on the beholder."

"Which one wins?"

"The one you feed."

5

THE PHONE JOLTED CLIVE LARSON AWAKE. *Who the hell calls at this hour?* The late news was on television. His arm toppled an almost empty wine bottle as he reached across the coffee table for the TV remote.

Like a fighter with an eight count, he struggled to get up from the couch, then fell back, letting the answering machine handle the call. "Probably just spam," he murmured.

The recorder beeped on. "Huh, yeah. This is Billy Strikeleather. You might not remember, but I worked with you on a research paper at University of Texas back in 1998. The one about the underground sea full of rare earth minerals. The thing is, now I need some help. It's about a mineral deposit. A big one. Just like in your paper. Please call me at—"

With a quick swipe, Clive punched off the apparatus.

Sitting with head in hands, he said aloud, "Of course I remember, you dumbass jock." He flashed back to those days at the fifth largest university in the country. A tenured professorship had been so close he could taste it—a geology department chair on the horizon. That was before he wrote the goddamn paper.

It had exploded like a bomb, destroying his marriage and career, as well as his psyche. A decade later he was still reeling. Now an assistant science professor at a Houston community college, bitter was too charitable a word to describe Clive Larson.

He hoisted himself up from the sofa. Lurching toward the kitchen with the bottle and a glass in hand, he paused at a wall mirror and shook his head at the reflection. The only remnants of that dashing redhead once poised to conquer the College of Arts and Sciences was an old man with an angry squint and a russet quiff, standing guard like a lonely sentry over an ebbing gray hairline.

In the kitchen, Clive poured himself the last of the wine. He leaned back against the sink with eyes closed. He was once more in his cramped office at Garrison Hall, the day the best football player on campus came looking for help. Billy had towered over him like the statue of Big Tex at the State Fair.

Clive knew he would have to give the star a passing grade or catch hell from the athletic director, but he would make him earn it. He needed a researcher on his thesis. Billy got the job.

The professor tried not to like him, but his work ethic and enthusiasm for the project won Clive over. Cocky and dogged, in Billy he saw a bit of himself. His fascination with this offspring of the West Texas desert was undeniable. Although he knew it was a long shot, Clive tried to convince his football star to put off a pro career long enough to get an advanced degree in geology. When Billy left for the NFL, Clive took it hard.

The babble of the ten o'clock talking heads brought Clive back to reality. He walked back to the coffee table and clicked them off with the remote. Draining his glass, he stepped to the front window. As he shut the curtains, he paused to watch insects buzz in futile orbits around the porch light, then drop to a spider web below. The prospects of his life, it seemed to him, were little better.

Leaving the living room, he saw the red dot flashing on the answering machine and considered listening to the full message. *Nah.*

Clive didn't bother turning on the hall light. The smell of dirty socks and stale newspapers drew him to the bedroom. He stepped over a pile of ungraded exams and fell across the sheets.

Sleep eluded him. While the call had sparked in Clive memories about the paper, it had also piqued his curiosity about Billy. They'd both been through hell, the vicissitudes of their professional lives played out in public like jagged EKGs. Until tonight, Clive had thought of Billy's career, like his, as flatlined into obscurity. The glow of the pulsing red light, however, stirred something long absent from his consciousness. Hope.

Clive awoke to a sultry Saturday morning in Houston's Montrose District, an enclave of gays, artists, and refugees banished from suburbia for refusing to say "thank you *sooo* much" or to attend their children's proms. The mix was weird, but it worked for most everyone, including Clive, because of the unwritten rule—no sad stories of previous lives.

Cafe Estrella was Clive's favorite coffee shop—close, cheap, and always open. Donning a pair of khaki pants, a blue work shirt, and a straw panama with black leather band, he headed there for breakfast. His sandals scraped along sidewalks warped by tree roots. Plastic flamingos stood watch over venerable bungalows.

He took a left at the corner and caught sight of himself in the plate glass of a Pakistani dry cleaners. He hadn't always looked like a cross between Burl Ives and the Wizard of Oz. *That's the thing about Montrose*, he thought, veering to miss a man on a bike bulging with bags of soda cans. *You move here to be on your own. The results are up to you.*

The tattooed barista must have spotted the professor at the newsstand a block away. He had eggs overeasy with a side of grits on the bar when Clive claimed his usual seat.

"Coffee black, right?" said the waiter.

Clive nodded and dove into the *Houston Chronicle*. By the time he reached the sports section, the next stool was filled.

"Professor Larson?"

From behind the box scores, Clive responded, "Who wants to know?"

"Billy Strikeleather. I called you last night, but you . . ."

"I know, I know."

"I went to your apartment."

"Huh," Clive grunted. "You get your kicks by stalking people?"

"Your neighbor told me where to find you."

"Figures. Which one," he snorted, peering over the paper, "the flaming flamenco dancer or Karl Marx?"

"He had a beard."

"Revolutionary. What do you want?"

Billy launched into fracking, rare earth mineral deposits, dysprosium, and what happened at the Rio Hot Springs. In two minutes, Clive reached the obits. In another, he folded the paper and threw it down with a ten-dollar bill. He spun around and headed for the door calling back over his shoulder, "I can't help you."

Billy scrambled after him. "You don't understand. This is exactly what you predicted in your paper. Don't you remember? The one we worked on together."

"Oh, I understand all right," Clive replied, pulling the panama over his forehead at a forty-five-degree angle. Their pace quickened.

"Then why won't you listen?"

"I understand you've found some minerals, got your uncle shot, and need some free advice. Is that about it?"

"I thought you, of all people, would get it."

Clive pulled up short and turned to Billy.

"Get what? Get into this mess with you? Go call the police."

"I did. But this is not about the shooting. It's about the minerals. The shooting only proves this is something big."

"How do you know?"

"I think it's dysprosium," Billy responded, his voice growing desperate. "You remember? The stuff you used to jack up the gas mileage in that riding mower?" He continued rapid-fire before Clive had a chance to escape. "I remembered the taste and smell and ran the basic tests with citric acid and baking soda. It looks potent as hell right out of the springs. I brought some to show you."

Clive's expression never changed, but inside his curiosity flared like the relief valve on a Texas gas well. His Pavlovian response scared him. This is exactly what he didn't need. Five years of grief, and the same of counseling, all at risk with the hint of redemption.

Affecting frustration, Clive pulled a white handkerchief from his pocket and wiped a dribble of sweat from the back of his neck. "If I give you fifteen minutes, will you leave me alone?"

"If you'll look at the sample," Billy risked, in a firm voice.

Clive considered his former student. His eyes were the same, dark and unblinking, but now with a hint of desperation. His countenance gave away little, but Clive could read between the lines on his face. He knew the story from his own image. Time was running out. *A fellow traveler.* The resentment Clive had harbored over Billy's departure for the NFL melted away in the Texas sun.

Clive motioned with his hand. Billy followed like a bloodhound.

They walked in silence the three blocks to Clive's apartment at the Hampton Arms, a one-story affair huddled under a canopy of post oaks. Green vines camouflaged the molded brick walls.

Clive opened an aluminum screen door, then unlocked the entry. It took a calypso hip bump to gain access.

"It's the goddamn humidity. I've been meaning to fix it." He raised the blinds and clicked on a table lamp made from a bowling pin.

On the tan carpet, Billy noticed a worn path even a white man could track across a small living room into a breakfast nook. A wooden table with curved metal legs and two matching chairs sat in the corner opposite the counter.

Clive swept pecan shells from the tabletop into a trash can, then stacked dirty dishes in the sink. With his face turned away from Billy, he surveyed the rest of the place and shuddered. *If you had any friends at all, you loser, this place would look half decent.* He glanced back at Billy whose mouth was turned up in a half smile. *Oh, what the hell*, he thought, *he gets it. He gets it.*

"Sorry for the mess," Clive murmured. "My cleaning staff is on vacation." He nodded at a chair. "Sit."

On the windowsill in the kitchen, a green parrot squawked from a dilapidated cage.

"This is Porter. We're engaged."

Billy took a seat. From the hip pocket of his jeans, he produced a silver flask.

"A little early for that, isn't it?" Clive sneered, pulling up a chair.

Ignoring the joke, Billy held it in front of the professor, stroking the shiny surface with his thumb. Clive alternated his stare between the flask and Billy's eyes like a metronome. He was hooked and they both knew it. *Okay*, he thought, *what's this going to cost me?*

"It took me a while to find you," Billy teased. "I figured you'd be running the show at UT by now. What happened?"

"I thought you wanted advice," Clive growled. "You're using up your fifteen minutes."

Billy laughed. "Okay, okay. I just thought you'd be a little more enthusiastic about a big mineral find like this. It could be worth millions."

"Millions, huh?" Clive answered with a smirk. He stood and walked the few paces across his kitchen. Gazing out the window, he began sprinkling birdseed to his closest friend. "They'll never let you have it, you know."

"Who?" Billy asked his eyebrows arching.

Clive turned back to Billy. "If you remember, my paper predicted an underground ocean in West Texas, miles deeper than drilling could confirm, moving inexorably toward the surface."

"Of course, I remember. That's the reason I'm here."

"I posited that an earthquake or underground explosion could force to the surface a tsunami of brine so rich with rare earth minerals, especially dysprosium, that petroleum would be obsolete overnight. My first faculty committee enjoyed the adventure, encouraged me to push the limits of scientific fact. What they didn't realize was I had proof."

"Sure. The seismic data."

"And the infrared satellite photos. That information was brand new back then. They hadn't analyzed it. I had."

Billy's eyes swept the dingy apartment. "That's about the time I left for the NFL. I thought you were on your way to the big time, too."

Clive looked at the young Indian and sighed. "Listen carefully, son." He sat and leaned across the table. "Once my paper was published, it scared the hell out of them. I mean they went apeshit. Just the idea that a cheap supply of dysprosium was readily available was more than they could handle. It could jeopardize the whole oil economy.

"Who were 'they'?"

"The oil companies, for starters. Think what would happen if a fuel additive made from your dysprosium hit the market. Demand for gasoline would drop by 75 percent. Overnight what had been an exotic energy oddity would become essential. Oil prices would tank and so would the value of oil company stock."

"Jesus," Billy whispered.

"And it doesn't stop there. Without gasoline taxes, the whole state would be in trouble. It didn't take long for the governor and his Big Oil cronies to size this one up. They turned the dogs loose on me right quick."

For a second, the only sound was Porter pecking his birdseed.

Clive rubbed his eyes and continued. "The final blow for me was the Permanent University Fund. You know what that is?"

Billy frowned. "Nope."

"It's a trust fund established under the Texas Constitution that controls better than two million acres, mostly in West Texas. Revenues can only be used to build facilities for State colleges. UT gets the biggest share. Last year it was worth over five billion. Guess where the revenue comes from? Oil and gas leases."

"Now I get it," Billy said.

Clive was on a roll.

"Once the faculty got the call from the university administration, my paper and I were history. I fought back until they fired me. Then I went to the private colleges and got a job at Rice. They told me I'd be protected and could continue my research."

The professor's voice began to crack. The two men sat again in silence. Billy waited.

Swallowing hard, Clive pressed on. His eyes brimmed with tears. "I was married then, you know. Sue was also a teacher and was helping me with my next paper on the underground sea. The day we finished, I took the draft to my office. When I got home, the place had been ransacked."

He rubbed the bridge of his nose, fingers trembling. "And Sue," he choked, "they duct-taped her to the bed and worked her over like a five-dollar whore. There were three of them."

Billy's jaws tightened and his pulse raced. He put his hand on Clive's shoulder.

"The security video from the parking lot showed the hooded bastards getting into a black SUV and a damn good image of the license number."

"God, Clive, I don't know what to say," Billy whispered.

"There's nothing *to* say," he responded, recovering slightly. "Sue went to the hospital, then the psych ward, then home to her parents. She never recovered, really, and neither did our marriage."

"What about the video?" Billy asked.

"You've got a lot to learn, son," Clive snorted. "Nothing ever happened. The police called it a random break-in, then reported the tape had been damaged beyond repair in the crime lab. What are the odds of that? Something stunk. Then I got a call. The caller didn't identify himself, but he knew about my apartment and Sue. He told me to forget about the break-in and the paper and there'd be no more trouble. Otherwise, they'd come for me."

Billy went to the sink, drew a glass of water, and handed it to Clive.

"I traced the license number of those bastards to an investigator in the Houston PD. You'd think they'd have been smart enough to hire it done. That's how brazen these Big Oil assholes had become."

"Think they'll do the same to me?" Billy asked.

"No question."

Clive scratched his head. "Fracking, huh? Didn't exist in '98."

"Yup. The perfect storm. Still want to see the stuff?"

"What do you think?" Clive responded, eyes ablaze.

Billy uncapped the flask. A poignant odor wafted across the table.

"Dysprosium nitrate," Billy whispered. "Straight from the springs."

Clive reached for the flask and took a sniff. His eyebrows lifted and his breath quickened. "What tests *have* you run?"

Billy answered with a sheepish smile. "Well, none. But from the taste, I've read enough literature on dysprosium to know this is different."

Clive touched his tongue to the liquid. His eyes locked with Billy's. Without a word he went to his bedroom, returning with a leather case. Inside was a collection of glass vials, each a different color.

Clive opened a cabinet, placed a bowl on the counter, and poured in a quarter inch of gray liquid from the flask. Until this moment, he thought, staring at the solution, his prospects had been just as dark and inert. But, now, with Billy's call, change was afoot.

He removed a cork from one of the glass vessels and tapped a tiny piece of white crystal into the bowl. As he swirled the mix, it took on a mustard hue and began to bubble and smoke.

From a small pocket in the case, Clive produced what Billy recognized as a chemical testing strip. The professor's hands shook as he peeled the wrapper. "If we've got dysprosium, this'll prove it. Red means we're right."

He caught himself slipping into the plural and glanced at Billy. The Indian's smile confirmed that he'd noticed.

The tip of the paper broke the surface and they waited.

Over the back fence, neighborhood children laughed. Out front, a Metro bus roared by. Porter pecked at the mirror in his cage. Life went on as normal in the Montrose, for all but two people.

The paper turned red.

6

WHEN MONDAY MORNING ARRIVED, Leslie Strikeleather sat at her desk in the LaCour Tower, dressed in a sleek, white Chanel pants suit, staring at the phone and drumming a pencil. Opening stock prices skidded across her computer screen like a crystal tide. Brochures for a client promotion lay on the floor.

She reached for the overnight sweep reports showing the latest account balances, but soon tossed them aside, instead dropping her fingers to the keyboard. Quick strokes brought up the website for Stasney Energy. She wrote down the telephone number then turned and closed the door. She sat back and looked at the scrap of paper in her lap. With her pointer finger, she slowly traced the numerals. Her face was stoic, but around her eyes her skin flushed. *I'm doing this for both of us*, she said to herself.

The fine down on her arms stood on end as she dialed the number. Brushing back her hair, she took a deep breath and came to attention.

"Luke Stasney, please."

"One moment."

"Mr. Stasney's office," a voice droned.

"Is he in, please? This is Leslie Howell . . . Strikeleather."

"Will he know what this is regarding?"

"Yes."

"Please hold."

After a long minute, she heard Luke's voice for the first time since she'd dumped him. "Luke Stasney," he said with an edge.

"Luke, it's Leslie Jean."

No response.

"Luke?"

"Yeah. How's it going, Leslie."

"Is that the best you can do after all these years?" she said, forcing a laugh.

"Well, to say I'm surprised would be the understatement of the decade."

Letting it pass, she pressed on, "How've you been?"

Luke refused to yield. "Well, it's hard to know where to start since I haven't heard from you in ten years."

"Come on, Luke. I was—am married."

"Right. I do recall that," he snorted.

His voice was tense, his words clipped.

Leslie knew Luke was used to being in control. He'd been that way in college, but she learned how to deal with it.

The Velvet Closer pulled at the gold earring hanging from her right ear and purred, "Luke, people make mistakes. Sometimes it takes a lifetime to figure them out."

"So, you've been working pretty hard at that, have you?"

Leaning forward across her conference table, Leslie chose her words carefully. "I'm sorry you feel this way, Luke. I have been thinking about you." *I've landed plenty of tough prospects*, she told herself. *This is just one more.*

"What do you want, Leslie?" Luke sighed.

"Just to tell you I'm sorry for how it all ended."

"Just like that, huh? I don't suppose Billy's mineral deal has anything to do with it."

"That's cruel, Luke, and it's not why I called."

Leslie hesitated then went all in. "Do you have lunch plans today?"

"Yes."

Silence, then Luke blinked first. "But, I'll change them. The Rainbow Lodge at noon. Ask the maître d' for my usual table. I'll give you one hour, tops."

"Done," Leslie said and hung up the phone. She leaned back with a smile, both hands laced behind her head.

"Client lunch," Leslie tossed off as she bolted past her Monday morning marketing meeting. The men at the conference table watched her leave with admiration and lust, in equal measure. The women seethed.

An elevator ride took her to the ground floor of the parking garage. Passing the bay reserved for LaCour top management, she walked quickly, her hips and arms oscillating like a runway model, to a second bank of elevators. Another ride down dropped her in the far corner of a cavernous parking area crowded with Fords and Camrys. She glanced up at red letters stenciled on the wall: *Lower Level – Employee Parking. That says it all*, she thought, *but not for long*.

Leslie climbed into her ten-year-old white Range Rover. With the air conditioner on full blast, she headed to the Rainbow Lodge. The swanky eatery was converted from an old fishing camp overlooking Buffalo Bayou. She accelerated onto Post Oak Boulevard, the main artery of the Galleria, an affluent shopping district. The area was a mix of office towers, high-rise condominiums, and luxury restaurants where Muslim millennials, fat with their daddy's oil money, had begun to nose out locals for the best tables, and Farsi was becoming the first language of valets.

From there she merged east onto Memorial Drive, a six-lane super street connecting the Galleria with downtown. The route was flanked by parks and running trails. A canopy of trees provided shade. The air was like a sauna, thick and hot. Tropical systems off the Gulf offered the only respite, but at a price. The storms either drifted through, washing away the heat for a day, or steamrolled across the coast, razing everything in their path. The city took its chances. Whether hurled down from the heavens by a hurricane, or gouged up from below by drilling bits, energy defined Houston.

Leslie pulled to a stop in front of the ivy-covered walls of the restaurant. She raised her chin and checked her lipstick. Inside, she knew, sat a man who could plug power and status back into her life. The attendant opened the door. She stepped down to the hot asphalt and pitched him the keys. Erect with shoulders back, she started up the walk, then paused to call out, "I won't be an hour."

The Lodge was made of wood. In the entry, pine handrails and oak plank floors were accented with mounted fish and an ancient outboard motor under a glass-top display. The staff wore white coats with black ties and spoke in muted tones.

The maître' d showed Leslie to Luke's table. Lean and tan, he stood to greet her. "Hi, Leslie," he smiled, helping her with her chair. No kiss.

"Luke, you look wonderful," she said.

He winked, sitting across the corner from her. "I'll bet you say that to all the boys."

Over iced tea and Cobb salads, Leslie covered her backstory with Billy. Luke did the same with his failed marriage to an actress who spent more time in Neiman Marcus than on stage.

"At least there were no kids for us to fuck up," he said, sipping the last of his drink.

"So, you heard about Billy's big deal?" Leslie ventured.

"Yeah. He called me last week, but I was tied up, so I told them to put him through to our head geologist, Jack Massey. He didn't tell Jack everything but said enough to get our attention."

Luke looked to his left and grinned, returning a wave from a blonde across the room. "An old friend."

"Of course," Leslie said, with a touch of sarcasm. "Could we have more tea?"

"Sure," said Luke, turning to hail a waiter.

Leslie dabbed her lips with a napkin while underneath releasing her top button.

When her glass was refilled, she continued. "I'm really happy for Billy. You can see things haven't gone too well lately, for him or us."

"Has he been working?"

"He tries, but he's seven years behind his contemporaries and not used to working nine to five. He wants so to make it in the oil patch, but he's worn out his welcome with the big companies. Dependability has been an issue."

Luke nodded. "It happens to these guys, Leslie." His thoughts drifted to the Billy of old—fearless and fun loving. "You know, after what happened between you and me, I tried to hate the guy. It was no use."

"I know what you mean," said Leslie, pretending to let down her guard. "If only he had . . . oh, well. It doesn't matter now."

"And you?" Luke asked.

"I've learned to survive. Billy will have to do the same."

"Doesn't sound promising," he said with a gentle smile.

Her lower lip trembled. "I've done all I can, Luke." She looked away, her eyes glistening.

Luke touched her hand. "Can I see you again?"

Without looking back, she nodded—then smiled.

7

IT WAS SATURDAY NIGHT. The Cave was crowded. The closest thing to a nightclub in a hundred miles, it was built underground in the shell of an old silver mine outside a ghost town called Terlingua. Thirty miles from Chinati Flats, the Cave was where the locals came to swap stories and drink beer.

Oliver had been to the Cave often, most recently when he was refurbishing old wells for oil giant Texas Trans-National Energy, Inc. It was there he had met Leland Vestal, an ex-hippie with long red hair and wire-rimmed glasses. He rode a Harley each day to his job rolling drill pipe onto trucks. In the evenings he trolled the Cave, trying to recruit oilfield workers for the AFL-CIO.

Oliver's faded green Karmann Ghia was the nearest thing to a sports car in the Big Bend. He rolled it to a stop outside the bar and swept back his hair with a rat-tail comb. When he stepped out, the shocks groaned.

Inside, the atmosphere was dank but lively. In this natural refuge from the June sun, the party was underway. Oliver ordered a Shiner Bock and drifted down the bar exchanging pleasantries. On the far end, under the snout of a stuffed javelina, he saw Vestal, deep in discussion with an

Indian girl. She was clearly underage, but dressed to kill. As Oliver approached from behind, he watched Leland lean in close to her. Standing a few feet from the couple, he heard Leland say, "So you see, we've all got the same needs and wants. Working folks can't be satisfied toiling for the man all their lives. We need to pull together," which he demonstrated by cinching his arm tighter around her waist like a copperhead.

"Hello, Lee," Oliver said.

Wheeling around, the redhead exclaimed, "Well, what do you know? It's Oliver Greentree. Big Bend's token playboy. Still driving that '54 Kaiser with a bamboo dash?"

"Karmann Ghia," he responded, extending his hand with a smile. Leland shook it.

"Right, right," he said, examining Oliver's grip. "I don't see any red lead paint under your nails. You retired from scraping tanks?"

"Got promoted."

"The hell you say! When?"

"Right after you got laid off."

"That's just great," Leland scoffed, slapping the bar with his palm. "I get canned, you get a promotion." He turned to the girl. "See what I mean? Those corporate fat-asses don't give a damn about fairness."

Oliver ordered another beer. When the bartender handed him the bottle, he took a long drink and faced Vestal. "If it makes you feel any better, they laid me off a month later."

Leland glanced down contritely. "Sorry, partner. I didn't know."

"No sweat. They did me a favor," Oliver said. "I got on with the Bureau of Indian Affairs."

"How'd you pull that off?" Leland asked with a curious frown. "You know somebody?"

"They needed an Indian who knew computers."

"You?" Leland snickered.

"I took night classes from Randy Kickingbird, principal of the reservation school."

"The hell you say! Well, I'll be damned."

"You still organizing for the unions?" Oliver asked.

"Let's say we have a working relationship."

"Can we grab a table for a minute? I've got something I think you'll want to hear."

They walked to the patio and sat down. Oliver told Leland about Clive Larson's paper, the fuel additive, and the Rio Hot Springs mineral discovery. He then explained the tribe's dilemma with a development plan.

"The key is financing. Trans-National has offered the tribe a joint venture deal, but the council is not convinced. There's room for alternatives."

Leland's eyes narrowed to slits and he stroked his auburn jowls. "How much do they need?"

"About three million to start. Enough to back off Trans-National and let the Chinati keep control of the minerals. It's the only way an additive will ever get to the market."

Leland's eyes widened and he sat on the edge of his chair. "I get it," he said.

Oliver continued. "I figured a tenfold increase in gas mileage, and a shot at unionizing the entire production operation, might be of interest to someone like the UAW."

Leland's head began bobbing like a toy duck in a water cup. "I guarantee you they would. Yes, they would, and I know how to sell it."

"I thought you would. So, here's the deal. You introduce the idea to the UAW. I'll provide a package with the technical information, a financing proposal for them to offer to the tribe, and deliver the votes on council to get it passed. I know who to tap."

"What's in it for us?"

"A fee, of course. Say, 10 percent? Split it fifty-fifty between us. But the funds have to run through me."

"That's fine," Leland laughed. "I know where you live. Waitress!"

8

A TWO-STORY BRICK RELIC WITH ARCHED ENTRY, the Gage Hotel guarded the main highway in Marathon, Texas, population 430. A porch with low iron rails and wooden rockers fronted the building waiting for the occasional tourist. The railroad station was across the road.

This was cattle country. By the end of the Civil War, as many as five million longhorn cattle, descendants of old Spanish stock, roamed wild in Texas. These rangy animals had horns with a spread of up to eight feet. In the beginning, they were hunted only for their hides since there was no way to get them to eastern markets. The Transcontinental Railroad changed that. It became possible to transport them back east where consumers had developed a taste for beef at a time when the effects of war had thinned eastern herds. Texan beef, though wild and tough, was in great demand.

In the 1860s, cattle barons came to the Gage to trade beeves pastured along the southern bend of the Rio Grande. Then they were herded north to the rail yards in Kansas City. Wranglers who brought in the droves were tough and independent, but their sinew was trust. The combination produced a unique code of conduct passed down by generations to the current residents of Big Bend. If a stray ended up on your land, you returned it. If you caught a rustler in your herd, you shot him.

On this hot afternoon, a visitor arrived in a dusty pickup with a low tire. The temperature would crest one hundred degrees until the sun slipped behind the mountains. Looking at the once lavish hotel reminded him there'd always been a double standard in this part of Texas. The Gage was for Anglos. The rest slept in their trucks or in the motel outside of town. He was ready to depart Big Bend for a level playing field.

Climbing down from the cab, he surveyed the parking lot. There was one other vehicle, a black SUV with a high shine, longhorn hood ornament, and chrome brush guard. *That's no working truck*, he said to himself with a dismissive grunt. *Probably a rhinestone cowboy.*

He donned his stained Resistol hat and walked to the front steps, the asphalt hot under his feet. After mounting the stairs, he reached for the handle on the wooden door, but paused. Images of weddings and parties at the hotel came back to him, events his family could attend only as hired help.

At these fiestas, he remembered mariachi bands stationed on the veranda to greet guests—ranch owners and their families from across the county, dressed in string ties and prairie dresses. In contrast to this West Texas aristocracy was a rough weave of blue-collar Mexicans, Indians, and itinerate farmers doing the dirty work. He had done his share.

The moneyed crowd, whooping it up at the Gage, had been his first glimpse of life outside Big Bend, he recalled. Thereafter, he knew the only hope for a better life was to leave. He was still trying to do just that.

As the visitor stood in the wilting heat, he knew the events of the next hour would be critical to his escape. With a deep breath, he pushed open the door.

The lobby smelled of leather and hardwood. The desk was straight ahead, under the staircase. A painting of a six-horse stagecoach at full gallop was propped above the hearth. Along the far wall was a glass-top display of six-guns and lariats. He'd not been in this room since his days of carrying suitcases to and from the train station. Guests would wait for him in high-back chairs. Lamps with rawhide shades cast shadows across the room.

He approached the hotel clerk and removed his hat. A woman in a denim dress with hair combed back into a tumbleweed looked up casually.

"Yes?"

"I'm looking for Buck Olmeyer."

"Is he expecting you?"

"Yes. I came from Chinati Flats."

"Your party is waiting for you upstairs in the Chaparral Room, number twelve."

He thanked her and climbed the stairs. At the top, an arrow directed him down the hall to the right. A maroon and gray runner, worn at each door, covered the passageway. Prints of cowboys and cattle drives lined the walls, reminders of Marathon's heyday.

The floor creaked as he walked to the room. Its double doors were adorned with a grove of mesquite trees etched into the wood. He knocked. There was no answer.

He tried the knob. The door clicked open.

At the same time the visitor entered, two men came in from an adjoining room. The suite was large with paneled walls and woven rugs. A speaker-phone sat on a low coffee table cluttered with newspapers and ashtrays.

The shorter man, wearing aviators and a two-for-one gray suit with paisley tie, pointed to the divan. "Sit down."

The guest did what he was told.

The second, a barrel-chested black man with a rumpled blue blazer and blank face, walked to the table and clicked on the phone. A dial tone buzzed.

Reaching past his string tie into his shirt pocket, he withdrew a business card and jabbed in a string of numbers. From the metal box came the sound of a telephone ringing, then a baritone drawl, "Olmeyer."

"He's here, sir," said the short suit. Turning to the visitor, he grunted, "Mr. Olmeyer in Houston."

Buck Olmeyer was CEO of the biggest player in the oil patch, Trans-National. At six-four and barrel-chested, he'd worked his way through Sam Houston State, a second-tier college in the pine forests of East Texas, as a honkytonk bouncer. Backwoods brawling was perfect training for the Big Oil jungle. He still had his father's roughneck hard hat and had reared his three sons with the single purpose of them becoming star athletes. None had, but he'd seen to it that they started every game.

"I'll make this brief," his voice growled from the speaker. "When you came to us, we were skeptical. We checked out you and your Rio Hot Springs mineral story. It added up."

The guest glanced at his hosts. Both held eye contact.

Olmeyer continued, "We asked you to keep us informed and made you a damn good deal to do it. Instead, at the first sign of trouble, you grabbed your rifle and started blasting away. Thanks to you, we've got a yellowjacket in the outhouse."

"What makes you think it was me?"

"Well, who else would be watching those springs?"

Silence.

"We told you to keep your mouth shut. Who the hell have you told?" Olmeyer snapped.

"Look, I worked for Trans-National for three years on half a dozen drill sites out here. You told me you were looking for more than oil and gas, so I busted my ass in your so-called training program learning about rare earth minerals. As soon as I knew what I was doing, you fired me."

"We had a layoff. Happens every day in the oil patch. Where are we going with this?"

"I'd been out of work for over a year when I contacted you about the dysprosium discovery. You promised me a $100,000 retainer and told me to start lining up Chinati council votes to deliver the project to you. I did that, but all I ever got from you was $2500 and a gasoline credit card. Who I spoke with is my business. You start paying and I'll start talking."

"Are you threatening me?" Olmeyer said coldly.

"What I'm saying is if you don't want to do business, I've got others who do."

The guest leaned forward as if preparing to leave. When he saw the suits reach inside their coats, he sat back.

Olmeyer resumed, quietly. "I don't think you understand what's at stake here." Then more forcefully: "More than your ticket back to civilization. If this job is screwed up, it'll mean the end of the line for you."

The visitor listened to the scolding for five minutes more without talking, but his face was growing tense.

"We'll kick your ass over the river and see to it that you never come back," Olmeyer concluded with a threatening hiss.

There was a lull while Buck caught his breath.

Suddenly the guest blurted, "I don't have to take this crap. I'm out of here." He grabbed his hat and headed for the door.

Both suits sprang into his path. The short one drew a snub-nosed pistol. The other one grabbed the guest from behind, crushing his throat with a forearm.

"What's going on?" Buck said loudly.

"Our boy wants to leave," the short suit grunted.

"You'd better call off these goons," the visitor said, choking. "I don't think a shooting at the Gage Hotel is the kind of publicity you need at the moment."

"Don't tell me what I need," Buck said.

"I don't think you've got too many options here," the guest wheezed.

"Turn him loose."

Oliver Greentree reached behind him for the doorknob. "I know about Clive Larsen's white paper. I know how long you've hidden the test results. And I know about the dysprosium discovery on the Chinati reservation. That's all I need to know. If you want me to work with you and keep my mouth shut, I need to be paid. I can line up the votes, but not until I get the rest of my money. Get it to me in forty-eight hours."

Seething, Olmeyer knew he was right. "Let him go."

When the door closed, Buck said, "Tail him. Get a tracker on his car."

The goons hurried out to the hall and down the fire escape.

From out of the back room, another figure emerged. "You still there, Buck?" he said.

"Yep. Is that you, Dolph?" Olmeyer asked.

"Right."

Dolph Barstow was the classic Texas governor, a silver-haired Aggie in an expensive suit who appeared to have all the answers, but in fact had only one—*In Texas, we solve problems with hard work, and we don't need pencil-necked bureaucrats to show us how*—and reframed every question into a bull's-eye for that bullet.

Guys like this, Buck knew, came from rich families with royalties, and split their time between mansions in Dallas or Houston and exotic game ranches in West Texas. Their components had been stockpiled years before their birth. Only assembly was required, which occurred in private prep schools, Ivy League colleges, and SMU Law School. Their wives were cloned from a secret blend of DNA harvested by the hairdressers of Barbara Bush and Farrah Fawcett.

Buck hated his guts.

"I thought you had this thing under control," the governor said, walking past the speakerphone toward the kitchen.

"We'll handle it," the CEO responded in an irritated tone.

A bar with stools on either side divided the kitchen from the living room. Barstow took off his coat, threw it on a chair, and headed around the bar to the refrigerator. On either side were glass-fronted cabinets at eye level. Spotting a tumbler, he opened the door, took it out, and placed it under the ice chute.

When cubes had clattered halfway to the rim, he set it on the sink and grabbed a bottle of Knob Creek from the next cabinet. The governor poured a healthy drink, turned back toward the speakerphone, and downed half in one gulp.

He ambled back to the couch and sank into the worn leather. After another belt, he cleared his throat and broached the obvious with the Houston fat cat.

"If that guy was under control, I'm Barack Obama. I think you better pay the boy and quick."

Olmeyer lost it. "Look, you pompous tick, when I need your advice I'll ask for it."

"Easy, big fella," Barstow cooed in mock surprise.

"You just keep your State fuzz off my ass and leave the rest to me," Buck shot back.

"The boys over in the capital are nervous, Buck. If the press gets wind of this dysprosium story, oil futures could take a beating."

"I said I'd take care of it," the CEO fumed.

"I hope you do. I'd like to see you finish out your career there at Trans-National."

Buck held his tongue. He knew he needed Barstow, and vice versa. Like he always drummed into his staff, politics and Big Oil were one in Texas. This unholy alliance with Barstow would have to hold until the Rio Hot Springs problem had been solved, or the election—whichever occurred first.

"How'd you find this guy anyway?" Barstow asked.

"He found us."

"How so?"

"That's a long story."

The governor finished his bourbon, belched, and stretched. "Well, time to head to the ranch, Buck. Call me when you've got this handled. I'll be waiting."

They hung up on each other.

In Houston, Buck took his feet off the desk and spun to his right where Colt Stone sat contemplating what he'd heard of the conversation.

"I don't like how this is playing out," Buck sputtered with an angry glare.

Director of Investor Relations was a handle contrived for Colt Stone to obfuscate his true role as hatchet man for the CEO. Tall and angular with dark hair combed straight back from a widow's peak, he was dressed tastefully in a blue blazer with red tie. Everything about him registered corporate, except for his eyes, which did not blink or stray under fire. He didn't intimidate easily.

"Maybe the best thing to do," Olmeyer tossed off with false bravado, "is just let those crazy redskins take a swing at developing the thing on their own. They've got no one to bankroll the job and no experience. They'll probably kill it for us."

Without moving or breaking eye contact, Colt replied coolly, "That might have been possible if the additive didn't work so well. With a ten-to-one increase in gasoline mileage, we can't take the chance. You said it yourself years ago. If anyone ever finds a ready supply of dysprosium, the game will be over."

"That was just to get the attention of the lab boys."

"I'd say you got it. Since then they've tried everything to find a flaw with dysprosium, something to make it too flammable, cancerous to inhale, anything. No use. Face it, Buck. This juice is the key to energy independence."

"How many people know about the test results?" Buck reached in his shirt pocket for a cigar. "Not counting the E-4 Group."

"Maybe five, and of that only a few grasp the magnitude of the problem."

"I'm sure we've played out the likely scenario if a supply of dysprosium ever surfaced," said the CEO, holding a match to the stogie and thrusting his chin up.

"We have," responded Colt.

"Well?"

"Roughly half of the oil produced today is turned into gasoline."

"I know that, goddamn it," Olmeyer volleyed, raking the hair on the back of his head with a vicious swipe. "What's it going to do to the price of crude and how quick?"

"It depends on how fast production and distribution of the additive can crank up," Colt replied, refusing to be stampeded. "But," he continued in a measured tone, "the market will see it coming instantly. Oil prices track sales. The math is easy to figure. If gasoline purchases drop by 90 percent, crude prices will follow. We're looking at ten dollars a barrel of oil within a month or so."

A stream of blue smoke spewed from his lips as the CEO gazed out at the evening lights of the energy capital of the world. He was a calculating man and, in his gut, already knew the answers to his questions. Big Oil corporate types survived by being a cross between cheerleader and pragmatist. The former was reserved for the office where every successful executive let on that they'd drunk the company Kool-Aid. "What's good for Trans-National is good for America," they told themselves with straight faces. No one questioned the company line, at least in public. But underneath, every decision was made first with an eye toward its personal political implications. Buck was now faced with the mother of all such challenges.

Winning was everything to Buck Olmeyer, but most importantly, winning with the illusion of class. Trans-National gave him the cachet he could never otherwise earn.

9

IN A TELEVISION STUDIO IN HOUSTON, anchorwoman Maria Cloud was coming back for her sign-off on the 5 p.m. news.

3-2-1 . . . her director mouthed in unison with his fingers, then pointed to the black-haired beauty.

"And finally, in Dime Box, Texas, population 375, a late model Ford sedan with emblems on the doors and flashing lights went missing tonight. That's right; the town's only police cruiser was stolen at a Dunkin' Donuts store when the sheriff went in for a refill of coffee. The vehicle was recovered on the outskirts of town. The donuts are still missing.

"For all of us here at News 7 Houston, this is Maria Cloud. Goodnight."

"That's a wrap," the director sang out. Bob Sharkey was a thirty-year veteran of WNBC in New York who'd come home to Texas to finish his career.

Maria plucked the mic from her blouse and gathered the news script. In three long strides, she was off camera and headed for her office.

"Good show, Maria," said the camera operator as she whisked by. She gave him a forced smile. He looked at the other cameraman and shrugged.

At twenty-eight, Maria Whitecloud, aka Maria Cloud, was the only Native American anchor in Houston. Tall, dark, and stylish, her look was a perfect fit for the most racially diverse city in the south. But the job hadn't come cheap.

She was a full-blooded Chinati Indian. After leaving the reservation for community college in the border town of Laredo, she'd gotten a job as a reporter on local TV. It helped that she had cover girl looks, a quick quip, and copper skin. There was no kind of car crash or drug bust she hadn't covered. After stints in Waco and Texarkana, she graduated to Houston.

Then came the night of the riot at Huntsville State Prison. She'd been waiting for her big chance and, with senior reporters covering elections, Sharkey sent her to cover the story. Armed inmates had taken two guards hostage and were demanding a TV interview in exchange for their release. Prison officials agreed.

Hungry for a scoop, Maria volunteered along with a cameraman and two armed Texas Rangers. The prison hospital was picked as a neutral site.

Midway through the interview, the inmates grabbed Maria and her cameraman. Shooting broke out. Three of the five inmates were killed by the Rangers.

Through a hail of bullets, the surviving inmates dragged their hostages into the depths of hell. With nothing to lose, and camera still rolling, they beat the cameraman senseless, then violated Maria in every way imaginable. The feed had been diverted from the air, but blared live through the TV studio as staffers watched in horror. Only an all-out assault by the Rangers, M16s blazing, had saved their lives—but not before the nightmare that would last a lifetime.

Among those at the studio that night was Vanessa Wilcox, wife of Edward Wilcox, the CEO of WILCO Communications. WILCO owned

Channel 7 and a string of thirty others along the Gulf Coast. Slim and tanned the color of creamed coffee, at fifty she was still a classic Texas queen, a style that worked well in her role as marketing director of the company. She was born and raised in Highland Park, a ritzy bedroom community of Dallas. It was only after a paunchy hustler from Houston named Ed Wilcox won a Houston television station from her father, by eagling the eighteenth hole at the Dallas Athletic Club, that he registered on her.

Although Vanessa's blood was bluer than Ed's, in Texas your financial statement does your talking. After picking up another station in a game of Texas Hold 'Em, Ed and his financial statement got a whole lot better looking to her. When his network reached three, the match was made.

It took Ed twenty years to parlay his holdings into a syndicate of thirty stations. Along the way, Vanessa rode her husband's largess to the top of the Houston social scene but lost interest in the marriage. The feeling was mutual.

When Maria returned to the air after the prison riot, Vanessa watched as she distanced herself from the staff. Despite her self-imposed isolation, over time, a few invited her to social events as a bridge back to a normal life. She refused.

Vanessa stayed clear of Maria but was intrigued by her resilience and determination. These were attributes she wished she'd possessed at that age. Through back channels, without Maria's knowledge, Vanessa got her on the short list for the evening anchor job. In the end, however, Maria won the position on her own merit.

This evening, after leaving the set, Maria stopped by her office for her purse, then headed for the parking lot. As she reached the exit door, she heard footsteps behind her.

"Want some company?" It was Bob Sharkey.

"Sure," she said with a quick nod. He pushed the door open for her. It was hot and muggy. When they reached her car, a red Corolla that had seen better days, she fished in her bag for the keys.

"See you later, Bob," she said, hurrying to unlock the car.

When the driver's door swung open, he caught it with his hand. "How are you doing?" he asked.

"Better. Better," she responded, slipping behind the wheel.

"I worry about you," he said with a gentle smile.

Her face softened. She looked up. "I know, Bob. It's only been six months. I just need a little more time."

"I understand," he said. "Don't get me wrong. Your work is excellent. When you got the anchor job so soon after . . . I was concerned. You've handled it beautifully."

"Thanks," she said, pulling the door closed.

Bob motioned for her to lower the window. "There's something else I want to tell you," he said, leaning down. "You have an admirer in Vanessa Wilcox."

"I suspected so. I suppose you know about the house?"

He nodded. When Maria had gotten the job of evening anchorwoman, Ed Wilcox had bought a high-dollar townhouse, fully decorated, from an Enron insider on permanent vacation in Ecuador, and leased it to her for a song. It was part of the deal, he'd told her. The arrangement worried her, but he'd insisted and he was the boss.

"Watch your step," Bob said, lowering his voice. "She and Ed are an ambitious pair. They buy and sell people every day and not just in the television business. What they want, they get. There's no angle they won't play."

"Thank you for the warning," she said.

When Bob left, she let her head drop back against the headrest.

What is it with this city? I've been through too much to quit, and now I've got to watch out for my own employers.

Maria turned the key, bringing the engine to life. The radio was set to her favorite station, NPR. The news was on. *Why can't I work for them?* she wondered. Reaching back with both hands, she pulled out her silver hair clip. A quick shake freed her black mane. It felt good.

After a ten-minute drive, she pulled her car into a wooded enclave with a dozen tony homes fronting Buffalo Bayou. A steel gate made of vertical bars, honed sharp at the tips, guarded the entrance. The spikes continued out either side atop an eight-foot sandstone wall, keeping the rest of the world out and the residents in. She lowered the window and punched in the access code. The barricade swung open. Once inside, it clanged shut behind her. That metallic sound would forever remind her of the night at Huntsville Penitentiary. The cell doors that closed behind her were intended to keep her captors in. Instead, they kept her rescuers out. The memory made her stomach wrench.

Now, as she pulled away from the gate, she was behind bars again. *What kind of people need to protect themselves from their own tribe? And why would I live with them? To prove I'm better? Perhaps.*

A breeze swayed the two trees flanking the front door of her two-story rental, red brick with a high roof and ivy-covered façade. As she pulled into the driveway, a horn honked. It was her neighbor and his girlfriend, leaving in a black convertible, top down. He motioned to her.

"Maria! Come out on the boat with us tomorrow. We're going down to Galveston Bay, then have dinner on the Strand."

"Thanks, Jerry, but I'm way behind at work. Can I have a rain check?"

"Come on. When's the last time you got of that house?"

Before she could answer, they waved and drove away.

He means well. And he's right.

The young broadcaster tapped the remote on her dash, opening the garage. After pulling in, the door closed behind her triggering an overhead light. She scanned the place. Unlike what she'd glimpsed in Jerry's garage, there were no kayaks strung from the ceiling, skis, golf clubs, motorcycles, or sports cars. Only a fat-tired bicycle with a broken basket, a coiled lariat, hiking boots, and an old pair of calf-high moccasins. *It may not be much, but it's who I am.*

She pulled the keys from the ignition. Her cell phone beeped with a voice mail. She checked it:

"Hi, Wa. It's me, Dad."

A smile crept across her lips—as if she wouldn't know his voice or his pet name for her.

"I hope you're okay. Can you give me a call? Bye."

He was never good at small talk, she recalled, laughing out loud.

She unlocked the back door and flicked on the kitchen light. The place depressed her. Stainless steel appliances, oak cabinets, and granite counters made her feel like she lived in a model home. That any minute a realtor would barge in with buyers in tow.

A stack of unopened mail lay on an old, red dinette table with metal legs and matching chairs. It was the only piece of furniture she'd brought with her and it was her favorite. She began sorting through the pile of letters, but her mind was on the chief. There had been something strange about his tone, like the time he'd called to tell her that her Appaloosa horse had died.

It was all junk mail and fluttered into the trash can. She opened the refrigerator with her left hand. A door full of low-fat yogurts reminded her of Bob Sharkey's warning: "Remember, kid, the camera adds ten pounds." *More rules*, she thought shaking her head. *Well, not tonight!*

She foraged through a forest of vitamin waters in search of an evil drink. Her mouth curled into a smile as her right hand brushed past a bottle of cab and clutched a full octane, red-canned Coke. As the door swung shut, she snapped the tab and took a defiant gulp.

Maria continued into the living room. It had high ceilings, soaring windows with white grills, and was appointed with gray and chrome furniture. It reminded her of a hotel lobby.

In retaliation, she'd hung Native blankets with rainbow stripes on the back of each chair. The contrast was stark, like her double life. A reservation girl posing as a media queen.

Her heels clicked past a glass-top table, then a sofa of gray chenille on the far side of the room. It was a long walk. A big screen TV she rarely watched hung over the fireplace, countered by a pumpkin-sized tribal pot on the floor.

Her cell phone rang. Opening her purse, she checked the number. Vanessa Wilcox rolled to voice mail.

She kicked off her slingbacks then climbed the spiral staircase. On the second floor, three bedrooms opened onto a tan hallway. The walls held framed photos of flowering cactus, alternating with beaded tribal shields.

Entering a bedroom converted to a study, she placed her purse and drink onto a desk situated beneath two wall-mounted shelves. On the top shelf, a collection of bound books by broadcasters from Cronkite to Walters stood in alphabetical order. On the lower ledge, a scrum of dog-eared paperbacks about Native American culture.

Crossing the room to a pair of French doors framed by long white drapes, she slipped her hands between each curtain and spread her arms like a symphony director. A brilliant sunset of red and orange burst through the balcony door, streaking the planked floor. Her memory flashed back to a bluff above Chinati Flats where the evening sunlight receded like golden lava flowing over the mountain ridge. It was a moment that reminds you of who you really are. *I love that girl.*

From the day she first stepped onto her balcony, Marie had been filled with wonder by the neighborhoods. Some, bordering lush green-belts, were fresh with emerald lawns and portecocheres. Others, cowering near freeway ramps, were treeless swaths of shotgun houses with perma-nent Christmas lights, blue tarp roofs, and makeshift antennas. The city's message, drummed in from the first day, was to seek the former. It troubled her. On the reservation, she knew, some had more than others. *But at least we're still one People.* Not in Houston.

She opened the door to the balcony and stepped out into the evening air. You could see over an oak grove beside the bayou, up to a sparkling cityscape. Across the water were pairs of mothers in running shoes, push-ing their babies in strollers along paths beneath the branches. At this age, she reflected, these fledglings were no different than their counterparts on the reservation. But their paths would diverge. After her experiences in the white man's world, she wondered, *Who would be the luckier?*

Maria retreated to the study and fell back into a couch near the desk. From her bag she retrieved her cell phone and tapped in her father's number.

"Hello," he wheezed.

"Hi, Dad. Sorry I didn't call back sooner."

"How are things in the big city, Wa-Xthe-Thomba?"

She smiled and responded with affected anger, "Stop, Dad. You're the only one who calls me that. No one even knows what it means."

"Nonsense, child," she heard him say. "Everyone knows Wa-Xthe-Thomba . . . Maria Tallchief, the Osage who went to New York City to be a ballerina."

"No, Dad. They don't."

He ignored her feigned protests. "Why then, when you were a little girl, would you not answer to Maria, only Wa?"

She closed her eyes and smiled. "Okay, okay." He was right. She remembered the story about Maria Tallchief's rise to fame. The chief would read it to her almost every night as she drifted to sleep, the mourning doves cooing outside her window. When she was lonesome or afraid, he would stroke her hair and say, *Doves are never lonely, Wa, because there are always two.* He promised her, as long as he lived, they would be like mourning doves. He would always be there for her.

Now, as if on cue, through the balcony door came the call of a dove. *Oo-wah.* Maria leaned back, her lower lip twitching. She loved the chief for that promise, but knew she was now on her own.

"Are you there, Wa?"

She sniffed and lifted her chin. "Yes. I was just wondering what happened to that little girl?"

"And to her father," he said wistfully.

"At least you're still the chief, just like always. The little girl . . . I guess she got lost somewhere along the way."

"She's not lost, Wa. She is you."

Is she? Maria thought, cradling the phone against her cheek as she had her father's hand. She pulled her knees up, curling into the crook of the sofa.

From the balcony—*oo-wah.*

"And what would you say to her today?" Maria asked.

There was a pause. "I would say, 'I'm sorry, Wa.'"

"Sorry for what?"

"For always telling her, 'Aim high, Wa-Xthe-Thomba. Show what the Chinati can do!' Ever since your bad time . . ."

77

"It's called rape, Dad," said Maria, jaw set, drawing herself tighter around the phone.

"All right. Ever since then, these thoughts have been with me. If I had not pushed you so hard, maybe, just maybe, you would not have volunteered to go to the prison that night."

Her stomach clinched. *It's true*, she realized. *His mandate to excel in the white man's world drove me relentlessly, like the beat of the sacred tribal drum.*

"Probably so," she said with an edge.

As soon as the sentence cleared her lips, she regretted it. She did not have to see the pain in his face. The line fell silent. Then muted sobs. The chief of the Chinati Nation was crying. Maria's eyes and lips compressed into thin lines. She fought back her own tears. She loved the chief. Her respect for him ran deep. She knew what a credit he was to her. There was little, if any, discord between them. They were solid. But now, as she pondered his words, she sensed a fissure. Was it possible her love for him had been compromised? With horror she dodged the question, asking herself instead, *In what way have I failed him?*

His voice cracked as he struggled to regain composure. "Something has happened on the reservation, Maria. It could change things forever. But it calls for someone with the strength . . . the experience to . . . to . . ." His voice drifted.

"Aim high?" she whispered.

"Perhaps," he responded with resignation. "That person is not, never has been, me. And because of that . . ." He could not continue.

In his voice she heard the deepest regret. But also, the resignation of an old warrior who doubted his nerve. According to tribal law, she knew such a fighter was never rebuked. Even if his failures had been costly to the tribe, unless from cowardice, they were condoned. Maria took a deep breath and brushed away a tear. Blame or regrets aside, she would honor that law. She could tell the key to assuage her father's guilt—true forgiveness—was in her hands alone. Only time would tell. Today something so serious was afoot the chief had pricked his most painful wound. She would help.

"Dad, let's deal first with the problem at hand. What's happened?"

"Do you remember Billy Strikeleather?"

Her eyebrows arched, and she shifted the phone to her right hand. "Billy? You know I do." Her pulse quickened.

"I'll tell it quickly."

The old chief related to his daughter the events of the past week. In most detail, however, he recounted his visit with Billy. "He's been through a lot. That can change a man for the better or the worse."

His choice of words, she knew, was prophetic. She'd met Leslie Strikeleather, even covered a story about her charity work as an NFL wife. She remembered thinking it was probably the only way Leslie could remain relevant since Billy was hanging onto his roster spot by a thread.

Whether it was provoked by Maria's prior relationship with Billy, her good looks, or her power to edit news clips, Leslie's cool demeanor with her was not lost on the Indian girl. *Whatever Billy's problems*, Maria thought, *Leslie had to be at the top of the list.*

The chief continued, "After our talk, I waited for Billy to come back to me with a plan for the minerals. After a few weeks, I figured he just wasn't up to it."

"Couldn't you find him on the reservation?" Maria asked.

"That's just it. He left without a word. But then one night he called and told me he had confirmed his suspicions. The minerals are the real thing, all right—rarer than any in the world."

Her reporter's instincts surfaced. She grabbed a pencil from the coffee table and began to jot down notes on the back of a *Texas Highways* magazine. "How did he know?"

"Well, that's the strange part. Seems like he knew a professor from his college days, a man named Clive, who helped him out."

"Last name?" she asked, tapping the pencil like a drumstick.

"I can't remember," he said. "But I wrote it down. It's here somewhere."

"Try to find it," she said.

She heard him fumbling through a pile of papers. Then a metallic clang as the phone hit the floor. "Crap!"

"Are you okay, Dad? I've never heard you swear."

"I'm fine. It's a bad habit. Don't do it."

"I won't."

"Aha. I found it. Clive Larson," he announced.

She wrote the name down with a question mark. Lying back, she sighed and closed her eyes.

With everything else in my life, why this? If God's giving me only what I can handle, she's sure as hell an optimist.

"I don't know Billy like you do," the chief said.

"That was a long time ago."

"I know, and that makes this request unfair. I just don't know how else to make a good decision."

Maria thought to herself how many times she'd gone to her father for help. How many times he had given the best advice he could. She'd try to repay.

"I knew Billy as a boy, Dad. He was kind and honest."

"It didn't work for you two, I know that," he said.

"And I was bitter for a while," Maria sighed. "When he left for college, we made all the usual promises about staying together. But in retrospect, I think I knew before Billy that it was impossible. I was right."

"I'm sorry to open old wounds, Wa. You have enough to deal with as it is."

"You can't just put life on hold when bad things happen or opportunities come along."

"I need to know if I can trust him. He's had some hard years since the NFL."

"What can I do?" she said.

"When I meet with the council to give my advice about the minerals," the chief said, "it will be the first time the tribe has had any hope of climbing out of poverty. But, with wealth comes compromise in principles. Billy was not immune."

"True."

"All I know is what I've heard in the media," she said. "But I can do some research. We have sources."

"I hope it's not asking too much."

"That's okay."

"There's something else in the back of my mind that's troubling me," the chief said.

"What's that?"

"Billy thinks the minerals surfaced by reason of a quake underground. Sam told him there had been fracking in the area."

"Like, for oil and gas exploration?" she asked.

"Yes. But there is also Massantipo."

"Who?" she whispered.

"My grandfather told me about a god of fire, the Devil's Soul, that lives deep inside the earth. When he's disturbed, there is thunder below.

He sends hot geysers of water—mineral water—to the surface. Other tribes, like the Utes in Colorado, know the story."

Maria smiled and sat up. "Those are wonderful tales, Dad, but we know these things aren't caused by gods."

"There's more."

The chief spoke about the Hopis from Arizona who predicted the future with ancient stone carvings. "One calls for a massive earthquake. The signs will be hot water coming to the surface in unexpected places, magical water that heals people."

"And you think this is such a quake?"

"Well, I can't help thinking the quake they predicted might not have been a literal one. Perhaps it was a violent shake-up of Indian values, threatening the foundations of our culture."

"Like the wealth that could come from the mineral discovery?" she offered.

"Maybe," the old Indian replied.

"Earthquakes come in all forms," she murmured, thinking of her life off the reservation. "Most without warning."

The lament of a mourning dove drifted through the balcony door. She waited for a companion call. There was none.

10

MARIA WALKED to the desk in the corner of her bedroom and switched on her laptop. As it blinked to life, she changed to khaki shorts and a pink T-shirt.

When she typed in "Billy Strikeleather," over twenty images appeared—touchdown runs, Mardi Gras parades, and finally, mug shots. She'd tried to avoid reading about him for the decade they'd been apart. With his exploits and her memories, it hadn't been easy.

She used her company password to run a background check. As the data flowed, her screen became a mosaic of Billy's life—a stained-glass window of triumph and tragedy. She felt lucky to have avoided the maelstrom, but also sadness for Billy.

Pictures of Leslie Strikeleather, some happy, most strained, confirmed the intensity of the storm. Maria wondered if she'd have fared better had their roles been reversed.

Maria couldn't deny her feelings for Billy. They remained locked away in a place she visited on lonely nights, or for no reason at all. He was for her, she knew, the 'might-have-been' that people hide—the dream they regret and cherish in equal measure.

She, therefore, also knew making an honest assessment of Billy for her father would be tough, maybe impossible. Resolving to approach it like a good reporter, Maria began taking notes.

Outstanding warrants: None. Lawsuits: None. Judgments: None. DWIs: Two. Worrisome, but not a deal killer. Otherwise, he was clean. The rest of the story would take more digging.

She jotted down the names of those in photos with Billy—most were before his decline. From senators to showgirls. Everyone had wanted a piece of him. The background service gave her his phone numbers and email addresses.

For the rest of the afternoon, Maria made calls. "We're running a story on retired NFL players," she lied. "What can you tell me about Billy Strikeleather?"

The responses were glowing. "Great guy. Too bad he got hurt. Should have run for office."

Maria logged out and stretched her arms behind her head. It was dark outside. She yawned and pushed away from the computer, then walked downstairs to the kitchen.

Leftovers in the refrigerator were turkey slices, low-fat cheese, and yogurt. Maria made a plate and opened a sparkling water. She returned to her study, sitting at a small table on the balcony. Aware of the quiet, she was more conscious of her solitude in the city.

Looking across rooftops, over storefronts, and up to the skyscrapers of downtown, Maria had never felt more alone. *It took years to get here and I've survived the worst this city can dish out*, she thought. *So, what is it that's troubling me? Maybe it's this business with Billy. He reached the top and look what happened. No. I'm smarter than that! I just need to keep plugging away. Aiming . . . aiming . . . no.*

The cold meat tasted good, clean. After a sip of water, she pulled a pencil from her pocket and began to decipher her notes.

When dinner was finished, she closed her eyes and leaned back, feeling the warm breeze. She thought about the last day she'd been with Billy—the Billy she'd known before he hit the big day.

It was graduation day from the reservation school. Maria had finished first in her class of ten, and the next day would be heading to the border town of Laredo to attend South Texas Community College. Billy, by then a rising football phenom at the University of Texas, was home from Austin for a visit.

Although they'd agreed to date other people while he was away, for Maria it meant any of the five boys in her class. For Billy, it was the pick of thousands of starstruck coeds. In his letters to Maria, he'd tried to diminish his social life, but neither believed it.

After ceremonies were over at the school, she changed into a white sundress made by her mother and waited for Billy on her front porch swing.

He pulled up in his new yellow Mustang, "on loan" from an alum. Dressed in faded jeans and a golf shirt, when he uncoiled from the car, she knew immediately that this muscled figure was now more man than boy.

Billy strode toward her, hands in his pockets, cool and chic. A lock of jet-black hair blew across his forehead. He casually brushed it back. His gait was the same, but with a subtle change of rhythm, just shy of a swagger. His grin was familiar, but now more confident—born, she knew, of experience.

"Hey there," he called out, as he approached the stairs. "You look great."

"Compared to those fancy coeds in Austin? I doubt it," she said with a desperate casualness.

He gathered her in his arms, "You know better than that."

If only that were true, she thought.

She knew she could not compete for Billy against his hordes of admirers in Austin. By season's end, he would be beyond her reach—a full-blown football icon. She had therefore decided to preserve her dignity by parting company with him as only a friend. But the sight of him elicited in her an animal sexuality, triggering a hot flow at her core. Her face flushed.

Sensing her excitement, Billy whispered into her ear, "Want to take a ride? Maybe out to the cliffs?" The thought of returning with him to the rim of Saint Helena Canyon made her heart race. They had lain there so many nights on a woven blanket, under a canopy of stars.

The temptation was palpable. The longer they embraced, the more her body yearned for his touch. Before, they had always stopped short of the ultimate intimacy. But now she was electric with desire, her body headed off on a path of its own. Willing to take any risk to possess him, if only for a moment.

Billy caressed her face, his gaze meeting her hungry eyes. She felt her breasts come alive against his chest. He responded by thrusting his hips hard against hers, confirming his arousal.

But then, somewhere deep within her, an alarm sounded. She realized that her most defining strengths—the will to make her own decisions, to stay in control—were slipping away. She weighed the risks of yielding to Billy before, and made her decision. She couldn't backslide now. With trembling hands, she pushed him away.

Billy looked hurt. Maria buried her face in her hands and began to cry.

After a long minute, she looked up. To her surprise, his frown had changed to a soft smile. "Don't cry, Maria. I understand," he said. It was something that would never fade from Maria's memory.

What a fool I am, Billy thought. *Of course, she can't give in. That wouldn't be the Maria I know*. As young men sometimes do before their judgment is clouded by a cynical world, Billy then made a choice that would bind him to her always. He walked away.

His car spun up a small cloud of dust that hung in the summer sun then drifted away—along with Maria's dreams.

Now, a decade later, as she sat on her balcony thinking of Billy, she felt the same familiar tension.

11

OLIVER'S PINK PUEBLO was carved into the wall of a small box canyon, along with four other dwellings. He slowed his Karmann Ghia to a stop in the driveway and checked his cell phone for messages. There was a text from Vestal with a phone number to contact, Alex Bronski of the United Auto Workers union.

He dialed and waited.

"Bronski here," a voice answered pleasantly.

"Hello. This is Oliver Greentree."

"Greentree, right," replied Alex Bronski, the union CEO, from his executive office at the UAW headquarters in Detroit. "We just heard the story about the dysprosium mineral discovery from Leland Vestal. Good union man. So, what's the latest?"

"Well, sir, the word is Trans-National is going to make a proposal to the Chinati at the next council meeting. The offer will be a joint venture deal with a substantial signing bonus to the tribe."

"Great," Bronski said sarcastically.

"If Trans-National wrangles a partnership with the Indians, those

Big Oil whores will see to it that the dysprosium additive is never produced at all."

Bronski was a career union man. At fifty-four, he was in his prime. But times had been tough for organized labor, especially in the south. The union, and Bronski, needed a break. Thirty-eight-cent gasoline, courtesy of a union mine in Texas, would be just the ticket.

"Look, Green," said the union boss, "for this to all work out, the council's got to come down right on this thing, get that additive on the shelves. That means nixing any deal with Trans-National. Vestal told us you had the stroke to make that happen."

Oliver turned off the engine. "It's Greentree, Mr. Bronski, and I don't know what Leland said to you. All I know is, there are some in the tribe who would prefer to look for outside financing. If that is of interest to the UAW, there is a chance the deal could be done."

"If we weren't interested, we wouldn't be talking."

"The council meeting is coming up soon. If you want my help, I need two things."

"Shoot."

"First, one hundred thousand dollars wired to my account, nonrefundable. Another hundred thousand if I can convince the tribe to turn down Trans-National and do a deal with you. Second, I need bait to bring around one of our council members—the principal of our local school. An administrative job with the union would do."

"You've got balls asking for that kind of money up front, Green."

"Greentree."

"Right. Let's just say this. If I decide to send the money and find out later that you never had the stroke Vestal represented, we'll be back to see you both."

Oliver's hands were damp. The line was silent.

"Well?" Bronski growled.

"And the administrative job?"

"Trustee of a regional UAW Education Fund. One hundred thousand a year. But only if the tribe borrows from us, joins the UAW as a union shop, and the additive hits the shelves within one year."

Oliver took a deep breath. "You've got a deal."

Bronski turned up the heat. "Just to be clear, Oliver—we get what we want, so do you. Otherwise, this will not be a positive experience for you or your principal."

"Understood," said Oliver.

"Good night, Green. We'll be watching."

12

DOLPH BARSTOW SAT SHOTGUN in a black Cadillac Escalade speeding down US 59 toward the Granger Ranch, twenty miles southwest of Houston. At the wheel was his chauffeur, Juan—a stocky Latino with a license to carry.

From the back seat, his legislative aide, the gangly son of a rich contributor, thrust the society page of the *Houston Chronicle* over the governor's shoulder. "Here's what's on the agenda tonight, sir."

Dolph fished some glasses from the breast pocket of his black suede jacket and read aloud. "In New York City, it's the Metropolitan Museum Gala, LA the Oscars, Houston the Cattle Baron's Ball. All are held in ballrooms. Only one doubles as a barn."

"That's just peachy," the governor scoffed and threw down the paper. "You know," he paused to light a Kinky Friedman Lone Star cigar, "I spent over ten million dollars of other people's money to get this job—just so I can fly around the state hitting them up for more at cattle calls like these."

As shopping malls and car lots whizzed by, Dolph remembered the early days of his political career. Fruit stands and gas stations in the South

Texas valley were the venues where he had rallied his first constituents. *Half were wetbacks and the other half dirt farmers*, he smiled to himself, *but every vote counted. We used to talk to them about real life issues like rain and boll weevils. Not the high-dollar horseshit sure to be slung around tonight.*

The governor lowered his window to vent smoke. "How much farther?"

"Ten minutes," Juan replied.

The Cadillac turned off the highway and snaked along five miles of farm road. It was dusk. Ahead a flashing sheriff's car marked the front gate to the ranch. Juan slowed and saluted the officer, then headed the limo up a private lane.

A mammoth two-story plantation house loomed from behind tall rows of oleanders. Eight white columns, each the width of a live oak, gave the place the feel of a Margaret Mitchell novel. Pulling into a circular driveway, it seemed to Dolph like they'd entered a time machine.

"Jesus," Dolph murmured, surveying the mansion. "Next it'll be Butterfly McQueen with a tray of mint juleps."

"Who?" the aide asked.

"Forget it."

Dolph put on his game face and climbed out. Waiting at the stone walk was a welcoming committee of Vanessa and Ed Wilcox, and Adriana Whitlock, the mayor of Houston. A step behind was her husband, Zach, a real estate developer.

"Well, Vanessa, it's good to see you, honey," the governor said with a plastic grin. "How long's it been? The Rainbow Room in Manhattan, right?"

"Why, I think you're right, governor. New Year's Eve of '07, wasn't it? The NBC party. Now that was a bash. We're glad you could make it tonight."

Vanessa, turned out in a low-cut top with frilly sleeves, a turquoise necklace, and designer jeans, was in her element. A silver belt-buckle the size of a Pop-Tart cinched her waist to seven-eighths of normal, storing enough potential energy to jump-start a Tahoe.

Pushing back her black Stetson hat, she stood tiptoed in her ivory ostrich boots with hummingbird inlays to give Dolph a hug.

Ed Wilcox, a squat man with a Texas tuxedo—a traditional tux coat and white shirt over wrangler jeans with a silver belt buckle—bobbed around the couple like a banty rooster.

"Whatcha know, Dolph?" he said in a high twang, drawing himself up to eye level with the governor's string tie.

"Not much, Ed," he replied, reaching down to pat his shoulder like a puppy.

Dolph turned to the mayor, a slender Latina in her mid-forties. His eyebrows arched and a smile crossed his lips. He admired how well she filled out her western cut white blouse spangled with blue stars. A leopard of a woman, she extended her hand with a slow, confident gaze. "Hello. I'm Adriana Whitlock."

He studied her angular face—cinnamon with high cheekbones, a strong jaw line, and onyx eyes. Her grip was firm but feminine. His first thought was, *A woman, particularly a brown one, should be cleaning—not holding—the mayor's office. But there can be exceptions.*

"This is my husband, Zach," she said. The rangy carrottop leaned in and, from a green plaid sleeve with pearl snaps, offered his hand.

"Evening, governor."

Dolph turned from Adriana to Zach. As he shook his hand, his eyes narrowed. He wondered, *How in the world was this match made?*

"Seems like you'd have run into each other before now," Vanessa said to the two politicians, taking Dolph's arm.

"I don't get down to Houston enough," Dolph said. "But, I'm glad to be here now."

"Me, too. Come on in," Vanessa said, leading the group down the sidewalk.

The path circumvented the house and ended at a party barn the size of an aircraft hangar. They entered through double doors to a yawning ballroom with soaring rafters and a wooden dance floor, rimmed by white linen tables. On the far end, an elevated stage with a podium overlooked the proceedings. The party was well underway.

"I hope you're hungry, governor," Vanessa cooed, pointing to a buffet table the length of an eighteen-wheeler, flanked by four open bars.

Country music blared from overhead speakers. "Nice spread," Dolph called to her over the steel guitars. "Who's the owner?"

"It's been in the Granger family for a century and a half—a working cattle ranch until the '50s. When the city limits closed in and land went to $10,000 an acre, they sold everything but the house, the barn, and the minerals. Since then the only herds have been two-legged."

The group strolled the length of the building, working the crowd. Scores of cowboy knockoffs, some dressed like Ed, others with leather coats and *bolos*, swore allegiance to the governor.

"I've never met a person yet," Dolph mused, "who hasn't claimed to have voted for me."

Waves of wannabe cattle barons wove their way through the throng like proud-cut geldings, with bleached blonde wives sporting all things sparkly and breasts a cup size larger than last year. The barn not qualifying as a homestead, cowboy hats stayed on.

Vanessa pulled Dolph's elbow, steering him toward the bandstand. "There are some folks I'd like you to meet," she said.

They walked the remaining steps to the head table where the diners stood to greet the governor. He started around the circle with a Jack Nicholson grin, chest puffed and head bobbing like a Texas horned toad. That is, until a tall, slender Native American woman with straight black hair and dark eyes extended her hand.

Vanessa took Maria's shoulder. "Governor, I'd like you to meet my friend, Maria Cloud."

"Why, yes . . . the TV anchor lady," Dolph said, grasping her hand for a split second too long. "It's a pleasure see you in person, Ms. Cloud."

"Likewise," she smiled.

"Do you mind if we join you?" he asked.

"Please do." As she turned, the stage lights ricocheted off her single strap black leather dress, belted with silver links. Nothing about Maria Cloud spoke of cowboys. *By comparison, she's a cut above,* Dolph reflected.

The governor held a chair for Maria then sat down beside her. A waiter in a white coat offered a tray of wines.

"Vanessa here says she'll buy us a drink," he said.

"How nice of her. I'll have cabernet."

"Make mine Jack Daniels on the rocks," said Dolph.

"So, governor, you've got a lot of supporters here. How do you get around to all of them?"

"I talk to the ones I like," he said with a wink.

"I've heard some buzz from Washington about a presidential run."

Dolph sat back and wrinkled his nose. "Oh, that's just whiskey talk. They'd take apart an old boy like me in a New York minute."

Maria sipped her wine, looking at him over the rim. "I'm not so sure. Jobs and energy are on people's minds. You might have a shot."

Snaking his arm around the back of her chair, Dolph tilted his head toward hers. "Well, it's tempting because all I'd have to do is tell the truth about what we've done here in Texas."

"Now, that might be a challenge for some politicians," Vanessa weighed in with radar hearing from across the table. It drew a polite chuckle from the group.

Maria pressed on. "How do you sell that in states not having oil and gas reserves?"

She'd thrown him a cantaloupe of a question and Dolph wasted no time bashing away at it. "One word—fracking. You've heard of it, I'm sure. They pump explosive fluids into rock formations and blast out the hydrocarbon gases. They come to the surface in a slurry where they're separated from the liquid and trucked off to market. There are shale deposits all over the country waiting to be tapped. When the gas starts flowing, so does the revenue—and revenue means jobs."

Maria's eyes narrowed as she recalled the chief's story about fracking near the Rio Hot Springs.

Buck Olmeyer and his wife arrived at the table just in time to hear the governor's pronouncement.

"Howdy, everyone!" said the oil executive. "Sounds like Dolph's got the energy crisis all worked out over here."

Niceties were exchanged. Buck sat to the governor's right, flanked by his wife.

Judy Olmeyer was a survivor. At fifty-seven she was close to Buck's age and a veteran of the corporate wars. Plain by contrast in her simple blue and white striped maxi dress, she tipped her big Texas hair toward Vanessa and whispered with a Mona Lisa smile, "Looks like plenty of fat stock to slaughter this year."

"Now, now, Judy," Vanessa replied, "it's all for a good cause. Who can argue with cancer research?"

"Not me. I'm sure they're all driven by philanthropic zeal."

Vanessa motioned to a waiter. "Have a drink, honey."

To Maria's left sat the mayor and her husband. Maria smiled and said, "We met once before at a Hispanic Chamber of Commerce lunch. It was one of my first assignments for Channel 7, and you were kind enough to give me an interview."

"I hope I had something newsworthy to say," the mayor replied in a self-effacing voice.

The waiter offered wine. Adriana took white. Zach asked for a beer.

"I've been admiring your necklace," Maria said to Adriana.

"Thank you," Adriana responded. The amethyst and silver choker lay flat across her neck catching the light as she sipped her wine. She tabled her drink and asked, "Where are you from, Maria?"

The question hung for a second. Maria Whitecloud traced a circle around the base of her glass. Though not a new question, it made her uncomfortable, especially around money. Adriana Sanchez Whitlock waited, her eyes fixed on the other dark-skinned woman.

Looking up, Maria answered softly, "I was raised on an Indian reservation in the Big Bend. Chinati."

Without waiting for the reciprocal question, Adrianna volunteered, "And I in the 'barrios' of East Houston."

Each considered her journey and the long odds of meeting in a venue like the Cattle Baron's Ball.

Maria scanned the table, then with raised eyebrow said to Adriana with a smile, "I think what's newsworthy is *us*."

"*Sí*," the Latina responded, to which Maria said in Chinati, "*v-V*." Yes.

Across the table, Governor Barstow was concluding his lesson in hydrocarbon economics: "So you see, in the end it's all about gasoline prices. Bring them down and it's like a tax cut. Folks will buy enough cars, homes, and iPhones to knock any recession in the head."

"And on that note," Buck announced, standing, "I'd invite those so inclined to step out for a cigar."

"Not for me," Ed declared. "Gave them up years ago."

"Same here," said Zach.

Figures, Dolph said to himself, dismissing both like Alamo deserters. Dolph stood and wheeled toward Buck. "Looks like you and me, pards."

They strolled toward a side door, pausing to shake hands at each table. On stage the emcee, a local country western deejay, was warming up the crowd for the auction by calling out last year's big bidders. As Dolph and Buck slipped out the door, they heard him bellow, "Now where the hell is Olmeyer?"

Buck scowled. That kind of familiarity, he believed, had to be earned. He'd paid his dues on the way to the top and so should they. He hated hangers-on, social groupies who made a living out of being "friends" with the moneyed crowd. He felt the same about the trust fund babies of which there was no shortage in Houston. People like Luke Stasney.

Dolph reached in the side pocket of his jacket for two Kinky Friedmans and handed one to Buck.

"You know, I've had enough of that gink," the oilman growled, hitching his right thumb over his shoulder toward the stage. He ripped the plastic off the cigar with his teeth. "Tomorrow he's history."

Dolph's lips sneered as he bit off the end of his Kinky and spit it between Buck's boots. He pulled out his lighter.

When both stogies were lit, Buck addressed the governor. "That was a nice campaign speech to the table, Dolph. Spreading it a little thick, aren't you?"

Putting his hand on Buck's shoulder, Dolph retorted with a toothy grin, "You just worry about your fucking earnings and leave the politics to me, Bub. By the way, what's new with your half-breed quarterback? I'm sure he's weaseled his way into this soiree."

"Strikeleather? What's it to you?"

Twirling the cigar between his lips, Dolph took a drag and spewed smoke past Buck's ear. "My boys in the Rangers tell me he's working on the dysprosium deal with the Indians now. And he's been talking to Stasney."

Buck coughed into his hand, masking his surprise. *How did he know?* he asked himself. "Well, Stasney's busted—couldn't beat his way out of a bag," Buck said. "And don't fret over that drunken Indian. We've got him handled, too."

"Like hell you do," Dolph said looking Buck in the eye. "Stasney would do anything to get back in the game and that redskin's crazy enough to give him a ticket."

Strains of "Cotton-Eyed Joe" wafted from the ballroom across the backyard where the men stood smoking. The governor of Texas swatted a mosquito from his neck and flicked away the corpse. A speck of blood smeared his palm. Clinching the cigar in his teeth, he brushed his hand on his Wranglers.

Buck had underestimated Dolph. It was the worst kind of mistake to make and he knew it. *I've just got to be calm. No reason to panic.* He watched lines of cattle in the pasture across the road, swaying as they plodded home to a real hay barn. A real cowboy leaned against a real pickup silhouetted in the sunset. The red dot of his cigarette confirmed he could likewise spot the cigar men weaving their web.

Dolph broke the silence. "Buck, you've got to put an end to this Rio Hot Springs shit, or someone else will do it for you."

"What the hell's the big rush?" Buck said. "These Indians have barely got the brains to string beads, much less develop rare earth minerals. This needs to be handled with precision, not a sledge hammer."

"Who do you think knows about this rare earth mineral thing?"

"You, me, Strikeleather, Oliver, and now Stasney."

The governor shook his head and sucked on his Freidman. "What the hell do you take me for? Strikeleather has already met with his old professor. We know all about your 'handling' of Larson's wife and the research you did on his mineral theory."

Buck clinched his jaw. He hated surprises as much as he hated this governor. *Wait till I get hold of Colt.* "You didn't ask me about Larson," Buck volleyed. "Besides, your boys were in on that, too. You knew we couldn't take a chance. Looks like we were right."

Dolph looked both ways, then hissed at Olmeyer from close range, "Don't you get it? If that whole cover-up gets out, and Larson's theory proves true, you and your company will be finished. I can see it now, 'Oil Company Scuttles Cheap Gasoline for Ten Years.' Trans-National's stock will be lining bird cages and you'll be playing gin with Bernie Madoff."

Buck never flinched. Instead, his face steeled like a Vegas dealer. "Now *you* listen. If we go down, so does the whole fucking state. Tax revenues from gasoline float the budget. If Larson is right and this miracle mineral dysprosium increases gas mileage tenfold, we're both out of business. So, don't lecture me about Strikeleather. I know what's at stake."

"All I know," Dolph said, flicking ash from Buck's lapel, "is if we don't get control of this, we'll be pledging allegiance to the Chinati flag— if they've got one."

They walked a dirt trail leading to the entry road and stopped. An auctioneer's banter drifted down from the barn.

Buck glared at Dolph. "Look, the Feds' tit is in the same ringer, they just don't know it yet. When their gas tax disappears, they can't fix roads. Gasoline revenues fund damn near all of that. You think there's a job shortage now, wait until there's no money to buy asphalt."

"Buck, you don't even know how much dysprosium they've got and how pure. What the hell's the hold up? I've got the big boys at bay, but I can't do it forever."

"We do know."

Dolph threw down his cigar and stomped it out. "What the hell?"

"Our man on the ground sent us samples. We scoped the site with magnetic resonance from high altitude, too."

"Well?" Dolph barked.

"It's the mother lode. We can't explain how it happened. Best guess is a freak earthquake so deep it wasn't detected—probably set off by fracking."

"So, what are you waiting for? Keep fracking that son of a bitch until it closes up again."

"It's not that simple. The quake opened a fissure winding close to twenty miles down. Solid rock on either side. There's no guarantee more explosions will do a damn thing."

"Can you seal it at the surface? Cook up an accident?"

Buck nodded. "We're working on it. But that trail would be hard to cover. It would have to be an inside job."

"You've got your man on the ground, right?"

"He doesn't have the expertise. We need to cut a deal with the Indians, a joint venture maybe, so our guys can get in there and wire it up right. Make it look like a real accident."

It was pitch black now and the men turned back.

"You know," said the governor, "while you're thinking about all this, Strikeleather and Stasney are liable to work a deal of their own with the Chinati."

They walked in silence. Dolph put his hand on Buck's shoulder and turned him face to face. "This thing goes higher than you know."

"What are you talking about?"

"I can't sit on this while you finesse Strikeleather."

"Who else is in on it?"

Dolph sighed and looked up at the stars strewn like diamonds across the Texas sky. "Let's just say there are organizations you've got no idea about that aren't going to sit around while you circle jerk with those redskins. Every oil producer in the country, hell, the world, is at risk."

"You're talking about E-4. We've heard about that group."

"It's not just a club, Buck—it includes the governors and their biggest contributors from Oklahoma, Texas, Mississippi, and Louisiana. Tentacles run to Wall Street and the Middle East. It's the closest thing to a cartel we've had in this country, dancing on the edge of anti-trust and racketeering. The only reason we haven't been busted is the attorney generals are in on it, too."

"Holy shit," Buck murmured, perspiration running down his neck.

"One thing is sure," Dolph said with a squint, "they're not going to be held hostage by a ragtag bunch of Indians, a drunken quarterback, or corporate fat cats like you."

The two men reached the head of the trail and veered toward the party barn. Live music was blaring and guests were drifting out for air. The two men paused short of the doors.

"Look, Buck," Dolph said, "we've known each other a long time.

You want to finish your career on top at Trans-National, and I want to be president. Neither can happen if this story gets out or profits evaporate."

"I know."

They walked into the ballroom to the sound of the Truck Suckers and their latest hit, "Chain Gang."

At the head table, all plates but two were filled with barbeque remains. The Suckers were hitting their stride and conversation was a challenge.

"Does he disappear like this often?" Maria called across the table to Judy Olmeyer.

"Constantly," she laughed, holding her wine glass up for a refill. She turned back to Ed and Vanessa who were belting out "Deep in the Heart of Texas" in time with the Suckers.

"Goes with the territory," Adriana smiled. "Politicians get used to it."

Zach leaned over.

"They've also got a different agenda than a poor little mayor's husband like me."

Maria threw back her head and laughed. She liked the Whitlocks.

"I always thought Big Oil drove Houston just like the rest of the state," Maria said.

"It does," Zach responded, pulling on a Shiner Bock. "The difference is we've got more than our share of the have-nots, too."

The reporter sipped her cabernet and asked, "Do you mean oil profits don't float all boats in Houston?"

The mayor glanced at her husband, then back at Maria. "There are some things you should understand about Houston politics. Mayoral elections are supposed to be bipartisan—no party affiliation. For the most part it works that way. This is probably the only city in Texas where Big Oil doesn't control things."

"Interesting," Maria said, cupping her ear against the Suckers.

"The irony is," Adriana continued, "Trans-National made ten billion last quarter—that's with a capital B—and their home office is here. Yet, all that revenue has moved horizontally. Not much trickles down."

"My God, look around," Maria exclaimed. "Seems like a lot made it down to this crowd."

Adriana glanced around then moved closer. "Look. It's not so much about oil. It's big money in general. Years ago, big money in Texas was new money. Most of it came out of the ground and made poor men rich overnight."

"Wildcatters?" Maria asked.

"A lot were," she responded. "Some were lumbermen from East Texas. Most remembered their roots. Families got rich, but never forgot to 'dance with the one that brung'em.' Folks looked out for each other."

"And now?"

"Well, you judge," she said. "Today I went to the top of the biggest bank building downtown, seventy stories up, to meet with a family company worth billions. Their money came from the land—mining, oil, and cattle. They said they wanted to increase their 'footprint' in Houston."

"I didn't know mayors made house calls," Maria said.

"Only the pretty ones," Zach said, putting his arm around Adriana.

The mayor took a sip of wine and continued. "So, in walks a thirty-year-old kid with a business degree from Ole Miss, rattling peanuts in a plastic cup, and hands me a card saying CEO. His plan, he tells me, is to buy houses cheap for back taxes, sell them on credit to folks who can't qualify for a mortgage, and wait for them to default—then take back the houses and do it all again."

The three sat silently.

"It's not the oil tycoons," Adriana said finally. "It's what the concentration of wealth has done to their children. At least that's my take."

Maria thought about her father's story. An earthquake of a different kind.

Zach put his hand over Adriana's. "You don't get elected governor with that speech," he laughed.

"Time for us to head home," the mayor announced to the table.

"Oh, come on now, Adriana, the party's just getting started," Vanessa slurred.

"I've got the early broadcast tomorrow. Can I bum a ride home with you two?" Maria asked the Whitlocks.

"Of course," Adriana responded.

"Now, now," Judy bellowed, sloshing wine in her lap. "You won't find a cowboy if you leave the roundup!"

Maria rolled her eyes and took Zach's free arm. The three walked toward the door. As they turned to thank their hosts, Maria caught sight of a broad-shouldered, dark-haired man across the room. His back was to her as he posed for pictures and autographed footballs.

While Zach and Adriana said their goodnights, Maria watched Billy Strikeleather ease away from the group of fans and drift toward the La-Cour table where his wife was sitting next to the lieutenant governor, Ben Hitchcock, a cross between a bull rider and a used car salesman.

As Billy approached, Hitchcock stood unsteadily and walked several steps from the table to greet him. He put an arm around Billy and held out his opposite hand. Billy shook it. The politician then began to talk while making throwing motions.

Adriana returned to where Maria was standing and, noticing the direction of her gaze, whispered into her right ear. "Do you know him?"

Maria tipped her head toward Adriana and answered from the side of her mouth, "Why would you think so?"

"Well, he is one of the state's most powerful politicians. I assumed you might have interviewed him or . . ."

"Billy, a politician?" Maria interrupted with a shake of her head.

Adriana frowned, nonplussed.

Realizing Adriana's confusion, Maria laughed and patted the mayor's arm. "Let's just say I've spent more quality time with Billy Strikeleather than the lieutenant governor."

Adriana's eyes opened wide. "Oh no. I'm sorry, Maria. I didn't realize."

"Don't worry about it. Are we ready?"

As they walked toward the front door, Maria glanced back one more time. Billy's back was to the LaCour table and Luke was leaning over Leslie. He put his hand on her shoulder. She set down her wine and looked up, flicking back her hair. He bent to whisper in her ear.

Maria's breath quickened. She felt her body come to attention.

From the circle drive, she heard Adriana call, "Are you coming, Maria?"

Billy turned, as if called.

Maria started to wave, but lowered her hand.

Seeing no one, he turned away.

"Yes," she replied, and walked out.

As she slid into the back seat of the mayor's car, Adriana smiled and handed her a business card. "If you ever want to talk politics again, give me a call. My cell number's on the back."

13

CLIVE SAT IN AN ARMCHAIR looking out the front window. It was Saturday, daybreak. The city was just waking up.

He saw a pair of runners, silent but for the sound of their shoes scuffing the pavement. Across the street, his pajama-clad neighbor came out for the newspaper. A dog barked.

Clive sipped coffee from a chipped mug. Billy had set a meeting that morning with Luke Stasney for eight o'clock to discuss the Rio Hot Springs minerals. He hadn't consulted the professor.

When Billy told him about it, Clive bristled. "How do you know he's right for the job?"

Clive thought, *I've taught rich kids. They're not worth spit.* But his real beef was with Billy acting on his own.

He drummed his fingers on the armrest. *First the big lummox comes running to me for help, then he starts peddling the idea on his own like a door-to-door snake-oil salesman. I wish I'd told him to go it alone.*

It was a lie and Clive knew it. The meeting made him feel relevant, alive for the first time in years. He checked his watch again.

In his lap was a profile of Luke Stasney from the *Houston Chronicle* archives. He studied it for the tenth time.

After another gulp of coffee, he stood and rolled his shoulders, then walked to the kitchen. The wall clock read seven thirty. He remembered Billy was always late—to everything. *Some things never change.*

He refilled his cup from a glass coffeepot. On the way back to the living room, he stopped and took stock in a hall mirror.

His bow tie was straight. His khaki suit was pressed. The cuffs of his yellow shirt were not frayed. And his chocolate wing tips were buffed to a high shine. He raised his chin with an approving nod. *Not bad.*

Clive's cell went off. He punched the answer button while looking through the blinds. "I see you. You're late."

Snapping off the wall switch, he slipped the Stasney clipping into his briefcase, and hoisted it to his shoulder. With his white fedora pulled low across his brow, he grasped the doorknob and pushed his way out. The sound of the aluminum screen door slamming behind him frightened a squirrel.

Billy swung open the passenger door of his truck. "Morning. You look like you mean business."

"Very funny," Clive shot back. "At least you could have worn a tie."

"Don't own one anymore," Billy said with a grin.

"Beautiful. Let's get going."

They drove down Clive's street and took a left onto Westheimer, the oldest artery into downtown. Once the heart of the business center, dilapidated buildings now hugged the street. Most were no more than two stories with the name of the original owner spelled out in brick over the door.

Clive laid his briefcase on his knees and looked at Billy as if he was calling on him in class. "So, tell me about Stasney."

Billy gave him the backstory about his college days with Luke and the history of Stasney Energy.

Clive squinted. "So why would he want to help you . . . us?"

"Well, we didn't get that far when we spoke. I think we'll find out soon enough."

The professor replied in the precise style in which teachers not only talk but think, and with the suspicious edge common to men who have lost it all. "So, we really don't know his motives, or do we?"

"He's never lied to me. That's worth something."

Clive turned back to the street ahead, scowling.

The truck pulled to a stop in a lot two blocks from One Trans-National Plaza. They got out and walked to the self-pay metal box. Billy stuffed a five-dollar bill into the slot—a third the price of the parking garage—and the pair set off for Stasney's office.

The sun was cresting the skyline. Clive strode ahead, pulling his hat down against the glare. As they approached the big revolving doors, he waited for Billy.

"Look, I'm not sure what to expect," Billy said, "but we might as well give it to him straight."

"Hell, we don't know enough to be coy," Clive growled. "If I'd had more than a day's notice, I could have been better prepared."

Billy glanced sideways at the professor. *Maybe I should have kept him in the backroom*, he thought. "Okay, okay. Just follow my lead."

"Like hell," the older man snorted. "There's something you're not telling me, and it pisses me off."

Billy spun the door open. Inside was a guard in a wrinkled uniform slouched behind a granite counter. He was thirty at best, with a snake tail tattoo slithering out from the neck of his shirt.

"I don't want to know where the head is," Billy whispered to Clive, tilting his head toward the guard's midriff.

"Sign in," the guard muttered without looking up from his tabloid paper.

Billy reached for the registration book. "We're here for a meeting at . . ."

"Just sign in."

"We heard you," Clive barked.

A faint smile crossed Billy's lips as he wrote down their names and destination.

Turning the register around, the snake man threw his paper aside and looked the professor over. Nodding, he droned, in a patronizing tone, "Okay, old timer. Stasney Energy. Seventy-fifth floor." He reached for the phone. "I'll let 'em know you're coming."

Clive strode off, calling out over his shoulder, "That won't be necessary, sonny boy. They're expecting us. You just go ahead and dive back into *War and Peace* there."

Billy caught up and hustled him around the corner to the third bank of elevators. Their heels echoed off the polished floors.

There was a sign that said, *Floors 50 to 80*. Billy pushed the button and they stepped into a mirrored car. The overhead television screen was blank.

"I feel like I'm about to be plucked," Clive murmured, adjusting his bow tie.

Billy tucked in his shirt and brushed a piece of lint from the lapel of his navy sport coat. He slipped his left foot from a black loafer and used the sock foot to shine the other shoe—then the reverse.

Clive studied the process with a smirk. *At least the shoes match.*

"What?" Billy asked, noting Clive's expression.

The elevator doors opened into the offices of Stasney Energy. A receptionist with a helium bouffant asked for their card.

"Billy Strikeleather and Clive Larson," Billy said. "We've got an appointment, no cards."

"Have a seat," the girl gushed, recognizing the football star. "Can I get you some coffee?"

"Yes. I'll have mine black," Clive butted in.

"Oh, of course."

"Dr. Pepper for me, thanks," Billy said with a smile.

She motioned them toward a black leather divan and oversized chair in the corner. The professor and his student drifted in that direction, taking in the soaring ceilings with ornate molding, the posh rugs, and pricy art.

Clive craned his neck over the couch to view the city below. Absent-mindedly, he buffed his shoes on the back of each calf.

He caught himself, but too late. When he stole a glance at Billy, his companion was shaking his head in mock reprimand.

"Fuck you," the old professor mouthed.

From the hallway Luke's secretary emerged, locking eyes with Billy. News traveled fast.

"Mr. Strikeleather?"

"Yes."

"I'm Nadia. Follow me please."

"My pleasure," he said with a half bow.

She giggled and led the way.

Exasperated, the professor put his palm on his forehead then pulled it slowly across his face. *Wonderful*, he thought. *Betting my future on a frat boy. Just wonderful.*

They followed her to the conference room. Billy winked goodbye as she closed the door. Clive walked around the mahogany table with a low whistle. "This is high cotton, son. Get your head back in the game."

"Right."

"Billy," they heard from behind. "How are you?"

Luke Stasney and two others entered the room.

Billy shook hands with Luke, then nodded toward Clive. "This is Professor Clive Larson. He's been working with me on the mineral project."

"Jack Massey, head of exploration, and Faisal Ahmad, chief geologist."

After greetings, they sat. The two Stasney men were opposite Clive and Billy, with Luke at the end.

Billy and Luke exchanged pleasantries about football, University of Texas, and the old days while the others sized each other up.

"So, Billy, tell us about the Rio Hot Springs," Luke said in a casual tone.

Billy related the story of the mineral discovery and the subsequent shooting.

"Okay, Billy," Luke said with a cavalier lift of his chin. "That's the craziest story I've heard in a while. Tell me why we should chase this rabbit?"

Billy leaned forward with a level stare. "You know, Luke, I'm feeling about as welcome as an outhouse breeze. Maybe this load's too big for your wheelbarrow."

Clive's leg was trembling under the table. *Don't blow this, Billy.*

Jack Massey began drumming a pencil on the table.

Ignoring the slight, Luke steepled his fingers under his chin and stared at Billy.

A few seconds passed, then Billy reached for his briefcase and said, "Well, thanks for the soda, Luke."

"Hold it," Massey said. "We've looked over the data you sent, Billy. We're interested."

Clive exhaled and leaned back in his high leather chair.

Luke shot Massey a scowl, but he ignored it and pressed on.

"We'll need more testing—a lot more," Faisal added.

"We can get more samples, but what I gave you should prove this is for real," said Billy.

"What we need most is proof of the properties of dysprosium," Faisal responded.

Billy turned to Clive.

"We tested it back in 1990 at UT, on a small scale of course."

"And?" Faisal asked.

"We confirmed the molecular composition of dysprosium is consistent with the other so-called rare earth minerals."

"Give me some examples," Jack said.

"Well, there are painite, grandidierite, and serindebite. Each is extremely rare. Like dysprosium, they all contain alkaline to peralkaline igneous complexes."

"So, what's special about dysprosium?" queried Luke, cracking his knuckles.

Clive pulled closer and looked around the table. In a deliberate tone that portended a revelation, he said, "What we found, quite by accident, was the atomic reaction of dysprosium was different than the others."

"How so?" Faisal asked, raising his eyebrows.

"During a routine analysis, Billy poured a solution of dysprosium and saline into a test tube that had been used in an experiment with light crude."

"I remember," Billy said, shaking his head. "You were steamed."

"We didn't have much of the stuff to work with so, yeah, I was pissed."

Turning to Luke, Clive continued. "Billy put the tube aside and we repeated the experiment in a new one. It wasn't until the next day that I noticed something strange about the petroleum tube. The color had changed, indicating a chemical reaction. When we put it under a microscope, we realized the petroleum molecules had begun to replicate."

Faisal frowned. "Divide perhaps, but not replicate."

"You be the judge," Clive responded. "For every one part of dysprosium we added, the petroleum atoms regenerated ten times. What's more, they replicated by an ascending power, meaning that each increase was a little greater than the last. If that trend continued, it would theoretically be possible to produce an infinitely greater amount of petroleum atoms with a very small increase in dysprosium. The more you make, the more powerful it gets."

"That's just not possible." The Pakistani geologist shook his head.

"Then what?" Jack said, peering over his glasses at the professor.

"We mixed them in larger amounts—about a quart of gasoline. Same result."

"You produced new petroleum in a test tube?"

"Not exactly. We converted other atoms in the petroleum chain to carbon."

"More carbon, more energy," Billy said.

"I sent Billy over to the maintenance barn for a lawn mower. We drained the gas tank and poured in a cup of our solution. It cranked on the second pull and idled for eight hours straight."

The room was quiet. Faisal stood, scratched his head, and walked to the window. He looked across the cityscape and said without turning, "Do you still have the research data?"

"We did what we could with the dysprosium samples we had," Clive replied. "I wrote up the results of our first experiments and ran some baseline tests to measure the stability of the new carbon under high temperatures. Solid as a rock."

"There's no proof this stuff will be a game changer," Luke said. "Hell, most of the big gasoline users are already moving to natural gas. There's plenty of that and it's cheap as a dime-store hooker."

"You just don't get it. Did you read the report I sent you?" said Clive, becoming agitated.

"Not all the technical stuff. But, enough to understand the play here."

"The play? You dickweed. This is not some marketing scam like premium gasoline. The mineral they've discovered changes the whole carbon chain reaction. It will work on anything with a carbon base. Gasoline, natural gas, oil, condensate, diesel—you name it."

Jack cut a glance at Faisal then back to Clive. "You told us it would affect gasoline prices. That was it."

"It's all in my report! Why do you think the petroleum consortium went nuts when my paper came out? They already knew dysprosium could slow down the reaction of any carbon-based fuel. Make them all burn slower."

Luke shook his head in frustration. "What paper?"

Billy glanced at Clive and nodded. "Okay, here's the backstory," the professor said. He explained everything about his research paper and how the majors had reacted when he predicted a breakthrough in MPG.

"Let me get this straight," Luke sighed, rubbing his eyes. "You want us to bankroll this party based on your lawn mower trick, and you've already given the information to Trans-National?"

Billy grimaced as he watched the professor's face turn red. Before Clive could respond, Billy slapped his palms onto the table and grabbed the lead. "It was no trick, Luke. We proved the theory. But, if you're not interested," the hard glint in his eye giving lie to the casual shrug of shoulders, "maybe there are others in this building that'll be happy to work with us."

The Stasney group looked at each other.

"If you mean Trans-National, sounds like they'd only give a damn if you had a way to control the source and produce the stuff yourself," Luke said in a condescending tone.

Billy's jaw bulged as he clinched his teeth.

There was a heavy silence.

"Okay," Jack said, coming to the rescue again. "If we didn't have confidence in you, we wouldn't be here now."

Clive cleared his throat. "What more do you need?"

Walking to an easel in the corner of the room, Faisal responded, "We'll need to bring in some refining guys to figure out how and why this stuff works. If we could just get our hands on their research, we could be sure about the feasibility of the product."

He picked up a felt pen and began writing formulas. "You see, when carbon is burned, it splits into atoms. If we could see the reaction of the dysprosium atoms, especially their regeneration into carbon at an ascending power—"

Now Clive flared. "Damn it, Faisal. If a frog had wings, he could fuck a bat. We don't have time to start over. We know the properties of dysprosium. So do the big boys. When word of the discovery leaks, and it will, they'll find a way to bury that spring so deep you'd need an H-bomb to frack it open again."

Billy leaned back.

"He's right. If you want in, we've got to go after it now."

"Look," Jack sighed. "You can't expect us to just take all of this on faith."

There was a pause.

Luke looked at Billy. "Let's let the technical boys talk this over." He stood and motioned to the Indian.

Jack and Faisal pushed back from the table with a look of relief.

Billy glanced at Clive and shrugged.

The two former college friends retreated to Luke's office. Luke motioned for Billy to take a seat in a low-back burgundy chair at a small conference table.

"Nice digs," Billy said.

"We get by," Luke responded, with a forced smile. "So, how's Leslie?"

The question hung in the air. They studied each other while Billy considered his answer.

Is he still angry about losing her?

Luke drummed his fingers, kicking himself for asking.

Does he suspect?

Finally, Billy answered. "She's fine."

"I think I heard she was with LaCour+Simon now."

Billy's eyebrows elevated. "Yes. That's right, for about a year now. There wasn't any announcement, though."

"Right. I must have heard it at the club. A lot of guys out there use that outfit," Luke parried.

Billy propped his left elbow on the arm of the chair and spun his wedding ring with his thumb. He let his head tilt down, then slowly raised his eyes up to Luke's. "Yes, I suppose so."

Luke broke the stare by stroking the bridge of his nose.

"So, what do you think about the Rio Hot Springs?" Billy asked.

The young CEO took a deep breath and exhaled. "It's one of those things that comes along in this business—it can make or break you."

"I understand the risk."

"Do you?"

The phone buzzed from behind them on Luke's desk.

"Mr. Stasney? Line two."

"Voice mail," he shot back over his shoulder, "and hold my calls." He turned his attention back to Billy. "A project this size would take a good bit of our resources, Billy. Capturing the stuff, refining it, shipping it . . . and all two hundred plus miles out in the desert. I'd need to bet the farm and bring in some help."

"I know. I thought it might be too big for you."

"It's not too big. We could arrange it. The question is, if you're right, what about the value of our oil reserves . . . everyone's oil reserves?"

Billy cocked his head and frowned. "What the hell do you mean? If I'm right, this dysprosium hot spring will be worth a thousand times more than any petroleum reserve. We'd be in the driver's seat."

"You don't understand, Billy. Our oil reserves are pledged to the bank to secure loans—loans we use to operate our business and drill for more oil, or finance projects like this. It's the same for everyone in the business. The second the value of that collateral goes down, the banks will call for pay-downs on the notes. The lower the value, the bigger the principal reduction. They've got no choice. The regulators will make 'em do it. They'll write down the value of those loans—think of them as assets of the bank—and the banks will need more capital to stay afloat."

"But we'd have the dysprosium mine to shore up those loans, right?" Billy asked.

"Not until it's up and running and the product is generating revenue. That's when the value of the mine will be well enough established to satisfy the regulators. In the meantime, the loans to all but the biggest producers go into default, banks go under, and we're in the mother of all financial meltdowns."

The Indian and the oil man sat quietly, each considering what was at stake. Luke stood and walked to the window. To the east he could see oil tankers sliding slowly down the ship channel headed to the refineries along the Gulf Coast.

Across the downtown skyline were a dozen buildings housing oil companies and their suppliers. Everything from hotels to sheet metal shops, all were anchored by the price of crude.

In Luke's office, the unthinkable hovered in the air—the first breath of a tornado strong enough to take down the city.

"So, what's the answer?" Billy said.

Luke's lips compressed. He turned and walked around the table, hands in pockets. Then in a guarded tone he said, "We may have to reach out to one of the majors."

Billy grimaced. "Luke, you heard what Clive said. They might decide to bury the whole thing, not develop it at all. Hell, somebody damn near killed his wife over this. Did you know about that?"

Luke blanched. "What?"

Billy recounted the story of the pro-oil thugs and what they did to Sue Larson.

"Jesus Christ. I'm sure they know he's over here meeting with us . . . you, too. It's a wonder the old guy's still got the stomach for it," Luke whispered.

"He's got something to prove. We all do."

There was a lull.

"You know," said Luke with a distant squint. "Trans-National is already out there, a half-mile from the Rio Hot Springs. If they think development of the additive is inevitable, they would want to be the first one at the party."

"I don't know if Clive would sit still for it."

"If he balks, could we do without him?"

"Look," Billy said, giving him a cold glare. "He knows the mineral and he's produced the additive. But, most importantly, we can trust him. He needs this as much as you and me."

"Okay. Talk to him and call me. If he says yes, I have good connections at Trans-National."

Billy nodded and stood up. "I'll let you know tonight. If it's a go, we really will have to get moving. This secret won't keep, and I don't have a lock on the Chinati."

"When Trans-National sees this, they'll swing into action," Luke said. "Can't tell you what kind of deal they'll want, but it won't be pretty."

"Is that a yes?" Billy asked.

Luke extended his hand. Billy shook it.

"I will leave the preliminaries to you," said Billy. "I've got to go back to the reservation to promote this adventure. Clive will be here to help with the technical stuff."

They left Luke's office and returned to the conference room. Luke joined Clive and Faisal who were poring over test results from the springs. Jack Massey was on the phone ordering lunch.

Billy looked at his watch. *It's time*, he thought, *to call Leslie. Arrange dinner. Maybe bring her up to date.* He reached for his cell, then glanced at Luke and cocked his head. *Or does she already know?*

14

LUKE HAD SCHEDULED A MEETING with Trans-National's top geologist, Robert Perkins, and invited Clive to attend. The professor arrived at the Trans-National Research Center early. Located in Bellaire, a sleepy suburb of Houston, the building was a sprawling two-story fronted by a concrete sidewalk and narrow lawn with boxwoods and emerald green magnolias. Its circa 1948 architecture resembled a high school campus complete with a flagpole flying American and Texas flags. The only corporate tell was a two-by-two Trans-National logo of black stone embedded above the door.

It would be Clive's first face-to-face encounter with Big Oil since their thugs beat his wife senseless a decade before. Although he felt certain Trans-National was not the only company involved, they were now the only face he had to put on that devil.

As he neared the revolving glass door, he recalled the words he'd written in his diary summing up his feelings about his wife's attack: *Big Oil's lust for survival is more ferocious than any moral margins can control. They will stop at nothing.*

"I'm Clive Larson to see Robert Perkins," the professor told the uniformed security guard sitting inside the entrance. As he waited, Clive reflected on his situation. *To settle the score, I've first got to make a deal with these bastards.* The thought of it turned his stomach, but his need for revenge and redemption prevailed.

The guard lifted the phone and buzzed upstairs. "Mr. Larson to see Mr. Perkins...Thanks."

"Okay, second floor."

Weathered briefcase in his left hand and panama hat in the other, Clive clicked across the gray granite floor to the elevator. Once inside, he took a deep breath, then pushed number 2.

The door opened into a sea of waist-high counters lined up along the right half of the floor like church pews. Serious-looking Trans-National employees with white lab coats stood at each station, studying charts and graphs on blinking monitors. Around the perimeter was a ring of conference rooms with inner walls of glass and outer walls overlooking the suburban landscape. Each had an oak conference table and straight-backed chairs.

In a room directly across the crowded floor, Clive spotted Luke Stasney. He was standing, hands on hips, poring over a partially unfurled roll of papers. Beside him was a lanky bald man in his fifties with sleeves rolled up and tie at half-mast. Looking up momentarily, Luke locked eyes with Clive and waved him over. The professor worked his way through the army of technicians and opened the conference room door.

"Morning, Clive. This is Robert Perkins, chief geologist in the Trans-National Exploration Department."

"Morning, Professor Larson," Perkins said, extending his hand. Clive shook it.

Professor! thought Clive, pulling out a chair. *What a suck-up.*

"We've been looking over these deep geophysical pictures you gave us on the Rio Hot Springs," said Perkins. "Remarkable. They show a clear fissure pattern down at least thirty miles, ending in a huge cavern of some sort. An underground lake, I'd say. Something big happened down there to open up those pathways. Where'd you get these photos?"

"I've got my sources," Clive responded with a wink, while sitting down. "Mostly government stuff—multispectral imaging—taken by satellite. Captures image data at specific frequencies across the electromagnetic spectrum. The wavelengths can be separated by filters or by using instruments that are sensitive to particular wavelengths, including light from frequencies beyond the visible light range, such as infrared. It allows extraction of additional information the human eye fails to capture with its receptors for red, green, and blue. I'm sure you're familiar with the process."

Perkins stood speechless. Luke dropped into a chair. Neither was sure what the professor was talking about, but both gave pious nods.

The hint of a smile crept across Clyde's lips. *Now these boys are going to find out who's really in charge.*

The Trans-National geologist walked around the table and pointed to a three-by-four-foot easel. Vertical rows of jagged seismographic lines streamed from top to bottom like lightning strikes.

"There's a hell of a lot of activity going on under those springs," Perkins said. "This is what we got shortly after we commenced our fracking program a half mile to the east. No one looked very closely at the situation under the springs themselves till now. Shows us pretty good detail down to a mile or so. Alone it wouldn't mean much, but with your images of the deeper fissures, it's compelling—very compelling."

Clive's pulse quickened. This was music to his ears. After years of unspeakable hostility and humiliation at the hands of the oil giants like Trans-National, it was payback time.

"There's more in my paper." Clive dug into his briefcase. "I have a copy here somewhere."

"Paper?" Perkins queried with a surprised look.

Clive stopped rifling and riveted his gaze on Trans-National's top exploration man.

He has no idea about my white paper or the Big Oil cover-up. Why would they keep their own management in the dark? I need to find out before I offer it up.

"I wrote it a while back. Guess I forgot to bring one along. Ask around."

Perkins cocked his head inquisitively. "I'll do that."

Clive turned his attention to the roll of deep seismic photos spread across the table. He stroked the paper like a favorite pet, lingering at intersections of what likely had been massive lava flows miles beneath the surface. "It's down there, all right," he declared with a confident wave. "All we need to do is stabilize the main fissure and bring the minerals up at a steady pace."

"I'm afraid it's not that easy," Perkins said, motioning for Clive to sit. "It's going to take a lot of work to verify this discovery. At those depths, we'll need to drill at least a couple of test wells to measure pressure and the porosity of the rock. Probably take a year."

Clive's eyes narrowed. "We don't have time for business as usual. I've shown you what's down there, you've tested it, and it's belching out of those springs stronger than bear's breath. This is no ordinary prospect."

"Look, Clive, you're asking us to dump millions into this thing. We can't do that on a hunch. Our board would have our hides."

Clive pulled off his glasses and hunkered across the table to speak.

"And what do you suppose they'll do when this deal walks down the street to ConocoPhillips?"

Perkins's jaws began to work and his face froze into an icy glare. Luke went pale. The number one man at Trans-National Exploration was not used to being threatened.

Without breaking Clive's stare, Perkins growled back in his best Dirty Harry voice, "Listen, *Professor* Larson, this is our house and we're going to play by our rules. You don't like it, you can take this porcupine and shove it up your ass backward."

"So be it," Clive flashed and reached for the papers on the table.

"Those stay," Perkins spit.

"The hell they do!"

Luke jumped up from his seat. "Now hold on, gentlemen!"

It was too late. Clive grabbed the photo rolls and pivoted toward the door.

As he reached for the chrome handle, it swung open. The CEO of Texas Trans-National Energy, Inc., Buck Olmeyer, strode in, turned out in an orange polo sport shirt, khaki shorts, and alligator loafers.

"Well now, you must be Clive Larson! I've heard a lot about you. I'm Buck Olmeyer. I work around here, too. Whaddya say, Luke?" He wheeled around the table, shaking hands.

Luke breathed a sigh of relief. "We were just going over the Rio Hot Springs project."

Buck turned directly to Perkins and asked with an insincere grin, "Well, when can we get started out there?"

Perkins blanched, his lips pressed into a forced smile. "We have some technical challenges to overcome, but I think we'll get there."

Buck wasn't satisfied. "So, what's the problem?" he snapped.

Perkins opened his hand and reached toward Clive. Taking the hint, Clive handed him the sheath of magnetic images and watched him roll it out on the table.

"We know what's going on shallow," Perkins said pointing to the easel, "and a pretty good idea of what's thirty miles down," sweeping his hand across the table. "What we don't know is how stable these fissures are that transport the mineral slurry to the surface. They opened suddenly and could close the same way."

"It was probably your fracking that did it," blurted Clive. "Just keep your crews the hell away from the springs. All we need to do is get in there and stabilize the pathway walls where they feed the springs, run a camera down the hole to map out the route to the main fissure, and install a valve to regulate flow rate."

Buck and Luke swiveled their heads to Perkins for a reply. His eyes cut to Clive, waiting with brows arched, then to Buck with his plastic smile. There was an awkward silence while the geologist judged the wind direction in the room. *This crazy geezer could get me fired!*

With a forced laugh he declared, "That sounds good, Clive. If anyone can do it, we can."

"That's what I want to hear!" Buck bellowed, slapping Perkins on the back. "Now, I've got a little bidness to talk with these fellas."

Clive glanced at Luke, then responded, "And the Chinati, of course."

"Sure, sure. But Strikeleather can bring them around, right? They can't pull this off on their own."

Buck took a stance and made a swing with an imaginary golf club. "Luke, I'll call you later. We've got to make an announcement about this project and get the PR boys on it. They'll need to interview each of you to get the story straight—I mean," he covered with a fake cough, "get the pertinent details."

Perkins, florid with angst, stifled his urge to protest.

"We'll wrap up the deal and announce it at a press conference on-site next week," Buck gusted. "Now, I've got a tee time in an hour. Any questions?"

Luke had the wide-eyed look of a kid ringside. *The fate of my company*, he thought, *is in the balance and all I could do was watch. A one-week deadline. And who knows where Billy is with the Indians?*

The cell phone in Buck's pocket went off with a vintage ring. He took the call, then gave the room an indifferent salute and left.

Luke caught Clive's eye and nodded toward the door. "Send us a draft of the presentation to review," he said to Perkins, who was now slouched in a chair, head in hands. "We'll be at my office."

Without looking up, the geologist dejectedly waved them off as they headed for the elevator.

As soon as they cleared the front of the building, Luke grabbed Clive's arm and snarled, "What the hell was that all about?"

"How would I know?" Clive responded with a shrug. "They're *your* friends."

"Look," said Luke, blocking his way. "These guys may be jumping the gun, but we need them. You don't walk out on Robert Perkins, ever."

Clive bristled as he brushed past the young oil man. "Don't lecture me, junior. The only thing these fat cats respect is power. Now I've got it."

Luke fell into step with the professor and snapped, "You're way out of your league. I know how these guys operate. Once the deal gets signed and Olmeyer gets his press conference, the go-to guy for Trans-National will be Perkins. You piss him off and there'll never be any development at all."

Clive forged ahead through the parking lot without looking at Luke. "Well, I hope your lawyers are smarter than that. Put it in the contract. They've got to help us produce or we walk."

"It doesn't work that way," Luke fumed. "No matter what the contract says, if we get crossways with Trans-National and they balk, this deal will be tied up in court for years. We don't have the resources to take them on."

When Clive glanced at Luke and saw the panic on his face, his anger waned. *I've been there*, he thought.

"Okay," Clive said, stopping in the shade of an ancient water oak by the parking lot. "There's one thing that does bother me more than Perkins. You know I want to get started as soon as possible. I think we all do. But what's the rush to make an announcement, have a big news conference? That could wait a few weeks, at least until we get better organized. Billy doesn't even have the tribe on board."

Luke rubbed his eyes, then pulled his hand down across his mouth and chin. "I'll admit," he said in a tired voice, "I was thinking the same thing in there. I know we agreed to the tight schedule, but with contract negotiations and the complexity of the seismic data, why box ourselves into a kick-off date? I suppose there could be political reasons inside Trans-National that we don't know about."

"Or," Clive murmured, taking a quick look around, "another agenda altogether?"

Luke cocked his head and answered in a low tone, "I can't imagine what it would be. Olmeyer knows if we're not happy with the deal, we'll find someone else."

"Maybe we should explore some other options just in case," Clive said.

"Word would get out and we'd be dead with Trans-National. Worse, they'd try to destroy the Rio Hot Springs altogether."

The last words had barely cleared Luke's lips when the men's eyes met and held. *Destroy the Rio Hot Springs*. Clive raised his eyebrows. Luke squinted at him in the morning sun.

15

AFTER HIS TRANS-NATIONAL MEETING, Luke headed home. Behind the wheel of his black SL550, he felt like a fraud. His father would have jumped on the deal. It was the stuff wildcatters dreamed of. As he navigated out of Bellaire, down Allen Parkway, and east along the greenbelt astride Buffalo Bayou, he pondered his hesitation.

He pulled into the driveway of his three-story mansion in River Oaks, the highest-end neighborhood in Houston. With six thousand square feet, five bedrooms, and guest quarters, it was enough for three families. Luke and his two cats rattled around inside like peas in a basketball.

Luke pushed the remote to open the garage and parked inside. *It's too clean*, he thought. His ex-wife had raised neatness to a religion, the last straw of a failed marriage. There were no man-toys.

As he unlocked the back door, his cell phone rang.

He answered.

"Luke? It's Buck Olmeyer."

"Oh, hi, Buck," Luke said casually, imitating the style his dad had used with Big Oil kingpins.

"I meant to tell you today that I'm sure sorry about your dad's passing. He was a good man. We went back a long way."

"I know. He used to talk about that."

"He did? Well, don't believe anything he said," Buck joked.

Luke walked through the kitchen into the den and descended into a leather recliner. A fat yellow tabby leaped into his lap, while a Maine coon made a question mark with his tail by the empty bowl on the floor.

"Didn't expect to hear from you so soon," Luke said.

"We're backed up at a three par, so I thought I'd give you a try. I'm interested in how your outfit's been doing. I like your style—reminds me of your dad."

Ignoring the inquiry, Luke responded to the compliment, knowing it was a ploy. "That's mighty kind of you, Buck. I don't always show too well against him."

"Now, now. No need for false modesty, son. How about dinner tonight? Petroleum Club, 7:30?"

Luke knew you didn't say no to the CEO of Trans-National Energy. "Sure. See you then."

The Petroleum Club occupied the top floor of the Exxon Tower, the oldest of the Big Oil buildings in downtown Houston. Walking in from the elevator was like a trip back in time. Tall ceilings accented by dark wood paneling and red carpet set the stage for an experience once removed from Tara Plantation. A black maître d' in a white coat welcomed each new arrival by name.

"Hello, Mr. Stasney. Haven't seen you in a while."

"Hi, George," Luke responded, straightening his tie.

George brushed a bit of lint from the lapel of Luke's navy blazer. "I'm sure sorry about your father."

"Thanks. I'm here to see Buck Olmeyer."

George walked a few steps ahead.

"He's waiting in the Spindletop Room."

They rounded the corner past an ornate floor-to-ceiling mirror and a floral display worthy of the White House. George opened double mahogany doors into a private dining room. At the end of the table in a white shirt and black smoking jacket sat Trans-National's top man, ready to hold court.

"Howdy, stranger," Buck proclaimed as Luke entered. The room was small with an oblong table and eight high-back chairs. The walls were papered with a collage of gushing oil wells and framed headlines announcing new discoveries.

Luke reached across the table and shook hands. Buck kept the end seat and motioned for his guest to sit to his left.

"George, bring this young man a drink."

"Yes, sir. What would you like, Mr. Stasney?"

"A glass of Stags' Leap cab will be fine."

"And you, sir?"

"I'll have another Wild Turkey on the rocks."

"Coming up," George said, pulling the doors closed as he backed out with a half bow. "Luke, I'll cut to the chase. I like your company and your style of management. You've had some bumps along the way, but every young CEO does."

Luke toyed with the butter plate and waited for the pitch.

"We're interested in innovation at Trans-National, Luke. Sometimes you have to look outside the walls for that talent. You've got it and we've got a place for you and your team."

"This is a little sudden, Buck. You mean you want us to come to work for you?"

"Hell, no. I want to buy your company."

"Buy my company?"

"That's right."

Luke stroked the back of his neck. "Just like that. You want to buy Stasney Energy?"

"Lock, stock, and barrel," Buck said with a grin.

The doors opened. The waiter served the drinks and left.

"My dad would roll over in his grave if he could hear this," Luke said, shaking his head.

"I think he'd be proud of us both," Buck waxed, clinking his glass against Luke's. "Now, I know what you're thinking. Independents like their freedom, like to call all their own shots. We'd stay out of your way, let you run things like you've always done. But this I promise you, with our resources we'll be able . . . you'll be able . . . to develop this new Rio Hot Springs mineral project right away. No waiting around for funding. No bankers to convince. Plus, we'll make you richer than you've ever dreamed."

"I don't know, Buck. This company's been in the family for fifty years. It *is* the family."

"I'd be willing to pay three times earnings for your production, and one and a half times book value for your reserves. With a premium for goodwill, I'd estimate that to top out at around thirty million. We'd also give you an employment contract, say a million per year, and the usual stock options and parachute."

The doors opened again, and the waiter appeared with the drinks and menus.

"I don't need that," Buck said, "Just bring me a ribeye, rare, and onion rings. And another bourbon."

The waiter turned to Luke.

"I'll have the same."

"That's my boy," Buck chortled. "So, what do you say?"

"I don't know. It's a big decision."

"Damn it, man. This is a world-class offer. Can't you recognize a bonanza when you see it? Your ship just came in, if you're smart enough to get aboard."

Luke thought about the sudden offer and considered for a moment what those millions would mean to him. *Not much,* he reflected. His father had left him with plenty. *But there'd be no more pressure to spend it keeping the family company afloat. And, more importantly, if we could get the additive to market, there would be no more comparisons to Dad, period. I'd be out of his shadow.*

In the back of his mind, another voice weighed in. *Is it worth undermining the industry Dad helped build? The one that raised him from the street to the penthouse . . . supported our family?*

"I'll need some time to think it over."

"Sure. Take a few days and give me a call. I'll have our lawyers start putting the deal together."

The waiter returned with the drinks, and the conversation turned to everyday fare, such as football and the stock market. Luke forced a smile while listening to Buck opine at length on each topic. He was glad when the dinner was over. Ready to go home to his cats, and the decision of his life.

Three days passed and Luke was no closer to a resolution. This morning he was pacing his office going over the alternatives for the hundredth time.

He was also dodging phone calls from Billy and Buck.

"Mr. Strikeleather again on line one."

"Tell him I'm in a meeting."

"I did. He wants to hold. And, Mr. Olmeyer called earlier. I put him in voice mail."

"Tell Billy I'll call him back."

At the lunch hour, Luke slipped out the back door and down the elevator to his car. He opened the door and slid behind the wheel. With the top down, he gunned out of the garage and headed to Memorial Park. He felt relieved to escape the pressure of the office and the decision he knew he'd have to make, if only for an hour.

Between the running trail and the golf pro shop, a burger joint squatted among the trees. Luke slotted into a parking space near the driving range and walked to the restaurant. He ordered a chef's salad and waited on the patio, surrounded by a blend of runners and golfers.

The running trail was crowded with noontime athletes. A few stopped at the water fountain near the patio. When the overhead speaker announced his number, he headed to the counter, lost in thought.

He weaved his way back between tables with his plate in one hand and iced tea in the other.

"Please don't spill anymore. Someone's got to clean that up, you know," said a familiar voice.

He grinned as Leslie Strikeleather pushed out a chair for him at her table. She was dressed in running gear—black shorts, tank top, and head phones pulled down around her neck, drinking an Arnold Palmer.

"I spotted you from the trail. Not exactly an executive lunch you've got there," she said with a smile.

Luke took a seat. "I didn't figure you for a runner. You come here for lunch a lot?"

"When I don't have client duty."

He looked her up and down. "Not bad."

Leslie blushed and slapped his arm with the back of her hand.

"I suppose Billy told you about our meeting," Luke said between bites.

"Only that you had one. He isn't home much these days, and when he is, there's not much conversation."

"Sorry," Luke said. "I remember when things got that bad in my marriage. We didn't last much longer."

There was a pause. Leslie sipped her drink and looked at Luke. "Enough of my sad story."

"I'm interested."

"No, you're not," she said with a giggle, arching to pull her hair back.

"He really hasn't told you about our meeting?"

"I presume he asked for your help," she said. "He told me he would."

Luke nodded. "That took guts."

Leslie twisted in her chair to face him. "So, what did you tell him?"

"That I'd think about it."

The speaker squawked out more food numbers.

"Have you?" Leslie asked.

"Yes."

"And?"

"It got complicated," Luke replied, averting his eyes.

"Okay. Let's talk about something else." She pushed back from the table and looked past him to the green golf course.

"Look," Luke sighed. "This involves Billy, and by extension you. I've probably already said too much."

Leslie reestablished eye contact. "It's fine, Luke. Really. If you'd rather not talk, I understand. I thought we shared a little something special at the Cattle Baron's Ball. Maybe it was the wine."

"I'm sorry. It wasn't your imagination, Leslie. I felt it, too. Only right now I'm not thinking too clearly."

"Can I help?"

"You remember back in college how my dad used to tell me never to sell out, to always to be my own man?"

She nodded.

"I've thought about him and his advice a lot lately." The more he spoke, the more he remembered how easy it was for him to open up to her. He recounted the events of the last three days.

When Luke was talked out, Leslie said, "Can we walk?"

They left the restaurant and moved slowly down a path leading into the forest, their shoulders touching.

"If you sold the company, you'd be free to start your own life, wouldn't you?" Leslie inquired gently. "I mean, you could live anywhere. Maybe you'd even invite me to visit."

Luke stopped and put both hands on her shoulders, turning her toward him. Leslie looked up at him, her lips parted. They kissed, tenderly at first, then with passion.

Leslie broke off their embrace and held his cheeks between her hands. Tears streamed down her face. "If you go, I'll follow."

Luke held her hard against him and rocked back and forth. In his stomach, he felt the old burning. Her shoulders heaved as she sobbed into his chest.

"We have to go now," Luke whispered.

"I know."

They turned and walked back up the trail. "I'll call you later," Luke said softly.

"I'll be waiting," Leslie replied and walked away.

Luke went to his car and opened the door. He got in and sat for a moment, letting what just happened sink in. *All this will do is complicate things*, he told himself. *Get a grip*. It was then he noticed a special brilliance of the leaves canopied overhead, the sweet smell of freshly mown grass from the golf course, and a pit in his stomach. He started the car and backed out. The road paralleled the running track, intersecting with Memorial Drive. As he drove slowly toward the corner, his eyes found Leslie standing with her back to the street. His senses were alive with anticipation. He needed to see her, hold her again.

She watched him from the corner of her eye and when he was safely past, put her cell phone to her ear. The line was still open. "How was that?" she asked.

"Beautiful. Just beautiful," replied Buck Olmeyer. "Now reel him in."

16

AFTER A DAY OF SOUL-SEARCHING about the Rio Hot Springs, and his encounter with Leslie, Luke was drained. Arriving home, he opened his refrigerator and took out a Corona. He reached for a bottle opener and snapped the cap. After a long drink, he dialed Buck's cell phone. *This has got to come to an end.*

A ragged voice answered. "Olmeyer."

"It's Luke Stasney. You okay?"

"Yeah. Let me get off this damn exercise bike." There was a grunt. "Luke, you're a hard man to reach. What's the verdict?"

"The answer is yes and no."

"What the hell does that mean?"

"It means I'll work with you, but only as a joint venture partner," Luke said. "25 percent for Stasney Energy, 25 percent for Trans-National Energy, and 50 percent for the Chinati. We'll bring the Indians to the table with the Rio Hot Springs minerals. You bring the money. That's it."

"25 percent to you. That's a hell of a commission," Buck said.

"If you think you can bring Billy Strikeleather and his tribe in without me, have at it. But I'm not waiting around. I've got alternatives."

"How much cash?"

"Ten million up front for the tribe, nonrefundable signing bonus," Luke replied. "The rest of the budget will have to be worked out."

"And who manages the work on the ground?"

"Stasney Energy, with the help of your engineers, of course."

"Are you sure you can bring the Indians on board?"

Luke walked from the kitchen to the den. *Here's where the fun starts.*

"We're working on it, but I can't be sure till you and I have firmed up our agreement."

"How fast could you pull it together?" Buck said.

"A month or so."

"That's too long. If you can do it in a week, we'll do the deal."

Luke swallowed hard and walked out to his patio. Pacing the perimeter of the brick pavers, he thought, *A week would be a miracle. I don't know where Billy is with Chief Whitecloud, whether they've even talked dollars.* Then from the back of his mind a picture of his father emerged. *He would show no concern. Give as good as he took, like a true wildcatter. He'd agree, then figure out how to pull it off.*

"All right. Give me two weeks," Luke said, plunking his beer bottle onto the patio table.

"Great. Oh, one more thing. It's your job to manage Strikeleather. I don't want any drunken Indians fucking this up."

"I'll work on it," Luke laughed.

"For this kind of money, you better damn well get it done," thundered Trans-National's top man before hanging up. His new partner wasn't laughing.

Luke downed the rest of his beer and dialed Billy Strikeleather.

Clive and Billy were sitting in Clive's apartment studying geological logs of the Rio Hot Springs area. When his cell phone went off, Billy checked the caller ID, then nodded at Clive.

"Hi, Luke. What's happening?" he said.

Luke gave him the news of the Trans-National arrangement.

"Sounds good, Luke. But holy shit. How the hell are we going to get this done in two weeks?" He put the phone on speaker.

Clive frowned and shook his head. "No way," he mouthed to Billy.

"Look, Billy," they heard Luke say, "something's put a burr under Olmeyer's saddle, but we can't afford to call his hand. His money, his schedule."

"Luke, Clive Larson here."

"Right."

"Who's in charge of the development?" Clive asked.

"We are," Luke responded. "You'll have to tip your hat to them, of course. But it's our baby unless we screw it up."

Billy broke out in a beam and extended his fist across the table. Clive bumped it.

"Well, I'd say daylight's burning, gentlemen," Clive announced.

"You're right. I've got to hit the road for Lost Pines, and quick," Billy said.

"Do you think the Chinati will go for this deal?" Luke asked.

Billy swept papers from the table into a leather briefcase. "I have no idea. But I think ten million will get their attention. They can't develop the minerals alone."

"You'll need some kind of basic development plan," Clive said. "I'll pull something together and email it to you."

"I'll need to borrow a computer," Billy grinned.

"Good God," Luke snorted from the speakerphone. "I'll have one delivered to you in the morning, early."

"And a couple of thousand in per diem," Billy said with contrived reverence.

"Goodbye," said the cell phone.

17

IT WAS EARLY EVENING IN CHINATI FLATS. Hot. Billy had flown his Piper in that afternoon, landing on a runway carved from a field of waist-high mesquite. He'd walked to the Petrified Forest Motel where Sam's truck was parked, then drove it to the Quonset hut that served as council chambers for the tribe. Heat shimmered off the building's metal roof.

Billy pulled open the large metal doors. On the walls were pictures of Indian warriors, some on foot and others astride painted palominos. Dressed in battle garb, their fierce countenances contrasted sharply with the stoic faces of their descendants now gathered in the room. The council members were seated in a semicircle of folding tables with the chief in the center. They were flanked by a half dozen elders representing three generations of Chinatis. *Spears for ballpoints*, Billy thought, *had been a poor trade*.

"It's good to be back," Billy said, approaching the group.

"I asked you to meet us here," said the chief, "so others on the council can hear what you have to say about the Rio Hot Springs."

Billy took a seat to the chief's right. The mood of the participants was cautious. This was not a normal meeting. "Good evening," Billy said, bowing his head.

They nodded in unison.

The old chief cleared his throat. "I've asked Billy to help us consider the best way to handle the mineral discovery at the Rio Hot Springs. Billy has a geology degree, which is why Sam Longbird asked him to visit the springs. We've been over the rest of the story. We will soon have to make a decision. As always, a majority vote of the council will control."

The chief glanced at Billy, who nodded, then addressed the elders. "Since you all know the background, I'll give only a brief summary." He described the mineral content of the springs, the shooting of Sam, and the potential of dysprosium as a fuel additive.

The chief broke in. "I've heard nothing from the sheriff about the investigation. Do you have any idea who pulled the trigger?"

"Not yet. The sheriff is working on it, but not too hard."

Billy watched the reaction of each council member carefully. On the far end, to his right was Patrick Red Eagle, tall and angular, dressed in a blue work shirt and jeans. "Red" owned the local restaurant.

Seated on the opposite end of the semicircle was the tribe's Methodist minister, Noshi Williams. He wore a clerical collar under a buckskin shirt.

As feeders of the tribe's bellies and souls, Billy reckoned these two knew best the tendencies of each man and woman in the room.

Reverend Williams fingered strands of beads around his neck, stopping out of habit at a silver crucifix. "No one shoots another man," he said softly, "except for anger or greed."

"Yeah, and Sam didn't have an enemy in the world," Red said.

Billy felt all eyes shift to him. After his roller-coaster life on the outside, he couldn't blame them for wondering if he had somehow put Sam in harm's way. *Still*, he thought, *if they want my help, they'll have to trust me.*

Sitting to Red Eagle's right was the lone woman on the council. Edith Landrum was a sinewy, full-blooded Chinati, black hair pulled straight back in a knot accentuating prominent cheekbones, a broad nose, and piercing eyes. Her late husband, Robert Landrum, had been a white man appointed agent for the tribe by the U.S. Bureau of Indian Affairs. He'd died in a hunting accident five years earlier, leaving his middle-aged wife to raise two daughters on his pension and her salary as a nurse at the local clinic. She'd been on duty when Billy brought Sam in.

"I've read about rare earth minerals," said Edith in the calm voice she used before giving an injection. "Tell us what they're worth, especially the dysprosium."

"Mrs. Landrum," Billy said with a level gaze, "if the mineral is mined and the additive produced properly, it will mean a tenfold improvement in the efficiency of every internal combustion engine in the world. We could name our price."

The council was silent.

"So," ventured Red staring in disbelief, "three hundred miles to the gallon?"

Seated to Edith's right, the principal of the reservation's only school, Randy Kickingbird, was agog. "This could mean a new school, right? New books—computers in the classrooms?"

"I remember about twenty years ago, coal was discovered on Choctaw land up north," Reverend Williams said, leaning back and narrowing his eyes in reflection. "The tribe got a new recreational center and jobs working in the mine."

Billy sighed and shook his head. It was clear to him that the council had not yet grasped the enormity of the tribe's good fortune.

"Let me try to explain it better," Billy said. "Think about all the things you've done without in your lives."

"A new truck," said Red.

"An overhead projector," said Principal Kickingbird.

"Give it to us in dollars, Billy," the chief said sternly, sensing a sales pitch.

Billy picked up a yellow pad, wrote the figure $368, then held it up. "This is how much the average American is paying for gasoline each month. With our Chinati gas additive, that monthly bill would be cut to . . ." he wrote the number, "$36.80." He continued writing as he spoke. "That's a savings of $331.20 a month, or $3974.40 per year. How much would you pay for that product? By our rough estimate, the deal could be worth at least a million dollars a year for every man, woman, and child in the tribe . . . as long as the dysprosium holds out."

Scratching his head, Kickingbird said what they were all thinking. "I don't see how that's possible. Sounds like just another empty *Yo-ne-ga* whiteman promise. The worst kind."

"I'm afraid I agree," said Red. "This is how we lost our land down along the Gulf Coast. It's the kind of promise that can't be kept." He re-counted a story told him by his grandfather about Indians from the tribe lining up at a little post office building at 8 a.m. to receive checks for their interest in a 25,000-acre tract "bought" from the tribe by the government. Instead, they were given government IOUs payable over twenty years and orders to move west into the desert. He reached for his wide-brimmed hat.

"I've heard that story from my mother, too," Edith said, pushing away from the table. "She was a little girl. It was the only time she saw her

father cry. I don't want that for my children. I've heard enough of this."
She rose and picked up her beaded purse.

"Wait," Billy pleaded. "Don't dismiss this out of hand. If we turn our
backs on it, someone else will find a way to steal it from us."

"He's right," Reverend Williams said. "We owe it to our kids to think
this through carefully."

"Look," Billy said. "I'm a football player with a geology degree, not
a speaker. I'm probably not explaining this very well. All I know is the
dysprosium is there and the world will beat a path to our door to get it.
Surely it's worth considering."

Red and Edith glanced at each other, then sat down.

"Go ahead, Billy," the chief said.

"I understand your skepticism," Billy continued. "I felt the same
way at first. And it's true, there's no guarantee we can raise the minerals
without damaging the underground source. It was likely opened up by
accident, probably the fracking operation next door. It could close just
as easily. But, if we do it right—stabilize the ground around the springs,
reinforce the fissure—we stand a good chance of producing dysprosium
for years to come. And remember, it won't take too long at a million per
Chinati to set aside enough money to support the tribe indefinitely. We just
have to be smart about it."

"Would we sell the minerals in bulk or do the manufacturing ourselves?" asked Red cautiously.

"We barely have running water in some parts of town," Edith scoffed,
shaking her head. "Just how would we build a plant out here in the middle
of nowhere?"

"Well, we'd need help," Billy responded.

"What kind of help?" she shot back.

"Someone with the know-how to get us started, not only with the mining and the processing, but with the financing as well."

"Whom could we trust?" Reverend Williams interjected.

"I've found a company willing to help us," Billy said.

"What kind of company?" Edith challenged with a squint.

"Stasney Energy out of Houston. I've known Luke Stasney since college."

"Not another football player, I hope," she grumbled.

"No. Fraternity brother," Billy replied with a sheepish smile.

The nurse rolled her eyes.

"Maybe you'd rather have a Big Oil company take over the whole shooting match as soon as you turned your back?" said a voice from the back of the room. It came from a tall man of tribal ancestry who had slipped in unnoticed. Dressed in a blue sport coat and gray slacks, his thinning dark hair was speckled with gray.

All eyes looked back at the new arrival, then shifted to the chief for an explanation.

"For those who don't know, this is Jim Blackwater from Dallas. I asked him to come because he's been a business lawyer on the outside and knows the ropes. He was born on the reservation, but moved away with his folks the year of the polio epidemic . . . 1951 or so, wasn't it, Jim?"

The guest nodded. The chief motioned for him to come to the council table. He shuffled toward the front with a limp, the metallic clank of a leg brace accenting each step.

"Sit down, son," Reverend Williams replied, patting the seat of an empty chair to his right. "I knew your folks. Good people. I was sorry to see them go."

"They didn't leave soon enough to avoid the epidemic," the lawyer said without emotion as he reached down to unsnap the steel sleeve around his right leg, allowing him to sit.

Billy shuffled his notes and looked painfully at the chief. *Why didn't you tell me about this guy?* Beads of perspiration dampened his collar. The chief took note and bought Billy some time with a question. "Jim, can you elaborate on your comment?"

"Sure. First off, the Chinati are a recognized tribal nation under federal law and that counts for plenty. Unlike a lot of others, the Chinati never agreed to have their land allotted among individual members. We retained the full ownership and control of our land, including the Rio Hot Springs. This was confirmed by a federal law signed by President Lyndon Johnson in 1968. What it means is *we* control the minerals, not the Bureau of Indian Affairs or any other federal agency. We may be a small Indian reservation, but we have the same rights as any other sovereign nation."

"That's all very interesting," Red replied, "but what does it have to do with how we develop our minerals?"

Blackwater frowned and fired back impatiently. "Look, just because we have the legal right to the land doesn't mean the government and everyone else won't be coming after us for it. They've been stealing land from the Indians for two hundred years. It won't stop now. There are two ways to deal with this. Both take money, lots of it."

The council leaned forward as Blackwater continued.

"We could find an oil company willing to partner with us, like Stasney. That means we'd donate all our minerals to what's called a joint venture. Our partner would raise the money and provide the drilling expertise. I'm betting we would get a modest cash distribution at first, that's all. It's called a signing bonus. The joint venture would develop the minerals and fight off any legal challenges. Our partner would be in charge. That's always what the oil companies want. If money was made on the minerals, we would get our share, after all expenses are paid."

The minister shrugged and said, "That doesn't sound so bad to me."

Blackwater responded, "As long as they do what's necessary to protect our rights and actually develop the minerals. If they don't, or just pay lip service to the project, all we'd get would be the bonus, or worse, we'd lose the land altogether. You've got to ask yourself just how eager an oil company would be to produce an additive that guts their most profitable product—gasoline."

"And the other way?" the chief asked.

Blackwater sat up straighter, warming to the task. "The other way is to finance it all ourselves."

A laugh fluttered across the room.

"The tribe could borrow enough money to begin development of the minerals using the Rio Hot Springs as collateral. It would take a lot longer, but in the end the entire operation would be ours."

"Who would lend us that kind of money?" asked Edith.

Blackwater drew back his shoulders and folded his hands on the table. "Any banker who understands a ten-to-one increase in fuel efficiency."

There was a knock at the door.

"Who is it?" the chief called out, looking past Blackwater.

"Ivan Stone," a voice responded from outside.

"Come in."

A tribal man of sixty or so, dressed in a gray tweed coat with elbow patches, entered and closed the door. He was clean shaven, bald but for a gray fringe, with thick steel spectacles. Under his arm was a leather portfolio.

"Please join us," the chief said.

Billy shook his head. Looking at the chief, a faint smile crossed his lips. *The old man is way ahead of me.*

Stone approached the council table locking eyes with Jim Blackwater. "Hi, Jim," he said, "it's been a long time."

The lawyer smiled and extended his hand as he spoke. "A lifetime, I'd say. I heard you'd left the village, too. Where did you end up?"

"Manhattan," Ivan replied, "by way of University of Cincinnati and Virginia Polytech School of Architecture. Had to serve a four-year hitch in the Air Force to pay the freight. Been in practice in New York ever since." He shook hands around the table, then settled into a chair to the left of Red.

"Ivan," said the reverend. "You probably don't remember me. I baptized you when you were a baby."

The newest guest laughed. "That might have been the last time we went to church. Dad wasn't a religious guy, but my mother didn't want to take any chances."

The chief rapped the knuckles of his right hand lightly on the table. "I've asked Ivan to join us, like Jim, so we can consider this matter with all the resources at our disposal. I'm sure the oil companies and others with a vested interest will be doing the same."

Chief Whitecloud acknowledged Ivan with a nod.

"When the chief asked me to think how we might use the mineral money to redesign the village, to improve the living standard of the tribe, it was like an architect's dream come true. A blank check with no limitations." From his briefcase he withdrew a fat roll of blueprints and held it shoulder high like a tomahawk. He waved it for emphasis as he spoke. "What's in these," he said, "is my first cut at a new Chinati city. It has every modern convenience and would transform the reservation into a living center of the future. The oil rich cities of Dubai and Saudi Arabia would have nothing on us."

All eyes were fixed on the roll of papers. Their author made no move to unsheathe his work. Instead, he pushed back his chair, looked at the chief, and said, "I'm sorry to report that I've failed."

"Don't you think the council should be the judge of that?" replied the chief.

"Oh, you're welcome to look them over. In fact, they're yours to keep," Ivan said, rolling the plans toward the center of the table. "But they're still a failure."

"Why would you say such a thing?" Reverend Williams asked gently.

Ivan took a deep breath and closed his eyes. "I learned something on this project, and not just about the design of a city."

The council sat motionless as Ivan Stone told his story.

"I've lived in New York City for thirty years. My company designed some of the biggest, most sophisticated buildings in the world. The closer I got to the top of the organization, the more important it became to conform, to make the Upper East Side my heritage. Along the way I tried to distance myself from my past, even denying my ethnicity on occasion."

He stood, removed his jacket, and laid it across the empty seat to his right. Grasping the table with both hands, he leaned forward and took a deep breath before continuing. "I can't say when it started. My life became a series of hurdles, each higher than the last. I could see the finish line ahead, but it had no meaning. I tried—" he stammered, "I tried to take stock of my life, to remember who I was. It was then I heard from Chief Whitecloud. Although I had ignored him and the tribe for years, he still asked for my help.

"As I worked on the design for a new Chinati city, something remarkable happened. I began to realize the importance of what was being left behind. I tried to find ways to incorporate the old and the new. It wasn't possible. What had disappeared in my design for a new city was more than a dilapidated village, it was our way of life. The same was true for the Rio Hot Springs. There was no way to lay out a mining operation and manufacturing plant, with all the necessary roads and housing, without destroying the natural terrain. I realized if we lost these things, even in the name of progress, we'd have nothing to bequeath to our children, except money. Our simple way of life, the one that fostered values defining me as a Chinati, and us as a nation, would be gone forever—our heritage sold to the highest bidder. What price would you accept for our nation?" His voice trailed off. The other Indians sat silently.

On a low hill outside of town, a coyote wailed. Ivan Stone had come home, and he bowed his head.

The architect sank into his chair and put his face in his hands. Billy's heart raced. Instinctively, he arose and slipped around behind the visitor. He held the man's shoulders. For a moment he pictured himself in Ivan's seat. *You're not alone.*

Recovering his composure, Ivan continued. "Consider this, too. If we construct a new city, as we surely would feel pressured to do, who would live in it? Plant workers? Oil company engineers? Do you think our people would choose life in the desert, no matter how luxurious, over any other city in the world?"

"I think you're selling yourself short," injected Randy Kickingbird. "First, what makes you think we couldn't have both a modern city while preserving our past? With the resources Billy described, we could protect the old village just as it is. It would always be there for our children to see."

The architect listened intently, his forearms in an A-frame with chin balanced on top. "What you're describing," he countered, "would be an exhibition, a place to look at an abandoned culture. Too many tribes have already done this. Religious ceremonies turned into tourist attractions, caricatures of themselves."

"Mr. Stone, you've spent the last thirty years in New York City," Reverend Williams said, defensively. "I've been here on this reservation. Never once have I denied our tribe the right to incorporate traditional practices into our worship services. They've simply chosen not to do so. Religion is not static. It evolves with its believers. You don't know that our people want to preserve, as you say, the old way of life. Our spirit will endure, Mr. Stone, even without the old village."

Eagle raised his hand. The chief invited him to speak with a come-hither motion of his right pointer finger. "If Billy is right, and that's still a big if, the mining operation would provide all the jobs we'd need. Full employment, right? We haven't had that, ever."

"Come on, Red. Wake up," snapped Edith with a scowl. "Why would a person making a million a year work at all? The real question here is whether we as a people would be able to survive the effects of unlimited wealth. Consider what happened to white society."

Jim Blackwater was annoyed. He made his discontent known by shaking his head and exhaling loudly through ballooned cheeks. When he could finally contain himself no more, he blurted, "This is just nonsense! Atomic power can either energize civilization or blow it up. But that's no reason to ban it. The issue here should be *how* not *whether* we use the money."

"Well, Mr. Blackwater," Edith responded coolly, "when you're elected to the council, you can make that decision."

The council fidgeted.

Billy stared at the chief. *Put a stop to this, old man! We need a consensus, not a stand-off.*

This time the chief stepped in. "All right, it's been a long day, particularly for our guests. I suggest we reconvene in a few days. In the meantime, with Ivan's permission, we can all look over his plans. I'll leave them here."

Stone nodded his approval.

18

WHEN RANDY KICKINGBIRD LEFT the council meeting, his head was spinning. *What will we do if there is no loan for us? The tribe will be angry at me and the council forever if we blow this.*

From across the parking lot, he heard his name and turned. It was Oliver Greentree.

"I'm glad I caught you," he said, approaching hurriedly.

"Oliver. Some meeting."

"Yes, it was. I heard it from the kitchen. Can we talk for a minute, privately?"

"I've got go over to the school for some papers. Can you meet me there?"

"Sure."

"Come to my office."

The principal's office was a cramped room, painted gray with a picture of the tribal council on one wall and a print of the Empire State Building on the other. His desk was piled high with test score reports and unopened mail.

"Excuse the mess," said Randy. "We spend more time testing than teaching these days." He cleared a chair and offered it to Oliver.

"Do you like your work here?" Oliver asked.

"It's a living," Randy answered with a tired smile.

Oliver laughed. "Reservation life wearing thin?"

"Is it that obvious?"

"I know the problem. That's why I thought of you when an opportunity came up that could change all that, for both of us. The tribe needs financing for the Rio Hot Springs mineral development. I have a source."

"Just like that?" Kickingbird said.

"Well, it would take us both to pull it off. Interested?"

The principal let his eyes drift over the desk and around the room. At every turn there were reminders of his discontent. He was a man, he knew, whose future was being dictated by circumstances rather than choices. Three children, a wife whose part-time salary, added to his own, didn't cover the mounting expenses of a family.

"That's not my line of work, but go on."

Oliver explained his inside track to the UAW, without disclosing Vestal's name. "My source tells me a loan could be arranged from the pension fund. It's a perfect fit for the autoworkers."

Kickingbird rocked forward on his elbows across the desk. When Oliver paused, he asked, "What would my role be?"

"You would convince the council that a loan from the UAW would be the best way for the Chinati to develop the minerals. You know, it would let the tribe keep control."

"And if I did that?"

"You'd be appointed as the administrator of a new regional UAW education fund to provide classes and education to union members and their families."

Kickingbird grimaced. "I—I don't know anything about unions or their training programs, Oliver."

"It doesn't matter. The job would move you off the reservation. Give you an office and a title in a place like Dallas and a starting salary triple what you're making now."

"How do you know all this?"

"You have to trust me, Randy. What do you have to lose?"

"Could it be kept quiet while we're working to make the deal? I can't afford to lose my job at the reservation school."

"Of course."

"And, how would I convince the other council members? I don't know anything about financing a mineral project."

"Don't worry. I do. I'll help you every step of the way."

"Can I think it over?"

"Sure. But don't wait too long. The union wants this deal. If you pass on it, they'll find someone else on the council to do their bidding."

As Randy Kickingbird drove home, in his rearview mirror he saw the run-down school building where he spent his days encouraging young Indians to learn enough English and math to escape the reservation. He felt guilty about the subliminal warning he'd been sending his students about the perils of being stuck in Chinati Flats. But in the end, he knew it was true. *I'm proof,* he said to himself, gripping the wheel tightly. *Do it.*

He reached for his cell phone and entered Oliver's number.

19

AFTER THE COUNCIL MEETING, Chief Whitecloud said his goodbyes at the lodge and walked to his old Suburban. Stonewashed blue and dusted with desert grit, on its rear window was a faded decal proclaiming in feathered letters *BUY NATIVE*. Few had.

He opened the door and stepped onto the running board. Using the steering wheel for leverage, he hoisted himself into the seat. The truck cranked on the third try and rattled onto the highway that doubled as the main street of town.

A pair of black horn-rimmed glasses clattered across the dash and onto the floor under the steering wheel. "Shit," the chief said, swerving to a stop on the apron. He fished around with his hand until he found the thick spectacles. After fumbling them onto his nose, the road came into focus and he pulled away.

A parade of disheveled bungalows and trailers passed to his left. Through the passenger window, the homes were modest but neat. The chief sighed. *What gives some people self-respect and others none?*

The events of the council meeting played back in his mind: Billy explaining the riches that lay beneath their feet; Ivan Stone warning about the price of instant wealth. *Poor choices*, the chief thought, rubbing his brow.

Instead of turning into his neighborhood, he held fast to the blacktop out of town. Behind him a full moon kept pace, silhouetting the truck in eerie shadows along canyon walls. Ahead, jagged gray mountains loomed in the lunar glow like a dinosaur spine. The old man shuddered as he considered what modern predators might be lying in wait for him and his people in the coming days. He rolled down the window and put out his elbow. A stream of night air helped clear his head.

As the elevation topped out, the stark formations gave way to open fields below. He depressed the clutch and slipped the gearshift into neutral. The engine idled as the SUV snaked down rolling hills, powered by gravity alone. To the cactus plants edging the highway, the swish of tread on asphalt was the only hint of the truck's passage. When its momentum was spent, the chief steered the machine to a halt on the shoulder and cut the power. The silence was sudden and complete.

He draped both arms over the wheel and looked out the windshield. The glimmer of stars backdropped the scene, then faded along the horizon into the faint lights of Alpine. He rested his cheek on the back of his right hand and considered his life. Twenty-five years as head of the council and what did the tribe have to show for it? A broken-down clinic. An old school. A people who had lost their way.

He opened the door of the Suburban and stepped down onto the desert floor. Around him were flora shimmering like ghosts in isolation so perfect the only trace of humankind was the sound of his own breathing. A soft wind blew—the desert's breath. With a callused hand, he bent to caress the flowers of a strawberry cactus, then its needles. *A blend of beauty and danger*, he thought, *like the choices facing the tribe.*

He put his hands in his pockets and walked back to the vehicle. With each step he questioned more intently whether he had the strength to lead his people through the challenges ahead. *It's a wonder they've stayed with me this long.*

But there was more to the story that only the chief knew. He stood by his truck staring down the highway toward Alpine, a cattle town where ranchers a century before had rounded up their herds for the drives north. In an instant he was back in the summer of his eighteenth year when he and his friend Sam Longbird hitchhiked this road to compete for the first time in the Brewster County rodeo.

The chief sat on the running board with elbows on his knees and face settled between his palms. A slight smile creased his lips. For two Indian boys whose only time off the reservation had been chasing strays on adjoining ranch land, visiting Alpine had been like a trip to New York City. They'd never seen so many people, white or otherwise. Some had trucks waxed to a high gloss with shiny bumpers. Others pulled tall trailers transporting the finest horses the young Chinatis had ever seen. In their eyes, all things seemed possible in this place.

When the truth came, it hit hard. As advertised by the city fathers, every rodeo contestant was provided a horse. But the Indians and Mexicans were allotted fewer by a measure of three to one. After half the events, their mounts were exhausted. The outcome of the remaining contests was never in doubt.

It was, he remembered, scratching a circle in the dirt with the toe of his boot, *a rude awakening.* They'd been warned by tribal elders of the double standard. But the depth of the prejudice and the lengths to which the white men would go to preserve their advantage would not be clear to the boys until later.

It had begun innocently enough. From the back of a borrowed pony, Angus Whitecloud had caught the eye of a rancher's daughter.

"Forget it, Angus," Sam had warned. "Even if you were the right color, she's too young."

"Aww, come on, Sam, she's smiling at me."

"I'm telling you. It's nothing but trouble. But you go ahead. Get yourself thrown in jail."

The old chief scooped a handful of pebbles and pitched them one at a time into the circle in the dirt. In his mind he relived the moment he'd spurred a tired palomino across the arena to try his luck with Miranda Sterling. Sam had been right. But it would be the Chinati nation that would pay the price.

He rose and spread his arms like a crucifix. With tears brimming in his eyes, he looked up and addressed the darkness. "If I were a religious man, I'd be looking to you for help. Since I'm not, let's not kid each other. I've got a lot of people counting on me. Can you do it for them?" He exhaled deeply and lowered his arms, chin dropping to his chest. After a moment he climbed into the SUV, wondering if his plea had been heard. *Guess it's time to find out.* The engine roared to life and a blast of gravel pelted the truck's underbelly as it lurched back onto the two-lane.

At the outskirts of Alpine, the chief spotted a tiny plane dropping out of the darkness. He arrived at the city limits in time to watch the aircraft make its approach. The streets were empty. He followed the plane's red blinking lights to the local airstrip where he parked in front of the portable building that served as a terminal. By the time the plane landed and taxied in, the chief was standing next to his truck. But for his headlights, the field was dark.

The propeller ground to a halt and the door opened onto the tarmac.

A worn canvas duffle and a leather grip dropped to the pavement. The pilot and two passengers crawled backward with deliberate steps down a narrow ladder. They stretched, picked up their bags, and walked toward the chief.

The first to approach was an Indian older than the chief, with long gray braids and skin like a dried stream bed.

"Whitecloud?" the man called out in a raspy voice.

"Yes."

"Charles Kaumudi from Lawton, Oklahoma—Cherokee." He motioned to the younger Indians behind him. "Winston Birdsong from Mescalaro, New Mexico—Apache, and Stephen Wolf from Livingston, Texas—Alabama-Coushatta. They met me in Ft. Worth. We took my plane."

Chief Whitecloud nodded toward his truck. "Please, get in."

The younger men walked to the back of the truck and loaded the luggage. Kaumudi sat next to Chief Whitecloud.

"Good flight?"

"It's a hell of a long way out here and I'm an old man," Kaumudi growled. "Just get me to a bathroom quick."

At 2 a.m., Waffle House was the only choice. The restaurant had operated in the same A-frame since 1969, fronted by a cramped waiting area with two sets of pink fiberglass chairs. Past the hostess desk, the room opened onto rows of plastic booths with yellow and orange headrests favoring giant Tootsie rolls and divided by particleboard partitions decorated in a Jetson motif. A short-order window was set along the back wall behind a counter with alternating orange and yellow swivel seats. Hot cylinder lights hung down over the serving ledge. A tattooed cook with a paper hat leaned his back against the counter, smoking a cigarette and reading the sports page.

Across the vacant dining room, a middle-aged waitress sat behind the counter rolling silverware into paper napkins. "Sit anywhere you like," she called out.

The Cherokee made a beeline to the men's room. The others walked to the back of the restaurant and slid into a booth.

The waitress sauntered over with menus under her arm, carrying a plastic coffee pot. After passing out the menus, she wiped her free hand on her blue coverall apron, which she wore over a maroon striped western shirt with fringe sleeves and a longhorn string tie. Her name tag identified her as Loretta. Without asking, she began pouring coffee into white ceramic cups.

"Hungry?" Chief Whitecloud asked the visitors.

They shook their heads. Loretta shrugged and retreated toward the kitchen, leaving the pot behind.

Kaumudi returned with a satisfied look and took a seat. Chief White-cloud sipped his coffee and leaned in. Kaumudi did the same, brushing back a braid to cup his left ear. The Chinati chief addressed the group in a low voice. As the story of the Rio Hot Springs minerals unfolded, the younger Indians became more animated. With each new disclosure, they whispered to each other and nodded. Kaumudi was different. His expression morphed from patient to concerned.

When Whitecloud had finished, the table was silent. Birdsong traced the lip of his cup with his ring finger and looked at Wolf. They both then deferred to Kaumudi.

"So, what does this have to do with us?" the Cherokee asked.

Whitecloud took a deep breath. "The Chinati were once a great people. So were the Alabama-Coushatta, the Apache, and the Cherokee. We all thought casino money would restore that greatness—give us back our independence." He shifted his gaze to the Cherokee chief. "Some fared better than others. But, in the end, was the money you made worth the price?"

Kaumudi held the stare, then broke it with an expression of resignation. "There were problems, it's true," he said in a low tone.

The other men at the table began to fidget. Whitecloud could see his words were hitting a nerve. He pressed on. "I saw these problems firsthand on our reservation. Drugs, alcohol, crime. I finally put a stop to it myself with a book of matches."

"So, it wasn't a lightning strike after all?" said Wolf, lifting his chin inquisitively. "I hope you at least got some insurance money."

"Not a cent. Never even made a claim. It was the money that caused the problems in the first place."

"We had one good year with our casino in Livingston," Wolf added. "Over a million a month until the governor shut down all gaming in the state. You watch," he said with an edge in his voice, "when it opens back up, it'll be the whites that get the permits. They'll squeeze us out."

"Well, we're a damn sight better off than we were before gaming," the young Apache said.

The elder Cherokee gave him a cold stare. "You've been lucky so far. Enjoy it, until it turns on you." Then he addressed Whitecloud. "I know you didn't call us here to discuss our problems."

The Chinati chief smiled. "All right. Hear me out before you respond. With the Rio Hot Springs minerals, our tribe has choices. We could partner up with a Big Oil company. They would either buy the minerals outright or lease them. The first way would mean a lump sum payment so big that, if it were distributed among our members, each could live in luxury for the rest of their lives. I doubt they would ever make any serious attempt at recovering the minerals or developing them into a fuel additive because it wouldn't be in their best interest to sell less gasoline. The result for us would be one generation of super wealth, with all that implies, and no long-term revenue to support permanent reforms for the tribe."

"How much would the oil company pay?" Wolf asked.

"I don't know exactly. But does it really matter? It could never match the potential for revenue if the minerals were developed, which brings me to the second option. Leasing. If we did that, there would be a smaller up-front payment to the tribe—a signing bonus—and the oil company would be obligated to make an effort to develop the minerals. As long as there was some development, the lease would stay in place. I imagine they would do the minimum required. And, even if they were successful, we would have little, if any, control over their methods of development. My guess is they would find a way to sabotage the Rio Hot Springs and choke off the minerals altogether."

"So, what's the solution?" Wolf asked.

Whitecloud paused. His eyes scanned the others at the table, then he began to speak slowly. "We could form an alliance among our tribes—operate in tandem to develop the minerals and loan the profits back to our members like a bank. They could use the funds to build real, lasting businesses, both on and off the reservations, instead of squandering them on luxuries that undermine our values and our spirit. The minerals would give us that power."

His words produced stares of disbelief. "And you would share your wealth with our tribes for this purpose?" asked Wolf. "What are you asking of us in return?"

"We would need your expertise and your money."

"Money? Ha. I knew there'd be a catch," the Apache scoffed.

Undaunted, the chief continued, "We have a small energy company willing to invest in our Rio Hot Springs. We think they will put up a million dollars."

"That doesn't sound like enough to me," the Coushatta said. "How much would it cost to capture the minerals and get to the market with even a small amount of product?"

"We're not sure yet. Probably somewhere north of four million."

"There's no way," said Kaumudi, sitting back.

"Hold on," Whitecloud continued. "If we can get this oil company to guarantee a bank loan secured by its own minerals, we could borrow more."

"That's a lot of ifs."

"We would use our control of the fuel additive to force the oil companies to support industries that the new American Indian Nation owns."

"Like gaming," Birdsong said, with a disconsolate look.

"More than that," Whitecloud countered, his chin higher. "New high-tech businesses with a future."

Kaumudi squinted across the table at Chief Whitecloud. He twirled the end of his right braid between a thumb and forefinger. Finally, he spoke. "Just how would we go about forming this new alliance of yours?"

Whitecloud sat forward, rubbing his palms together slowly. "Domestic Big Oil companies know about dysprosium and what it can do. They have for years. We'll give them a choice: Do as we say, or we'll partner with the Mexican company, Pemex. They're right across the river from the Rio Hot Springs. I think the Americans will come to the table."

Kaumudi looked sternly at Whitecloud. "They'll fight back. They'll not want to swallow down what we've lived on for two centuries."

"To hell with them," Wolf hissed, his eyes blazing. "This time they'll be the ones to capitulate."

"So, you believe," Whitecloud replied to the young Indian, "that victory over the white man should be our goal, our natural destiny? That reclaiming dominance, if we've the skill and power to do it, would bring about a different result in our lifetimes?"

The Chinati chief leveled a steady stare.

Wolf leaned back and looked up at the ceiling. He exhaled, bubbling his cheeks.

Whitecloud continued. "Why would a future with a victor and a vanquished turn out differently this time? Wouldn't each side still be waiting for the counterattack?"

Wolf brought his right fist to the table, rattling the saucers. "Don't be naïve. It's a dog-eat-dog world. There are winners and losers. All I'm saying is, it's our time again. We should seize the opportunity."

Birdsong nodded and cut his eyes over to Whitecloud. The silence was uncomfortable.

Kaumudi broke it by touching the Chinati on the sleeve. "Let's go for a smoke." The two elders slid out of the booth and walked toward the door.

The old chiefs sat on a bench in front of the restaurant. Kaumudi reached into his shirt pocket, withdrew a pouch of tobacco, and offered it to Whitecloud. When they had filled their pipes and lit them with wooden matches, they smoked in silence.

A smile crept across the face of the Cherokee leader. "Remember when we were that smart?"

Whitecloud blew a fusillade of smoke. His lips curled into a grin.

"This idea of yours is intoxicating, at first," Kaumudi said in a kind voice. "A unified Indian nation. However, I fear it would degenerate into a power struggle just as it's always done among us."

"Of course, there's risk," Whitecloud said. "But we're not new to this game. Look at the Iroquois. They've had a democratic government longer than the USA. Don't you think there's a chance their approach, or something like it, would work on a larger scale if we had some strong economic glue?"

"Who knows."

"It would be a dream come true. Lord knows this country needs something new to help bring it back."

"You talk as if it was really *your* country," Kaumudi said with a trace of sarcasm. "When did you or your Chinati ever enjoy the American dream?"

"I'm both an American and a Chinati," Whitecloud said softly.

Kaumudi nodded toward the door. "Our young friends would argue it should be in the reverse order."

"And perhaps, in the end, they'd be right. All I know is another round of racial power mongering on this continent won't serve anyone's interests. We might find ourselves on top again for a while. But sooner or later, everyone, including the whites, must feel like they've got an equal chance at success, at happiness. We, above all, should know this."

"Like the chance the whites gave us?" Kaumudi said, rapping the rim of his pipe against the bench leg.

Whitecloud tapped out his pipe on the bottom of his boot. "Truly great nations are not built by force," he said, looking at the Cherokee chief. "They are built by consensus. We have a chance here to rise above petty racial and class differences. We can show the whites, and the world, we are bigger than that. We can show them all how Indians from multiple tribes can come together to forge a great initiative. Who knows what it might develop into? Think what it would do for our children."

"And when the additive is stolen, or dysprosium deposits discovered elsewhere, what will become of your grand experiment? Unless we've kept enough of the wealth for ourselves while it's here for us, we'll just end up in the same place. Tricked out of our heritage again." Kaumudi looked out across the parking lot. His eyes lifted to the canopy of stars. "I'm sorry, Angus. Have you ever felt like the world is looking to you alone for an answer? I just don't want to make a mistake with this."

"I can imagine how that feels," the Chinati whispered.

The old chiefs rose and shuffled toward the front door.

"Well," said Whitecloud in a kind but resolute tone as they reentered the restaurant, "there's no time to debate the matter. We must move quickly or not at all." He paused, touching Kaumudi's shoulder. He saw the young Indians watching them intently from the booth in the back. Then speaking directly to the Cherokee chief, he asked, "Will your people join with us?"

Kaumudi raised his chin and extended his hand. "I think you know the answer."

20

TWO DAYS AFTER HIS MEETING with Oliver, Principal Randy Kickingbird invited Chief Whitecloud to meet him at an old campsite outside
of Chinati Flats. It was late afternoon and the September sun was hot.
He watched the dirt road from under a wooden shed, hands folded on a
picnic table.

The desert floor was tinged green with autumn grass and dotted
with mesquite. In the distance, an outcropping of brown granite, veined
white from ancient lava flows, rose abruptly from the plain like the cap
of an enormous mushroom. At its base, you could see drifts of pale stones
gouged from the mountain by the seeping magma. A hawk patrolled the
flat land in graceful orbits, silhouetted like a black dot against the upthrust.
Kickingbird closed his eyes and breathed deeply. A part of him loved this
land. He thought, *Would I really be happier on the outside?* The sound of
an approaching truck broke the spell.

Chief Whitecloud pulled off the highway and parked his truck next
to the principal's old minivan. His boots stirred up tiny puffs of dust as he
shuffled toward the table, shook hands, and sat down.

"Thanks for coming," Kickingbird said.

The chief nodded. "What's on your mind?"

"I'm a member of the Texas State Teachers Association. We're not an official union, but we have friends in organized labor. I was contacted by the United Auto Workers union. They know about the Rio Hot Springs minerals and want to talk about a financing arrangement."

"Why?" the chief asked.

Kickingbird looked down, took a breath, then raised his eyes. "Well, as they explained it, they see the additive as making automobile ownership more affordable and the cost of operation lower. It will create jobs in their industry and more union members."

The chief smiled. "And that's it?"

"There's one more thing," the principal said, remembering the talking points Oliver had given him. "The UAW is weak in the energy industry, especially in the South, and sees our fuel additive facility as a way to get established. It's automotive and energy. A perfect fit for them."

The chief noticed Kickingbird's hands were trembling slightly. *There must be something else*, he thought.

"So, do they have a proposal of some kind?" he asked.

"They are willing to consider a development loan for four million dollars from the UAW pension fund."

Whitecloud sat back and cocked his head, fingering the beads around his neck.

"What's the catch?" he asked.

Kickingbird squirmed. "They want to organize our tribe into a local branch of the UAW."

Ah yes, thought Chief Whitecloud, remembering the casino. *Griev-*

ances. Strikes. The only thing worse than real prostitutes were the union bosses. But . . . four million.

"How do they know how much our minerals are worth?" the chief asked.

"I enlisted the help of your grandson. I hope you don't mind. Oliver pulled together a copy of Clive Larsen's white paper and a current sample from the springs. I sent them to the UAW. They said they would have to make a site visit and do some tests of their own to verify, but it looks good. They want to make this loan."

The two men sat in silence for a minute. Kickingbird finally drummed his hands on the table and said, "I can see you've got concerns, Angus. Maybe this wasn't such a good idea."

Chief Whitecloud gazed over the principal's shoulder at the circling hawk.

"Tell them we'll do it."

The schoolteacher's face went white and his jaw dropped. "Okay. Okay," he stammered.

"Only one condition," Angus Whitecloud added. "They must conduct their tests, give us a copy of their appraisal, and make their decision within one week. That's it."

The chief stood and extended his hand. "Send their report to me when you receive it."

He got into his truck and drove away, leaving Randy Kickingbird alone.

As he watched the chief leave, the principal's mind raced. *He must have wondered if there was anything in it for me. If he'd asked, I would have had to tell him about the job the union offered me. And what about Oliver? How much is he getting paid to set this up?*

He buried his face in his hands and exhaled audibly.

Don't think so much.

21

THE COUNCIL ROOM WAS PACKED. The members took their seats around the tables, arranged in a U-shape. Three days had passed since the first counsel meeting. Joining them were the lawyer, Jim Blackwater, and the architect, Ivan Stone. The audience, now ten rows deep, settled in, facing the open end of the horseshoe. There was a nervous buzz. The chief's knuckles clicked against the table. "Okay. Let's get started. We've got decisions to make. I wish we had more time to consider alternatives, but circumstances have overtaken us. So far, we've talked about several approaches: We can make a deal with an oil company partner, like Stasney Energy, to help us develop our minerals. We can try to find financing on our own and go it alone, as Jim Blackwater suggested at our last meeting. Or we can do nothing at all, as Ivan Stone proposed."

"That's not quite accurate," Stone interjected. "I just pointed out what we would be giving up for a major development operation."

"I understand," replied the chief. "There are no bright lines here. Your comments were valid."

The chief took a deep breath and looked around the room. "Before

I offer my opinion, I would like for Billy Strikeleather to tell you about another kind of offer he received only last night."

He looked at Billy, who shuffled a pile of papers and cleared his throat. "Yesterday I got a call from Luke Stasney," said Billy. "He has been talking to Trans-National Energy, who is willing to make a deal with us to capture the Rio Hot Springs minerals, refine them, and produce the additive."

"They've already figured out how to make the stuff?" asked Red.

"Looks like they've known for some time," said Billy. "They just didn't have enough of the mineral or didn't want to find it. The ramp-up would take a while, but they would pay us a bonus up front of ten million dollars just for signing the agreement."

The room went quiet. Finally, the silence was broken by Edith who said, "And when the product is sold, how much do we get then?"

"A percentage of the net profit. A royalty."

"And who would be in charge of the project?" asked architect Stone.

"Trans-National has said Stasney Energy could run the day-to-day operations."

"But the funds would be coming from Trans-National, right?" the lawyer interrupted. "So, the funding schedule would be dictated by them."

"Well, I suppose."

"If no money flows, neither do our minerals."

Billy shrugged, but continued, "It's not that simple, Jim. I'm not a lawyer, but surely they would have some duty to hold up their end of the deal."

"What you're describing is really two deals," Blackwater responded. "A lease of the minerals and an agreement to refine and manufacture the additive."

"Couldn't we include deadlines to force them to move ahead with funding the recovery of and development?"

"Sure. There are a million ways to draft this," said Blackwater. "But, in the end, it's all just words on a page."

"What do you mean?" asked the school principal, Randy Kickingbird.

"Once they have the minerals under lease, the only way to force Trans-National to develop them is to sue. Hire lawyers and go to court."

"What's the problem with that?" Red inquired.

"The problem is, you can beat the rap, but you can't beat the ride," said Blackwater.

Frowns ringed the table.

"Sorry. Left over from my criminal defense days," Blackwater smiled. "We'd have a winning case, but a rich defendant like Trans-National would make us earn it. You have to understand something. Justice is for sale in Texas. Only money counts. That includes the cost of lawyers, which they can afford, and we can't, and the price of the right decision upheld in court."

"Like the worthless IOUs my mother was given for her land," Edith hissed.

"Yes."

"What do you mean?" Principal Kickingbird asked, raising his palms up in an inquiring fashion.

Blackwater scratched his neck and leaned forward on his elbows. "Think a minute about what our minerals could mean to the oil business, and not just in Texas. A ten-to-one increase in gasoline mileage would undermine the value of every oil field in the world. Oil money controls Texas. Without it, the economy collapses. Think also about the fact that judges in Texas are elected, not appointed. To get elected takes money, especially to the most powerful benches in the state, like the supreme court."

"You mean the judges are paid to rule a certain way?" the principal said, eyes wide.

"Let's just say those who rule against Big Oil never make it past the next election. And, there is the matter of what they do after they leave office. The usual routine is to go to work for a big law firm, using your influence with the court to bring in fat-cat clients. It's part of the unofficial retirement package for supreme court judges. Buck the system and you'll never work for a major law firm, ever."

"I can't imagine our case would go all the way to the supreme court," Red said.

"The supreme court hears the cases it wants. Believe me. Any case threatening the underpinnings of the oil business in Texas would end up there."

Quiet settled over the chamber. Billy shivered as he felt the first threads of his proposed alliance with Trans-National begin to unravel.

After a short pause, the chief spoke. "There's yet another way," he said, glancing from face to face. "After our last meeting, I went to Alpine."

He reported on his discussion with the other tribes, a possible alliance with Stasney, and developing the Rio Hot Springs minerals with an Indian economic development foundation.

"They didn't commit to the investment of a specific dollar amount, but were open to the idea, and to guaranteeing a loan," the chief said of the other Indians. "We would also need Stasney's backing to get additional financing."

"So," said the principal, "we'd just be selling part of our minerals to them to raise money, right?"

"Not exactly," the chief replied. "Their money, and any loan funds, would go to develop the minerals, and the profits would go to the foundation. It would be owned by all the tribes and used only to provide seed money and loans for new projects that create real jobs and build a long-term economy."

The chief scanned the table, then turned back to Billy. *Jesus*, Billy thought, *he wants me to get on board right now. What the hell will Luke say?*

"Well," Billy stammered, "this is not how I expected the deal to work out. I'm not sure what Stasney would say about diving into the project without Trans-National's financial support."

"So, you're suggesting we pass up, what is that, fifty thousand dollars for every member of the Chinati tribe?" said Edith. "And hope for the best from Stasney and the other tribes?"

The crowd began to murmur audibly.

"What kind of money are we talking about to produce the first drop of this stuff?" Red asked in a skeptical tone.

"We'd need a pump to pull water from the springs," said Billy. "Also, a distillation plant to separate the dysprosium, and a cracking unit to refine it a number of times until we find the right density of carbon molecules. The right circle."

"How much?" Red repeated.

"We figure about four million dollars."

"All that to produce a pint of gasoline?" Edith asked with an edge in her voice.

"We're not making gasoline. Only additive and in small amounts. Maybe a pint for each twenty gallons or so of gas. We don't know yet how much spring water that will take."

"Sounds to me like we've got a lot of unanswered questions," Edith said.

"It's true. We have some work to do," Billy responded. "But we know it works and so does Trans-National. What will Luke Stasney say to going it alone without a Big Oil backer? I don't know. I would need to flesh out the details some more before going to him."

Blackwater raised his hand. "I'm not an engineer or manufacturing expert, but I know business deals. We need Stasney's money and production expertise and his financial statements to get the loan. That's worth a percentage of the profits. The money has to be up front, so we are in charge of the pace of development."

"How would that work?" Billy asked.

"We'd need Stasney and the other tribes to contribute, together, a million and a half dollars to get started, and borrow the rest."

The group fell silent for a long moment.

Finally, Edith asked the obvious question. "And who would make a loan like that to us?"

"Like I said last night, the same banks that stand to lose big when the value of oil reserves drops like a stone, which it's certain to do when our additive hits the market," said Blackwater.

"How would Luke fit in?" Billy asked.

"I don't know his net worth or his company's," said Blackstone, "but I know their credit's been good enough to keep drilling dry holes for the last three years. I'd bet with his guaranty, along with ours and the other tribes, we could borrow enough to get us to market."

"If he was willing to do it," said the chief.

"That's right," the lawyer responded, looking at Billy.

"Exactly what would be in it for him?" asked Billy.

"An override on all the profits we make."

"You mean he would own an interest in the economic foundation like the Indians?" Edith asked.

"No. Only a right to receive a portion of the profits. No ownership in the minerals."

"And no control over what we do?"

"Well, I'm sure he'd want some sort of budget and timetable for development. The lender certainly will."

"Would he do that?" Edith asked.

"He'd have to," said Blackstone.

"So, as I understand it," Edith said, "we have to decide whether to take the Trans-National money and give up control, or reject it and raise enough money to go it alone with Stasney and the other tribes."

"Yes," said Whitecloud in a cautious voice, scanning the table. The room was silent. "I would need the authority to make the best deal I can on a loan to the new Indian foundation for at least three million dollars."

"I think we've discussed this long enough," said Edith.

The chief stood and cleared his throat. "All in favor of approaching Luke Stasney with the idea of developing the minerals on our own, with the help of Stasney Energy and the other tribes, please raise your hands."

The vote was unanimous, except for Red, who avoided eye contact with the rest of the council.

Whitecloud nodded and turned to Billy. "Can you please discuss this with Luke Stasney and get back to me right away?"

"Yes."

"Meeting is adjourned."

After the meeting, Billy cornered the chief.

"This all sounds good in theory, chief. But you've got no idea what Buck Olmeyer and the rest of the Big Oil goons will do when they figure out you've two-timed them."

"I didn't deceive anyone, Billy. I never told you or them we had a deal. Olmeyer just presumed he could buy his way in with a multi-million dollar buyout offer. He was wrong. The council wanted more independence and gave me the authority to pursue that with Stasney and the other tribes as our partners.

"Olmeyer needs to control the minerals, Billy. He's desperate. Otherwise, his business model will die. That's not the kind of partner you want."

"What makes you think Luke can, or will, go it alone?" Billy asked.

"He also needs the deal, but for personal reasons. I think he'll come onboard."

"Well, that's just great," Billy said. "And I suppose you want me to convince Luke?"

"I think you are the right person to do it."

"Do you have any idea how angry Olmeyer will be when he hears this?" Billy said.

"I don't see how he can stop us."

"Like hell he can't, you old fool!" exclaimed Billy, his eyes wide. "Right now, he's prepping for a news conference announcing his partnership with our tribe. Without that deal, he's in trouble. There's no telling what he'll do. It damn sure won't be pretty."

"Think about it a minute, son. What's he going to do?"

"What does an animal do when it's wounded, trapped? It fights back, and that's what will happen."

"He has no legal right to the minerals."

"I tell you, you're playing with fire."

"Answer my question, Billy. What would you do in his place?"

"I'd make sure nobody ever developed the goddamned minerals."

22

BILLY KNEW CONVINCING LUKE TO MOVE FORWARD without
Trans-National's money or credit would be a hard sell, so he'd traveled to
Houston to make the pitch in person.

"Good God, Billy," said Luke with a trace of panic in his voice. "I
agreed to help you with this deal when Trans-National was going to be our
partner, not our enemy. They were supposed to fund it. Now you want me
to put up virtually all the money and borrow the rest?"

"Not all of it," Billy said, looking at Luke across the CEO's desk.
"We think a million and a half would be enough cash to get us started. The
tribes would put up two hundred fifty of that."

"Have Clive and my guys figured out what it will take after that, all
in, to get the first can of additive to market?" Luke asked.

"Probably close to four million," Billy responded tepidly.

Luke looked past Billy and out his office window at the Houston
skyline. "So, tell me if I've got this right. Stasney Energy pumps in
a million and a quarter bucks to get the project started. Then we wait
for a bunch of Indians we don't know to show up with a quarter of a

million more. Then we borrow three million more from a lender we don't know. Brilliant."

"It's not like that, Luke," Billy responded. "These tribes don't operate like your company. If they say they'll help, they will. It just takes time."

"Well, I've got plenty of that," Luke said, wagging his head sideways for emphasis. "We'll get in when they do."

Billy lowered his head and said, "We don't have that kind of time."

"What are you talking about?" asked Luke. "Those minerals have been down there for a million years. They're not going anywhere."

Billy raised his eyes. "Our sources tell us Trans-National has been at work among the Chinati, pushing to take over the entire deal. Another two weeks and they'll have bought enough support on the council to do it."

"Billy, we don't have that much cash on hand to dump into this thing right now. With Trans-National as a partner, I could have borrowed my share. Without them, I don't know."

"Do you have a lender who could help?" Billy asked cautiously.

"Our best bet would be Hugh Gantry at Texas Commercial Bank. He financed my dad for years when Stasney Energy was a start-up."

"So, he's comfortable with oil and gas lending?" asked Billy.

Luke rolled his eyes. "TCB is the lead lender for Trans-National and half a dozen other majors. But Gantry's likely to be more than a little worried about a project like ours. If we are successful, it would be a real blow to all their other oil and gas customers."

"I understand," Billy said. "But wouldn't it, at least, be worth asking?"

"Look, Billy. No lender would even consider making this kind of crazy loan without a corporate guaranty from Stasney Energy, my personal guaranty, and a pledge of all my company stock. That means if the project failed, I'd be ruined."

"There's one more option," Billy said. "Chief Whitecloud has a friend at a Midland bank, Plains Savings. He thinks she'd have an interest."

A cloud cast a shadow through the window. Luke's thoughts drifted to his father, the wildcatter. *For him these decisions had been routine. All or nothing. He'd thrived on them. They'd defined him.* Luke's pulse quickened.

"Do you have her name and number?"

"I can get them."

The cloud passed.

23

BUCK OLMEYER SAT AT HIS DESK and thought about his meeting with Luke.

Across the room, Governor Barstow crossed his legs and leaned back into the leather chaise lounge. He took a pull on his cigar through oval lips and launched a formation of smoke rings toward the CEO. "Where are you with the Rio Hot Springs joint venture?"

Buck rubbed the back of his neck, then looked up. The halos drifted across the room like vultures. "It's in the works."

"It's been a while now," the governor said. "Time to get the deal inked before any more surprises."

"We're on it."

There was a knock at the door. "Mr. Olmeyer?"

"Yes."

His secretary looked in. "Are you available for Hugh Gantry?"

"Sure. Put him through. Dolph, can you excuse me for a minute?" said Buck, glancing at the open door.

"Of course," Dolph responded, standing. "Tell that fat son of a bitch

I'll be looking for him at the Houston Republican Party fundraiser to-night." He pivoted around the coffee table and strode into the hall.

"This way, governor," Buck's secretary said. "You can use the guest office next door."

The latch clicked shut.

Buck turned and put the receiver to his ear. "Gantry? Olmeyer here."

"Hello, Buck, how's it going?"

Olmeyer could picture the balding fat man, sitting behind his over-sized desk at Texas Commercial Bank.

"Can't complain, you?"

"Fine. Fine."

"What can I do for you?"

"Buck, I got a package in the mail this morning. No return address. It contains a report on something called rare earth minerals. There's a paper in here by a guy named Clive Larson presented at the Texas Drillers Association convention back in 1968."

"Never heard of him," Buck said, a plastic smile frozen across his face.

"Larson's paper predicts the discovery of these minerals out in West Texas. According to him, one mineral—something called dysprosium—has some pretty special qualities."

"I'm listening," Buck said, never changing his expression. "I love a good story." His pulse quickened.

"It's probably nothing, but these days, you know, I've got to check out everything," the banker droned.

"Sure. Sure."

"Now here's a pretty interesting section in the report called 'Trans-National Test Results.' It says Trans-National has run tests on dysprosium going back to 1968, showing it can enhance gasoline mileage tenfold."

"And if you put it in your coffee, it probably makes you ten years younger," Buck snorted. "Even if it were true, there's not enough of that stuff to fill a thimble."

"I'm sure you're right," Hugh said with a laugh. "But there's something else in the report that's got us interested."

"What's that?"

"It's about a dysprosium discovery in West Texas," the banker said slowly. "Let's see, looks like only a few weeks ago. If this is correct, and we're checking it out, there might be a hell of a lot of this stuff out there."

Buck stiffened in his chair. "And where was this so-called mineral find?"

"On an Indian reservation, of all places. Chinati, I think."

"And you believe this nonsense? I'm surprised you'd be taken in by it. Oil futures traders will go to any length to manipulate the market. Why else do you think this bullshit would show up like magic on your desk?"

"We thought about that, Buck," the fat banker said. "But here's the thing. If all they wanted was to spook the market, they could have sent it to the newspapers. Instead they sent it to us—and you know we're duty bound to inform the bank regulators and the SEC. That guarantees a government investigation. No stockbroker would want that."

"What the hell are you talking about, Gantry?" Buck barked. "This is nothing but a ploy to set up a short sale. These pricks are trying to drive down the price of crude so they can cut a fat hog. I assure you they've already shorted oil futures. You spread this nonsense, even to a regulator, and they'll get away with it."

"Settle down, Buck. I'm sure there's a good explanation for this. All we need from you is a denial about the Trans-National test results, and a sworn statement that you've got no knowledge about a new dysprosium discovery. You know, just something for the loan committee."

"The loan committee?" Buck said in an icy tone. "Are you threatening me, Gantry?"

"Look, Buck," the banker replied, his voice a pitch higher. "I can't just ignore this. All I need is your input before it's presented to the committee this Friday. With loans the size of yours, everything's got to be squeaky clean."

"You idiot," Buck said. "Don't you see what you're doing? What do you think the bank's board of directors is going to do when they hear you're screwing with their biggest customer? They'll have your job."

"Buck. Put yourself in our shoes for a minute. If there's even a possibility that gasoline mileage could go up by 1000 percent, the price of crude's got to come down accordingly. No banker could ignore that kind of devaluation of collateral."

"We're current on our credit lines," the CEO seethed. "Hell, we're the best goddamn credit risk on the planet."

"Read your loan documents, Buck," Hugh replied in a steady voice. "If the value of your reserves goes down, we'll have to call for a principal reduction on your credit lines—a big one. Worse still, if we know about it and don't call those loans, somebody's going to jail. I can assure you, it's not going to be me."

The line went silent.

"Are you there, Buck?"

"Yep."

"Please, just get something to me by Friday," Hugh said with a sigh.

"That's only four days, Hugh. I haven't even seen what you've got."

"I've told you enough," the banker responded. "If you want more specifics, have your lawyer call. We'll give him a copy and tell him exactly the language we need in your statement."

"Who knows about this at the bank, Hugh?"

"So far only me. The package came to my desk. But I can't keep it quiet forever."

Buck took a deep breath and fell back into his chair. His cheeks expanded as he exhaled hard. "Hugh, we've known each other a long time. Trans-National's got a lot of money at Texas Commercial. We made your bank, and we can break you. I hope we can work something out."

"Goodbye, Buck."

★ ★ ★

The CEO of Texas Trans-National Energy, Inc. was sweating. Dark circles crept from under the arms of his blue dress shirt. His lips pressed into a straight line. He turned to his computer and clicked on the directory of the Trans-National Board of Directors. Scratching his head, he moved on to his personal lawyer. Finally, he stopped the curser on LaCour Financial. He reached in his pocket for his cell phone and dialed the number.

"LaCour Financial," came the greeting.

"Jerry LaCour, please. This is Buck Olmeyer."

"Yes, Mr. Olmeyer. One moment."

"Hi, Buck. How's it going?" said the managing partner of LaCour.

"Jerry, I've decided to make some portfolio changes."

"Sure," the middle-aged accountant responded in his usual accommodating tone.

"I want you to liquidate my Trans-National stock in blocks over the next four days. Also sell any REITs that have real estate holdings in Texas."

"I'm sorry, Buck. Say again?" Jerry responded smoothly.

"You heard me. Just do it," Buck shot back.

"If you don't mind me asking," Jerry probed, his brow knotted, "why the sudden decision?"

"I've got some investment opportunities," Buck parried. "Put half the proceeds in my trust account in the Caicos Islands, a quarter in T-bills, and the rest in Ford Motors."

"Okay, Buck."

"And one more thing."

"Yes?"

"I want all the funds in the Trans-National Employee Pension Plan converted to T-bills. Do it over the next four days."

Buck heard the headman at LaCour cough nervously. "Buck, that's over a billion dollars."

"Do it, Jerry."

"It'll raise some eyebrows. We may need a corporate resolution from your board," he responded meekly.

Buck bristled.

"Listen carefully, Jerry. You do exactly as I instructed, or I'll move the whole goddamn shooting match over to Dick Scanlon at Dain Rauscher."

"Yes, sir."

As soon the line went dead, Jerry called out to his secretary, "Get me Leslie Strikeleather on the phone, now!"

On the top floor of One Trans-National Plaza, Governor Dolph Barstow sat quietly in an overstuffed chair near the wall in the guest office. His right pointer finger looped around the butt of a smoldering Kinky Friedman cigar. With his left hand, he held a gold cigar case to his ear like a cell phone. Inside, a red light blinked as the directional recording device played back the conversation between Buck and his banker.

The governor expelled a stream of smoke, then crushed out the embers in a marble ash tray. He slipped the case into his coat pocket and walked to the door.

In the hall, Barstow met Olmeyer emerging from his office. "Shall we grab a bite to eat, governor?"

"Love to, Buck, but duty calls. League of Women Voters lunch over at the Hilton."

"Lucky you. Let's talk later."

"You can bet on it."

24

LESLIE SNAPPED OFF THE LIGHT IN HER OFFICE and swung her briefcase over her shoulder. It had been a long day. Rumors were flying about a big trade, but no one knew the details. As she wheeled out of her office toward the elevator, she noticed a light down the hall. *What would keep a blueblood broker from the LaCour firm working this late?* she wondered. She reversed course and headed back to Jerry LaCour's office.

"Burning it pretty late, aren't you?" she said with a half-smile, peering around the door.

He was hunched over his desk, tie loosened and sleeves rolled. "Nothing special," he responded without looking up.

"Sorry I wasn't available earlier when you called. Trans-National?"

Her statement drew a glare. "How'd you guess?"

"Olmeyer's the only client I know so important to LaCour that you'd still be here at this hour."

"That's all?"

"Well, there's been some office buzz."

Giving in, Jerry leaned back, running his fingers through thinning gray hair. "I just can't figure out what the hell he's up to."

"How so?" said Leslie taking a seat.

Jerry related to her the sell order from Buck that afternoon, causing her to whistle under her breath. Even she hadn't guessed at the magnitude of the trade.

"Something big must be cooking," Leslie said.

"That's what I was going to ask you," Jerry said. "Any idea what?"

"No," she lied. "But I don't think you want to know all that Olmeyer does. Insider trading can get you five to ten these days." Leslie's mind was racing a thousand miles per hour as she began putting two and two together. *It has to be the Rio Hot Springs minerals. The damn additive must be for real to scare him into taking such a risk. And he must not have a lot of confidence that Billy Strikeleather and Luke Stasney can bring the tribe to the table for a deal with Trans-National.*

"Have you made the trade yet?" she asked.

"No. You can't dump that much in a day. The market would tank and the SEC boys would be on you like stink on shit."

"Be careful, Jerry," Leslie said, standing.

"I'm trying. And, of course, this is all confidential. Got it?"

"Of course," she said with affected concern and walked out.

On her drive home, Leslie barely saw the road. Buck Olmeyer had given her an opening. All she needed were a few more details, something that would stand up in court. She reached in her purse for her cell phone and punched in Buck's mobile.

"Hi, baby," she heard him grunt.

"Long day?" she asked.

"You could say that."

"Can I see you tonight?"

It hadn't been difficult to get into Buck Olmeyer's pants. When powerful men are under pressure, they reach out for reassurance from anyone who will give them a positive stroke. For the last month she'd been that person for the CEO of Trans-National. Initially hired by Olmeyer's goons to herd Luke Stasney and the Chinati tribe into a deal with Trans-National, she had quickly impressed him with her total lack of moral boundaries and her willingness to prostitute her prior relationship with Luke to her own advantage. They were two of a kind.

"Good idea," Buck said. "I'll meet you in an hour."

Leslie veered off the freeway to a side street leading to the Montrose District. The Trans-National guest quarters were in a fancy three-story complex called La Petite Retraite, a high-end restaurant and bar on the first floor servicing Houston's elite. Above, Upper East Side apartments were available for desserts of all kinds.

She pulled up to the garage and opened it with a gray remote entrusted to her by Buck. That, and an electronic keycard to the apartment, had been a signal of her acceptance into the Trans-National hierarchy where the air was rare, and secrets kept.

By the time Buck arrived, Leslie had showered and donned his favorite white lace negligee. As the door rattled open, she propped herself on one elbow in the turned down bed. "Want a drink?" she heard him call out in a gruff tone. Some women might have been put off, but tonight she was on a mission.

"Sure."

The sound of clinking ice preceded him as he came down the hall. He entered the room and walked to the bed where he set her usual scotch and water on the nightstand. Without a word, he took a long swig of Knob Creek from the other glass and kicked off his Tony Lamas. In less than a minute he had shed his clothes revealing a golfer's tan and a pot belly thick with gray hair. *No prize*, Leslie observed, contemplating the view over a sip.

For Buck Olmeyer, lovemaking was like food. When he was hungry, he ate, mostly out, and he expected the service to be prompt. This time, however, Leslie made him wait. Instead of touching him in her usual fashion, she rolled him on his stomach and began massaging his shoulders.

"You're tense, honey," she whispered. "Anything wrong?"

"I've had better days," he muttered into the pillow.

She lifted her glass, capturing an ice cube in her mouth, then brushed her lips down his spine stopping just short of his white buttocks. The cold liquid made him flinch. Pulling back, she laughed and reached for his whisky on the opposite nightstand.

"Come on, Leslie," he groaned, but then rolled toward her, accepting the drink and the fact that some conversation would be required.

"So, what's the big news?" Leslie cooed, toying with his belly fuzz.

Buck took a deep breath and summed up the day's events with Texas Commerce Bank. As he described how Hugh Gantry threatened to call Trans-National loans unless Buck could refute the dysprosium gas mileage report, Leslie's pulse quickened, and her lips replaced her fingers.

Buck drank off his cocktail and lay back.

Leslie looked up through the gray forest which was now rising and falling more rapidly. "Does he have that right?" she asked between kisses.

"Yesss, baby. Who cares?"

"I do."

"Why?"

"I worry about you, honey. You know that."

He reached down with casual confidence and pushed her head farther down. She resisted.

Buck sighed and threw his hands aside like a crucifix.

"I took care of that situation. Once we get the minerals under our control the report will become irrelevant. Problem solved."

"So why did you decide to sell off your Trans-National stock and go short on crude futures?" Leslie said, looking up at him with a level stare. She felt his muscles tighten.

"Who says I did?"

"Have you forgotten where I work?"

The CEO propped his right forearm under his neck and returned her gaze with dead eyes.

"I didn't have any choice. I can't let a fortune ride on the business sense of a band of fucking Indians, a drunk quarterback, and a trust fund baby," he said, closing his free hand around her neck.

She felt the pressure increase like a tourniquet.

"Of course, once you've convinced Luke to take our deal, none of this will matter, right?" His cold stare and unrelenting grip brought a flash of fear to her face.

"Sure, baby," Leslie said before lowering to deliver the main course.

Buck freed her head as she went to work. Her mouth began its calculated routine, but her brain slipped into overdrive. *What the hell has he gotten himself and Trans-National into?* She brought him to the brink over and over while she pondered her next move. *I need more information. More details.*

The president and chief operating officer of the world's largest oil company was moaning and grinding like a pipe yard pumpjack when Leslie heard the beep of an incoming text. It came from Buck's phone on the nightstand. With a flick of her tongue she unloosed from him a bull bellow, carefully milking it till the phone went quiet.

When Buck began snoring loudly, Leslie slipped from the sheets and walked to the bathroom. After brushing her teeth, she took her clothes from a hook behind the door, dressed, and crept back to the bedside. With her right hand, she snapped off the light, then stooped to read the new text: "DA ready to roll on Chinati rape charges if necessary. Plan B frack can be ready in forty-eight hours. Colt."

My God, there's no end to this. What rape? What in the world is the Plan B frack? She considered the options, then took a chance. "What was the date of that rape again?" she asked Colt electronically. "June of 1960," came the reply.

Buck grunted and rolled toward the opposite wall. Leslie replaced Buck's cell phone and reached under the bed. A green light blinked to red as she stopped the recorder on her own phone. Slipping it into her purse, she blew him a kiss and left.

25

ACROSS THE STREET from the mammoth David Crockett Pavilion in the Galleria District stood the Aria Centre, a sparkling midrise office complex purchased by LaCour Financial at foreclosure during the 1986 oil bust. With free rent, the firm had made it through the recovery and still occupied the top three of ten floors.

Leslie arrived at 8:15 a.m. Trudging into the blue granite lobby, past the baby grand with tuxedoed pianist and onto an elevator, she struggled to overcome another sleepless night. Her companion had been, once again, a nagging doubt. The kind you try to forget at 3 a.m., but can't. Since Billy's final downfall, her goal had been to solidify her position at LaCour. Now she wasn't so sure.

The elevator doors slid shut and she was surrounded by a gaggle of lawyers, CPAs, and wildcatters wearing thousand-dollar boots who inhabited the lower floors. Pitching deals to LaCour clients over ribs and sweet tea at Buster Bill's Basement Bistro was their long suit.

Most were survivors of the 1986 depression, when oil prices had dropped by two-thirds in less than six months. The energy engine that pumped capital from the ground into the veins of the Houston economy ran dry. The ripple effect—from top to bottom—was swift and deadly. Aside from the petroleum industry, the worst hit were owners of real estate, large and small.

Leslie stepped off on the top floor and headed down a hallway with gray cut pile carpet. On her right was a maze of cubicles where young analysts awaited their manager's arrival, gratuitously shuffling papers. Leslie knew the game and pitied them. Overpaid and pampered, they could run computer programs on modeling bonds but couldn't write a sentence. Most were still unaware they'd been hired for their family connections and once the referrals stopped, they'd be gone.

Farther along, on her left, a double door opened onto a maze of windowless offices where stock traders, wise to the eyes of management, worked world markets in private. They were the bell cows of the firm, producing over 50 percent of LaCour's revenues. The best got back half as commission.

Leslie stopped at the far end of the corridor. Account executives who handled daily relationships with clients officed here. They rarely arrived at their Henredon desks before nine. Her work area was a small converted conference room with burgundy walls and a view of the parking garage.

She shrugged off her bone white blazer and tossed it across a large glass table that doubled as her desk. Settling into a black captain's chair, she jettisoned her Jimmy Choos and ran her manicured toes across the fake Persian rug. As marketing manager for the firm, she resented the setup, but understood the rules. Perks went to those who controlled the business. She knew customers by their first names and they by hers. It was enough to make their Christmas card lists but not, however, to direct their investments.

Part of her job was to monitor fluctuations in client accounts and learn the patterns. The date of a customer's annual bonus was information she was paid to know. Thus armed by Leslie, the account exec would call the next day with a friendly reminder about new financial products. *I tee them up*, she thought. *They get the credit and commissions.*

She scanned the pictures on the walls in her office. Most were of her at posh restaurants with wealthy investors. There was a time, she recalled with a sigh, when she and Billy had been the guests. *We were everybody's best friend. I knew they weren't sincere, but I pretended.*

Billy was in only one picture. It was the night LaCour made the winning bid on the Houston Rodeo grand champion bull. The $360,000 purchase price, which all went to charity, had been her entry fee to a clique of good old boys who picked the investment firms for the richest philanthropies in Texas, like the rodeo. It had also bought access to the state's political elite such as Governor Dolph Barstow and Houston Mayor Adriana Whitlock. In the picture, they flanked Billy and Leslie, like old friends. *Those were heady days*, she thought, *until Billy's off-the-field shenanigans made us damaged goods.*

On her desktop computer, she began scrolling down a client list. *I suppose this is pretty much my portfolio*, she said to herself sarcastically. The big-time nonprofits were her favorites. *The Armstrong Family Trust, The Houston Livestock Show and Rodeo, The Medical Center Foundation*, the *University of Texas Endowment*—they were the Who's Who of Houston's nonprofits. Millions flowed through these accounts daily. So much that even their account executives could not always pinpoint balances.

Twisting a lock of her hair, Leslie considered her options at LaCour. What once seemed a ticket back to the good life, now mired her in a world of corporate politics, disproportionate compensation, and ass-kissing. Her recurring nocturnal notion was correct. *I can do better, but how?*

Her thoughts turned to a three-whisky soliloquy on investment strategies delivered to her a few weeks before by Buck Olmeyer. "Futures," he'd gushed, "are how you make a killing in a crappy market. A sucker agrees to purchase certain stocks, bonds, or commodities—deliverables—from you at a specified amount on a future date. It's called a *futures contract*. If the market value of the deliverables on the scheduled sale date has dropped below the contract price, you buy them at market and sell them for more under the contract. Simple."

"The parties don't actually deliver the real products, do they?" Leslie had asked. "Like a railcar of oranges?"

"No," he chuckled, pinching her backside. "The contracts are netted out to determine profits or losses for each player based upon market prices. What changes hands then is money, not fruit."

He went on to explain that to enter into a futures contract, you must put up a fraction of the contract price, usually around 25 percent—a margin—which requires cash.

Her mind fast-forwarded and her eyes widened as an inkling tickled her brain. *OF COURSE. If Billy's dysprosium additive gets to market, oil prices will take a huge hit. A correct futures bet could make someone a bundle. Why not me? What would be the smart way?* she pondered, looking out at the morning sky. *Something not easily traceable. A big enough play to make the return worth the risk. But how could I fund the margin?*

She leaned forward in her chair, one elbow on an armrest supporting her chin, and began researching futures contracts online. Buck Olmeyer's description had been accurate in principal. However, there were variations and a language unique to the investment. She began taking notes. When she looked up, it was noon. Skipping her lunchbreak, she began reviewing recent futures trades in the company transaction logs. An unfamiliar name caught her eye. *The Estuary Fund.*

The executive assigned to the account was a former trader named Ron Bossier, a third-generation financier from Galveston with an appetite for the good life. She knew him as a crafty tactician with a client base of high-end trophy hunters and fishermen from his hometown.

Bossier was around fifty with salt-and-pepper hair combed straight back, his custom-made suits accented by alligator belts, and Italian shoes polished to a high shine. He had a deep tan year-round, teeth a shade too white, children in private school, and a condo in Aspen. All were calculated to inspire confidence in, or intimidate when necessary, his blueblood clientele.

Although a fair marksperson, being of the wrong gender and not *born on the island* had limited Leslie's marketing options with Bossier's Galveston crowd. New shotguns for Christmas was the best she'd come up with.

LaCour client records labeled The Estuary Fund as a nonprofit for the preservation of coastal wetlands. Bossier was the treasurer. He'd gotten himself appointed as both the account executive and equities trader for the account when the fund was a sleepy start-up. Leslie was gobsmacked when she discovered the fund had churned out $225,000 in commissions this year alone, half of which went to Bossier. She looked deeper.

The balance in The Estuary Fund now stood at two million dollars, off a high of twice that amount earlier in the month. The pattern had repeated itself for two years. Scratching her head, she called up an annual activities report on Bossier's ten top accounts. When she made a graph of the deposits and withdrawals, they matched those of the Estuary Fund. She made a print.

Trading department records did not show the outcome of all Estuary transactions since they were handled by Bossier direct. Client records revealed, however, that Bossier had purchased $2,000,000 in gold futures with contract dates in two months. The margin alone was $500,000. Leslie pushed away from the table and cocked her head in astonishment. If, as in the past, he had guessed wrong on the direction of gold prices, Estuary and Bossier were in trouble—serious trouble.

She walked to the door and closed it with a click. Returning to her chair, she sat and gazed out the window at the David Crockett Pavilion, drumming a staccato rhythm with a pencil on her glass top. *Any futures trade on my own behalf would require a sizable margin deposit, and, if discovered by auditors, could lead to an investigation by LaCour and possible criminal charges from the SEC, for insider trading.* A smile began to creep across her lips. *I don't need to worry about any of that. With what I know about Bossier and his Estuary Fund monkeyshines, to keep me quiet, he'll have no choice but to keep playing the futures markets—this time betting on the collapse of oil prices—and cutting me in for a healthy chunk of the profits. All I need to do is make sure Buck Olmeyer never gets his hands on the dysprosium.*

Then there was the matter of Billy. In her mind she knew the marriage was over. Although Billy probably felt the same, he could never bring himself to end it. She'd have to be the one to file for divorce. The offshore company would remain a secret. No reason to split the short sale profits with Billy. He and the Indians would make enough from the sale of the fuel additive. And, he's so trusting, it would never occur to him that she would keep such a secret from him.

She lifted the receiver from the phone on her credenza. On a firm roster scotch-taped to her computer screen, she found Bossier's extension. Her finger trembled as she dialed the four-digit code.

"Ron Bossier."

"Hi, Ron. It's Leslie. Have you got a minute?"

"Sure. What's on your mind?"

"The Estuary Fund."

He cleared his throat. "Of course. Give me fifteen minutes and come down to my office."

The receptionist greeted Leslie as she walked by on her way to Bossier's office. She smiled and returned the pleasantry. Her heart was pounding.

"Hey there," Bossier chirped when she peered in. "You're looking mighty sharp today! Stalking a big client tonight?"

He'd intended it as a compliment, but it fell flat. *Women as anything but bait is more than he can comprehend*, she thought. *Today he'll get a lesson.* She took a seat on his leather couch. He sat across from her, opposite a brass coffee table.

"So what's got you interested in my fishing buddies at The Estuary?"

"I follow all major accounts. Today was the first time Estuary came to my attention."

"Oh hell, Leslie, they're just a bunch of trust fund babies who like to dabble in the market. Haven't done too badly, if I do say so myself. Made a big contribution to Galveston Bay Preservation Project a while back. Maybe you saw it?"

"I don't recall that I did."

"Well," he said energetically, standing and reaching for his desk. "Just happen to have a copy here."

"Ron, please . . . sit down."

He complied. His mood sobering.

"There is a lot of unusual activity with this client. In fact, if you weren't the account exec, I would have already reported it to the auditors."

Ron looked her squarely in the eye. "I don't know what you're talking about." But the color began to drain from his face.

"Its balance is $2,000,000."

"So?"

"Two days ago, $4,000,000. The pattern continues for the entire month."

"There's nothing unusual about that, Leslie. A lot of customers have systematic deposits and withdrawals. What's this all about anyway?"

"Until six weeks ago Estuary's top balance was $53,000. At that time, it made a major bet in gold futures. Within a week the market moved away, and the exposure went from $275,000 to over $500,000. Instead of settling out and taking the loss, the account doubled down three more times. Total commissions paid to you, while the investment grew more and more tenuous, were $176,000."

"Look, Leslie," Bossier said, "I don't know what you're implying, but I've had just about enough of this."

From between the pages of the yellow pad, she withdrew the graph print and handed it to him. "The Estuary deposits match, to the penny, withdrawals from your other customers' accounts. Were they loans, Ron? Maybe to cover margin calls?"

He examined the paper then laid it on the table and looked out the window. The only sound was the ticking from the ship's clock on his bookcase.

"We could ask them," Leslie said.

Ron turned back and locked eyes with her.

"Okay. What do you want?"

"I want in."

"How?"

"Simple. When I give you the word, you raise and bet $5,000,000 in the futures market on the collapse of oil prices. You lay it all on the line in the name of Estuary. When the trade settles, the first $2,500,000 to hit the account is wired automatically to my offshore company. The next disbursement goes to cover all the losses you've rung up for Estuary over the past six months. The rest we split after paying the standard commission to LaCour."

"Why should I get in any deeper?" Bossier said, his voice quivering. "I could trade out of this in a few days. The market's ripe for a turn."

"Because in ten minutes I'll be on the phone to the auditors and you'll be locked out of your office."

"You wouldn't do that. You're in too deep already."

"Who do you think they'll believe, Ron. You or this printout?" As her statement registered with him, Leslie swept the report from the table, folded it, and stuffed it into her blazer.

Glancing at her watch, she stood, and looked him in the eyes. "So, what will it be, Ron? Go to the well once more to short the crude market," she patted her blouse, "and make enough to take care of us both? Or go to jail?"

Wheeling toward the door, she heard him say, "How do I know you've got a winner with crude?"

Without turning back, she answered, "You don't."

The door tumbler clicked open as she turned the knob.

Bossier heard it. Staring at the floor he said, "Okay, I'll do it."

26

BUCK'S CELL PHONE RANG between bites of porterhouse at the Petroleum Club. Instinctively he reached into his shirt pocket and glanced at the screen.

"Can you excuse me for a moment?" he said to the curvy SMU grad interviewing for a job as his administrative assistant. She smiled and left for the ladies room.

"Olmeyer," he answered.

"Mr. Olmeyer, this is Oliver Greentree."

"I told you not to call me, Greentree. If you've got something to tell us, talk to Colt."

"This is important. I need to speak to you about it."

"Oh, you do? Well, make it fast. I'm having dinner." He stifled a belch.

Oliver related the events of the last council meeting when the tribe decided to seek an independent loan rather than a joint venture with Trans-National.

"They did what!" he roared. "Have you spoken with Colt about this?"

"No sir."

Olmeyer swiveled toward the window and snarled, "You little prick, we're paying you plenty to handle this thing and you damn well better do it. If not, I'll personally dunk your ass in molasses and hide-strap it to a fire ant mound."

"Circumstances have changed," Oliver said evenly. "You've got competition. I think I can reverse the tribe's decision, but it will take money."

"What kind of money?"

"A hundred thousand now, and the same when the Trans-National joint venture is signed. I know the votes that can be bought."

Buck leaned back picking a piece of meat from his front teeth with his pinky nail. "Now look, Green . . . Green . . ."

"Greentree."

"I know a shake down when I see it. You're out of your league."

"Mr. Olmeyer, it's your decision. But I'd advise you not to delay. Things are moving fast down here. I need the money in my account—Colt has the wiring instructions—by tomorrow. Otherwise, you may be too late."

"That sounds like a threat," Buck said coldly.

"No. It's a fact." Buck heard the line go dead. He rattled the ice cubes in his whisky glass and thought about the call. *Little bastard*, he said to himself.

Buck dialed Colt. He recounted the conversation with Oliver. "What's your take?" he asked.

"So far we've used him to get information from Red Eagle about what's happening in the council meetings. Looks like he wants to be a player now."

"That's the problem with kids today," snorted Buck, waving his empty glass at a waiter for a refill. "They don't want to pay their dues. When I was his age, I was rolling drill pipe all day, and throwing drunks out of bars at night. Can't we just fire his ass?"

"We've got no one else on the ground right now, Buck. Red Eagle has been dealing strictly with Oliver. I don't know what kind of money he's been promised. I think we're going to have to play ball, at least for now. A hundred thousand in the overall scheme of things is peanuts, if he can deliver the votes."

"That's a big if," said Buck. "Pay him." The CEO hung up.

The applicant returned. "Did I miss anything?"

27

JUAN PULLED THE BLACK ESCALADE into a tunnel beneath the State Capitol building. It was a hot August day. Leaving the motor running, he got out and reached for the passenger door handle. The governor picked up his briefcase and stepped out.

Waiting for him in the lobby was his young assistant, Mallory Cellers, clipboard in hand. "Morning, governor," she chirped as they walked to the elevator. "First up at 10:30, Buddy Smith, lobbyist for the Texas Mortgage Bankers Association—thirty minutes. Here's a rundown of the legislation they're opposing and why."

The doors slid open and they stepped in. Dolph glanced over the report and put it into his coat pocket. "Tell Buddy to come back at two o'clock this afternoon."

"All right," Mallory replied. "At eleven o'clock, Randy Erskin, representing the Texas Drillers Association—thirty minutes. Here's the story." She continued filling him in as the elevator crept upward. The doors opened onto a third-floor hallway with thick red carpet. The oak walls were adorned with heroes of the Alamo.

At Sam Houston, they turned right into the governor's office. Now trailing the chief executive, Mallory said, "Then at eleven thirty—"

Dolph turned to her. "Cancel everything till noon."

She raised her eyebrows. "Yes, sir."

"That will be all for now."

"Shall I close the door?"

"Please. And hold my calls."

He threw his coat on the side chair and looked at his watch. Five minutes to go.

On either side of his desk stood flags in heavy brass stands, Texas on the right, United States on the left. He sat in his high-back chair and reached into his shirt pocket. On a white card was a handwritten telephone number, followed by a series of letters and symbols.

At 10 a.m. Dolph picked up his cell phone and dialed the number. After each prompt he entered a new configuration of letters. Finally, after pressing a string of symbols, he was added to a conference call.

"Barstow here," he announced.

"Hi, Dolph. Jimmy Breaux here, with Al Simmons."

"Gentlemen," Dolph said to the governors of Louisiana and Mississippi.

A new attendee entered. "Butch Baker here."

They all greeted the Oklahoma governor.

"I called the E-4 alert number last night because of a family emergency," Dolph said. "You're all familiar with the potential problem out in West Texas—the code D issue."

The line was silent.

Dolph continued, "The situation has deteriorated. We're looking at a major breach."

"How'd it happen?" Jimmy Breaux asked with a Cajun twang.

Dolph relayed the results of his cigar case eavesdropping, and the reaction of Texas Commercial Bank to the anonymous delivery of Clive Larson's white paper.

"What are our options?" drawled Governor Simmons.

"I think we've got to make it go away," Dolph replied, "until the larger issue is resolved."

"I'm on board," Simmons said. "Just don't tell me any more about it."

"Same here," Breaux added.

"Butch?" Dolph asked.

"I don't think we have a choice," the Oklahoma governor grunted.

"Then we're agreed," Dolph said. "Now for the big picture."

He recounted Buck Olmeyer's recent dealings with Luke Stasney, concluding, "I'm not sure he can handle this thing."

"Boys," Butch said, "we've been dancing around this problem for months, years really. Ever since Trans-National figured out the dysprosium additive really worked, we've known a big discovery of the stuff would be a disaster. Well, now it's happened, and right in our backyard. Our friends in the Middle East have been calling me. Russia, too. These guys are nervous as whores in church, and they're not going to wait long for us to deal with this."

"Who contacted you?" Dolph asked.

"Yamani from Saudi. Fedun from Rukoil in Russia."

"How did they get their information?" Breaux asked.

"We don't know yet," Butch replied, "but it's pretty damn accurate."

"Okay. What's next?" the Mississippi governor asked. "We can keep that bank quiet for a little while. But word's going to get out sooner or later. When oil prices tank, so will our economy. I can't balance the damn budget with what I've got now."

"Same here," said the Louisiana governor.

"And here," Butch echoed.

The line went quiet as each man considered what was at stake.

Dolph closed his eyes, and let his head fall back against the chair. He took a deep breath. "There's an alternate plan. I heard about it just this morning from Buck Olmeyer."

"I'm not sure how much faith we should put in that," Simmons snorted.

Dolph's voice changed to church timbre. "If you want to know the details, stay on the line."

Outside, a group of school children walked up the capitol steps to see democracy in action. Lobbyists chatted with legislators in the halls adjoining the House Chamber. And in the basement cafeteria, the chef prepared tacos al carbon.

The governor of Texas waited. The line went dead.

28

HUGH GANTRY SAT AT HIS DESK in the offices of Texas Commercial Bank and thumbed through the mystery package about dysprosium. Company protocol required that all incoming mail be scanned. So volatile was this missive, he had elected not to comply.

He kept coming back to the white paper by Clive Larson. It set the stage for everything.

In paragraphs that read like a history book, Professor Larson had casually predicted exactly the course of events that would transpire at a hot spring on Lost Pines Reservation. He hadn't named the specific location, but even in that respect, he came remarkably close.

Hugh studied the graphs in Clive's paper describing how a freak underground fissure in the bedrock could be opened by a minor earthquake. *Back then*, Hugh remembered, *no one would have dreamed that any quake could be manmade.*

He turned to a short paragraph on the mining of oil shale. Amazingly, it had forecast advances in the technique of fracking which would allow the use of subterranean explosives over an ever-expanding distance.

Horizontal directional drilling, Hugh read, combined with more powerful fracking, would put enough stress on existing fault lines to open pathways deeper than any before. Through these corridors, Larson foretold, would gush forth a witch's brew of the rarest minerals in the world. Previously trapped in an underground sea, this treasure trove would redefine the balance of power in the world.

Stuffing the report into his briefcase, Hugh headed for the door of his office. On the way out, he stopped to scribble a note to himself and drop it on his desk. *Call Buck Olmeyer re fracking.*

The portly banker walked out of the corporate offices of Texas Commercial Bank on the ninth floor of the building bearing its name. While he waited for the elevator, he looked out across the cityscape. The buildings were dark with only occasional office lights marking an overtime real estate closing or preparation for an early morning trial.

When the doors swished open, he entered and pushed the button for the garage. The car stopped on five where an elderly woman, carrying a pink shoulder bag, stepped on.

"Evening," Hugh said to the lady.

"Evening," she responded. "Beautiful night out there, isn't it?"

"Indeed it is. Too bad we're still stuck in this office building," Hugh quipped with a wink.

When the door opened, he stepped back, inviting her to exit first. They walked together down the white stucco hallway to the underground parking area. As they approached Hugh's parking space, he reached in his coat pocket for the keys to his silver SUV.

She smiled and walked past his vehicle, then fell forward with a gasp. The heel of her right shoe had caught an expansion seam along the floor, throwing her to the concrete.

"Goodness!" Hugh exclaimed, rushing to her side. "Are you all right?"

Her bag had spilled its contents of books and assorted pencils and pens. She struggled to get up.

"Oh my," she wheezed as she began collecting her things from around Hugh's truck.

"Let me help," he said, gathering her belongings from the garage floor.

"Thank you so much," the old woman said, reaching into her purse. "There's a notebook that slid under the next car over. I can't get down that low anymore."

As Hugh knelt to retrieve it, she withdrew from her purse a silver box the size of a deck of cards. She slipped it under the back bumper of Hugh's truck where it clamped on with a magnetic snap, hidden from view except for a slender antenna.

"Thank you so much for your help," the woman said to Hugh as he returned her items.

"I hope you're all right. Better soak in a hot bath tonight!" he called out as she hurried to her maroon Mazda. He thought it strange how quickly she started the engine and pulled out. He waved as she sped past.

Hugh opened the door of the SUV with his electronic key. Slipping behind the wheel, he tossed his briefcase onto the seat beside him. After fastening the safety belt, he reached down and pressed the ignition switch.

As he left the garage and drove to the traffic light at the corner, he was surprised to spot the Mazda parked along a side street. When the light turned green and he passed the old woman, they exchanged smiles.

He couldn't see her push the button on the end of a blue plastic ball-point pen. A split second later, Hugh Gantry, his SUV, and the dysprosium report were incinerated in a fireball so intense it set off the sprinkler system on the first floor of the Texas Commercial Bank building.

29

MARIA SAT AT THE DESK IN HER STUDY considering what she knew about the Rio Hot Springs minerals and Billy Strikeleather. *Why should I get involved at all? Sure, Dad asked. But I think he's sold on Billy anyway.*

She spread her notes out across her desk. Assembling a dossier on Billy Strikeleather had been an easy job. All that was left was to connect the dots.

Why was Billy so blind? His wife was one of the biggest financial whores in town. She was at every ostentatious fundraiser on the arm of a different "good friend" like Luke Stasney. Was he incredibly naive or did he have a plan?

The phone rang, disrupting her thoughts.

"Hello."

"Maria Whitecloud?" said a muffled voice.

"Yes."

"Please listen closely. I won't repeat."

"Who is this?" Maria asked, leaning forward across her desk.

"Never mind. It's about your father."

"How did you get this number?"

"Don't interrupt. Your father is in danger. It's about the minerals. I will tell you where to start looking. Any more would put us both at risk."

"What kind of risk? How do I know you're telling the truth?" Maria said.

"You don't. Now stop talking. Trans-National knows all about dysprosium and what it can do. When the deal with the Chinati didn't make, Olmeyer had to find a way to stop the minerals from being developed."

The pen in Maria's hand was flying across a yellow pad. "Okay. Where do I go next?" Maria asked, a quiver in her voice.

"Whatever you do, don't contact Strikeleather or Stasney. Now that they're closing in on a ready source of dysprosium on the reservation, they represent the biggest threat to the oil industry since atomic power. Big Oil has got to stop them, and they won't like you sounding a warning. They're being watched day and night."

"Why are you telling me all of this?"

"I have my reasons."

"And you knew I couldn't stand by and watch them cut my tribe to pieces."

"Exactly. Start with the Houston police investigation of an old rape charge against Chief Whitecloud in 1960, case number 73251 R-1960. Trans-National is threatening to use it to discredit your father if he doesn't cooperate with them. I'll send you more on it." The voice continued, "There's more—a kickback scheme involving Trans-National's top management funded by fracking contractors. If the truth comes out on any of this, Buck Olmeyer and his cronies will be fired by Trans-National, and probably worse."

"How can I reach you?"

"You can't. I'll be in touch."

The caller hung up. Maria spun away from the desk and lowered the phone to her lap.

Just what I needed. The last big exposé on the energy industry landed the reporter and the station manager in jail on trumped-up DWI charges, and cost them their jobs. What should I do? What would Dad do? If I ask him, Big Oil may find out and realize I'm onto them.

She looked at the bookshelf over her desk. There were pictures of her with her father when she was small. Most were in the backyard. He was always teaching her something. Painting, pottery, astronomy. Then it came to her. He had already taught her what to do now, by example. He knew the alliance with other tribes would draw the wrath of Trans-National. But he'd pressed on because self-reliance was best for the tribe.

It's one final lesson, she reflected, gazing at the photos. *I've got to write the story.*

30

IN THE CHANNEL 7 STUDIOS, the evening news theme blared, and cameras advanced on Maria Cloud.

"Good evening, I'm Maria Cloud. We open with an exclusive story about executive compensation in a major Houston oil company. Channel 7 has learned about a vendor pricing scheme that has siphoned off millions of dollars from the money paid by Big Oil to service companies. The final destination of that money may surprise you."

After the broadcast, which singled out Trans-National executives as the recipients of the kickbacks, the young anchorwoman gathered her things and headed to the parking lot. Once in her car, she pulled out onto the service road of Loop 610 and gunned into the center lane. Barely audible over the din of the engine and the music from her radio, she heard her cell phone go off.

"Damn," she murmured as she moved her right hand off the wheel into her purse, sifting for the phone. She got it on the last ring.

"Hello?"

"Hi. It's Vanessa."

"I know that," she said, smiling. "I know your voice by now. How are you?"

"Very well, thanks. Congratulations on your Trans-National exposé. Our ratings have spiked, and the website is swamped. Your blog on the investigation has also taken off. Good work!"

"Thanks."

"Say, I'm at a little get-together of a few friends at the Ritz Carlton Hotel, you know—over on San Felipe?"

"Wow, nice. What's the occasion?"

"Nothing special. Thought you might like to stop by."

"I don't know. I'm not much on parties. Maybe another time."

"There are some people here who want to meet you—from the network," the older woman offered. "I think it would be a good idea for you to come, just for a minute."

Maria sighed. "Okay. What room?"

"The penthouse."

"I should have known. I'll be there in fifteen minutes."

Maria made a U-turn under the freeway and headed toward the posh side of town. The Ritz was on a prominent corner in the Galleria. She drove through the intersection and pulled under the porte cochere. A valet in a white jacket and gloves opened the door.

"Good evening, ma'am," he said. "Staying with us tonight?"

"No," Maria said, swinging her long legs out to the pavement. "I'll just be an hour or so."

"Very good."

The Ritz Carlton was one of the swankiest hotels in Houston. Twelve stories of white granite. Every door was manned and every floor polished. When oil sheiks came to town to cut deals, they stayed here.

The doorman welcomed her through the glass double entry. On her way to the elevators, she veered into the ladies' room.

She pulled out a brush and swept back her hair. Like preparing for a broadcast, she powdered her cheeks, dabbed on lipstick, and practiced her smile. When the starched collar on her blouse was straightened and wrinkles from her blue silk jacket smoothed, she turned to leave.

On her way out, Maria caught a glimpse of herself in the mirror. Her disdain for this posh scene showed. *But*, she thought, *I've got to do it. Time to get on with my life.* She strode to the elevator and pushed the button.

The elevator doors opened and she stepped in, selecting "P" for penthouse.

When the car reached its destination, the daughter of the Chinati chief steeled herself and stepped out. The atmosphere was not at all what she expected. Instead of the usual cocktail scene—men in suits and women in little black dresses making small talk—the lighting was subdued, and soft music was playing from speakers on either side of a small wooden dance floor.

On the far end of the room, a server stood behind a long table covered with white linen, arranging plates of hors d'oeuvres. Black leather settees bracketed the dance floor. The walls were glass, floor to ceiling, with curtains open to display the twinkling cityscape.

Everywhere couples and foursomes were drinking and laughing, some swaying to the music. *What is Vanessa up to?* she wondered. This was no ordinary party.

"Hi there," said her hostess, who had obviously stationed herself by the entry. Vanessa wore a white silk shirt and black slacks with a black patent leather belt cinched tightly around her waist. Her shoulder length hair was swept back closely and secured with a bone clip.

"My goodness. This is some little get-together," Maria said, mockingly.

"Now, now. Be open-minded. They're all friends of mine," Vanessa whispered into Maria's ear.

"Let's have a drink," Vanessa said, taking Maria by the arm. On the way to the bar, she steered Maria toward a love seat where a woman was sitting alone, holding a glass of red wine.

"Maria, I'd like you to meet a friend of mine from NBC corporate."

She was around forty, New York sleek with jewelry and clothes to match.

"Hello, Maria," the tall brunette said, taking Maria's hand. "I'm Sunny Langford. I've heard a lot about you—seen some of your clips. Can we talk a bit later?"

"Of course," Maria smiled.

Maria and Vanessa moved on to the bar and ordered martinis. "Are all these network people?" Maria asked.

"No," she laughed, putting her arm around Maria. "Some *own* networks."

Maria took a long sip and adjusted her jacket.

"You might want to take that off," Vanessa said. "You're a bit over-dressed for this time of night."

"I think I'll stay as is," the young anchor replied, blushing.

"Suit yourself, but now is your chance to do some good with the right people. Look at me," she commanded, playfully taking Maria by the lapels. "There's only one way to make it to the big time in this business. These are the folks that can make it happen. I suggest you have another drink."

For the next hour, Vanessa taught the young anchorwoman how to work a room. With each martini, it got easier for Maria. This had been her pattern since the attack. Liquor was the only thing that calmed her fears, allowed her to mingle. Luckily, most of the attendees were women. It was men she feared.

Sunny Langford had been eyeing Maria. Finally, she made her approach, touching her lightly on the arm. "Nice party, huh?" said the executive, moving closer.

Vanessa smiled and backed away. "I'll get another drink while you two talk."

Brushing back a strand of hair from her brow, Sunny spoke slowly and deliberately. "Maria, we think you have a future at the network level. Your ethnicity is right for the times, and your look is . . . well . . ." she reached out and stroked Maria's cheek, her fingers trailing down the front of the younger woman's blouse, "fabulous."

"You're very kind."

"I want you to come to New York for screen testing. Would you like that?"

"I don't know what to say," Maria stammered.

"I think you should try 'Yes,'" Sunny smiled, guiding her by the elbow to the hors d'oeuvre table where Vanessa was waiting.

"So," Vanessa said, "what does our young anchor have to say?"

The two women watched Maria, gauging her reaction.

Old demons came to life in Maria's brain. What about the crowds, the subways, the strangers? Her heart pounded.

The older women exchanged glances.

"Maybe we had the wrong idea," Sunny said to Vanessa, arching an eyebrow.

Maria felt Vanessa's hand, warm and firm, against the small of her back. "What do you think, Maria?" her mentor said softly.

Putting both hands together over her lips as if in prayer, Maria took a deep breath, looked up with a smile, and said: "When do we leave?"

"Excellent," Vanessa crooned. "I'll make all the arrangements."

Maria's head was spinning. This time it was Maria who took Vanessa's hand.

31

OPENING HER EYES, Maria grimaced and rolled onto her back. An unfamiliar ceiling came into focus. To her right, long white curtains were drawn against the morning sun. *Where am I?* she asked herself. *Not home.*

"Well, the goddess awakes," came a familiar voice from across the hotel suite.

Maria rubbed her eyes and sat up, clutching a blanket to her naked body.

Wearing a white silk robe, Vanessa padded toward the bed.

The reporter fell back into the pillows with a moan. "God. What time is it?"

"Just past nine," Vanessa said, sitting next to her guest. "But a girl should be able to sleep in on her day off, don't you think?"

Maria arched her back and yawned. "Preferably at her own place."

"Well, sweetheart, after your fourth martini, there weren't too many options."

"I suppose," the reporter replied, eyeing her hostess with suspicion.

"If it makes you feel better," Vanessa said with a wink, "I slept in the other bedroom."

Blushing, Maria returned her gaze. "Thanks."

Vanessa reached across the bed and stroked Maria's hair. "I only want the best for you. Do you believe me?"

Considering her answer carefully, Maria replied, "Yes, I do."

For a long moment, they sat in silence. Vanessa studied the young woman, whose dark hair now fell in a tangle across the pillow. What was it about her, she wondered, that had loosed a passion so long dormant? In her heart she knew—the hunger was for the girl she herself had been. Strong, striking, and independent. But that was before the compromises.

The Wilcox's success was not entirely self-made. In an industry as tightly regulated as broadcasting, you didn't make it big without help from Washington. Favors had been granted to them by lobbyists and influence peddlers which, in Houston, translated to Big Oil. Dues were still owed. Now it was time to pay them back.

Maria's oil company exposé, Vanessa knew, had ruffled some feathers at the highest levels of energy firms. Her husband had assigned the problem to Vanessa to fix, one way or another.

"I've got to get going," Maria said, gathering the sheets around her and heading to the bathroom.

Vanessa returned to her room and dressed. She called for Maria's car and went down to meet the valet. After parking the car, she reentered the hotel through a side door.

Inside the suite, Maria was dressed and ready. "Thanks, Vanessa . . . for everything."

"No problem. I think you can make a clean getaway now."

Maria stepped into the hall and then the elevator. They both smiled at each other as the door closed.

32

RED EAGLE'S RESTAURANT, MI CASA SU CASA, was on the edge of town, set back from the highway in a box canyon. Pulling into the parking lot, Billy and Clive came to a stop between Luke's black Mercedes and Chief Whitecloud's faded blue Suburban.

The western sky was streaked crimson as the September sun set behind the Chisos Mountains. A hot wind was blowing. Dust swirled low across the ground.

Inside they joined Luke and the chief, seated at a wooden table in the corner, under a hanging lamp. Without waiting for an order, Red brought each a plate of enchiladas and refried beans, then a basket of corn tortilla chips and a bowl of salsa for the table.

"You fellas need anything else, just holler," he said over his shoulder, returning to the front counter.

"So what's the problem out there?" Luke said. "We closed the damn loan with Plains Bank six weeks ago."

"Who said there's a problem?" Clive answered, his eyes narrowing.

"Well, the project is slipping farther behind schedule every week. If we don't get back on track, the money will run out before we produce one thimble of additive," said Luke.

"Finances are not my department," the professor shot back. "Why don't you ask your man Massey. He was supposed to have the experience to make this baby hum. So far, all he's done is have meetings and take shots at the science. What he needs to do is pump the goddamn mineral water out of the spring. I'll handle the rest."

"For one thing, we can kick the damned Indians off the job," said Luke. "My superintendent tells me he can't trust them with even the simplest jobs. They don't bother to show up, but when they do, they're too drunk or hungover to be of any use."

"You think it's their fault they don't know how to build a refinery?" Billy flared, throwing his hands up. "You knew we had to hire them from the very beginning. They needed jobs and training. We needed their money."

A tense quiet settled over the group. The chief stared at his plate, hands trembling on the edge of the table and lips pressed into a rigid line. Without looking up, he said in a low tone, "Look. This is just what the oil companies were hoping for—infighting. What can we do to fix things?"

Clive sat back, arms crossed. "You don't just flip a switch and start bottling product. It's taken longer than we thought to find the right process for extracting the dysprosium."

"That's why we needed more testing before launching off into a production facility," Luke murmured out of the side of his mouth.

Clive scowled. "Bullshit! It's easy to coach from the goddamn bleachers. I've got better things to do than listen to your crap. Why don't you just put your boys in there and see how long it takes them to start from scratch?"

"At least I'd have a realistic idea of where we stand," Luke fired back.

An awkward silence followed. They began to eat.

Chief Whitecloud put down his fork and leaned forward, pinching the bridge of his nose between his left index finger and thumb. Under the table, his right hand began twitching uncontrollably. Light from the overhead lamp reflected off a sheen of perspiration on his brow.

"Are you okay?" Billy asked the old man.

"Sure," he said, reaching under the table to clutch his stomach. He rose unsteadily. "I just need some air."

The chief of the Chinati Nation started for the exit, but then doubled over and fell forward. He was dead before he hit the floor.

Behind the counter, Red cupped his cell phone to his lips and said, "Ok. it's done."

33

IN THE CEMETERY PARKING LOT SAT TWO OLD PICKUPS. One was Sam's, the other Chief Whitecloud's. Inside the first, Billy Strikeleather sat watching a lone figure, shaded by a mesquite tree deep in the field of crosses.

Maria Whitecloud stood beside a newly covered grave, her head bowed. Billy stepped from the truck and approached quietly. When he was near, he said in a soft voice, "He was a fine man."

"Billy," she said, recognizing his voice. As she turned, she was struck by how the years had aged him. But his smile was still as comfortable as a slipper.

He took her elbow and guided her toward the trucks. Arm in arm, eyes straight ahead, they left the chief behind—for the last time.

"It's been a while," Billy said.

Looking up she answered, "Yes, it has. Thanks for helping him. It meant a lot."

"I'm not sure how much help I was."

"He thought of you as the son he never had."

"Warts and all?" Billy asked, shaking his head in disbelief.

"I suppose."

They walked on.

"How's Leslie?"

His forearm flinched.

"Too busy to make the funeral," Billy said.

Maria let it pass. "You know Dad was aware of the tough times you've had. He even asked me to look into all that before trusting you with the Rio Hot Springs minerals."

"And what did you tell him?"

"It didn't matter. He'd already decided to accept your help," she said.

"And did you agree?"

"I couldn't find any dirt bad enough to change his mind," she said with a shy smile.

"You must not have looked too hard," Billy laughed.

His eyes locked with hers for an instant. Something turned over inside him. The kind of feeling you discover with your first love, then spend a lifetime trying to find again.

Maria opened the door to the chief's truck and climbed in, pushing aside an old book on the seat.

"How long will you be staying?" he asked her.

"Not long. I've got to get back. I looked through the house this morning for a will, not that there's much to inherit."

"And?"

"I found it. I'm now the proud owner of a broken-down house and this twenty-five-year-old truck."

"He left you a lot more than that," Billy said gently. "He lived his life with a special passion. I think he passed it down to you."

"Maybe. Some call it stubbornness," Maria said.

"I saw it when I met him again after all these years. He still had something to prove, something he wanted more than anything else."

"The minerals?" said Maria.

"Indirectly. He had a vision they could help Native Americans reclaim their greatness. Redemption, if you will."

"I found something I would like you to have," Maria said.

She picked up the book and handed it to Billy. "I found it by his bed. *The Final Circle* by Chief Black Bear of the Navajo Nation. Dad wrote your name on the inside cover."

Billy held it delicately, like a bird. The pages were worn. As he examined the volume, a folded paper fluttered free. Billy plucked it from the red gravel and sat on the running board to read:

Dear Chief Whitecloud,

You don't know me. I served in Vietnam with a soldier named Jimmy Littlebow from your tribe and his friend Burt Cole. Once, before we headed out on a jungle patrol, I told Jimmy I had an ominous feeling. He loaned me his good luck charm which was a leather necklace with the enclosed gray feather attached. That's the kind of guy he was. It turned out he needed it more than me.

That night we were ambushed. There was confusion. Jimmy and Burt grabbed our heavy machine gun and called for the rest of us to fall back. Everywhere we looked, the Viet Cong were closing in. A few of our guys began to break and run. When we heard the machine gun open up, we knew it was our only chance. Those two men held off probably fifty VC while we made our escape. At dawn, we went back with reinforcements. There was only one body there hunched over the gun, burned beyond recognition. The dog tags said, Burt Cole. Jimmy was never found.

I thought Jimmy's family should have his lucky feather, but it took me years to track down his hometown. Army records just said 'Chinati Indian, Big Bend, Texas.' Thanks to the internet I finally located your name, as chief of the tribe, and the location of your village. It's not on most maps. When my letters to the Littlebow family were returned, I sent this one in care of you. I hope it has found its way to you, and you will pass it along to the family.

Jimmy used to tell me that, in his culture, life was likened to a circle. In the end, we would all return to where we started. Kind of a balance, I suppose. He also told me if your journey was cut short, you could still complete the circle through a ceremony involving a feather. I hope you can help Jimmy do that. He was a brave man. He and Burt Cole saved my life and nine others. Jimmy deserves to finish his circle.

Billy looked up at Maria through moist eyes. She was curious about the letter but waited for Billy to offer.

"It's about my father, Burt Cole." He read her the contents. "He went to war with Jimmy Littlebow. I remember, even though they never found Jimmy's body, they had a memorial service for him on the reservation. My father's body was burned beyond recognition. The only identification was his dog tags. My mother read about his funeral in the newspaper. She made the trip to his hometown, Lamesa, by bus. From a pew in the back of the church, she said goodbye for both of us. In those days having a half-breed, bastard grandson would have dishonored his parents. Mother never said a word."

"He was a hero," Maria whispered.

"I know. It's just I'm certain he wouldn't have been very proud of me."

"You can't be sure, Billy," she said, putting her hand on his shoulder. "He'd certainly approve of what you're doing for the tribe now."

"Maybe so," said Billy, standing. "Maria, for the record, I don't have a clue how to handle the Rio Hot Springs situation. There are already people on the reservation trying to undermine the chief's plan. I'm not sure I can hold all this together." He kicked at the sandy gravel of the parking lot, rough and unsettled, like his state of mind.

For the first time, Maria saw vulnerability in the Chinati hero. *And why not?* she thought. *All he did was carry the hopes of a nation. So, what if he stumbled? He'd aimed high, hadn't he? Why does the world demand so goddamned much?*

She started to close the truck door but paused to let her lips brush Billy's cheek. Out of the corner of her eye, she saw him tuck the book under his arm. With a weak smile, she backed out and slowly navigated the length of the parking lot to the edge of the highway. In the side mirror, shoulders stooped, Billy's image seemed diminished by more than the distance she'd covered. His left hand gave her a tentative wave. Her mouth went dry and her lips began to quiver. In her stomach, she felt a familiar longing. *God, don't let this happen. Please.*

34

THE WINE BAR WAS RAUCOUS, so the two women headed to the patio. Leslie led the way. Maria watched her scan the room nervously. They sat at a corner table beneath a vine-covered arch and ordered drinks from a waiter.

"Thanks for coming," said Leslie.

"Of course. How's Billy?"

"He's spending a lot of time in West Texas these days," she answered dismissively.

Raising an eyebrow, Maria continued, "I saw him briefly at my father's funeral."

"Yes, he told me. I'm very sorry for your loss and that I couldn't be there."

With a polite shrug, Maria sat back and waited for Leslie to announce her intentions. Instead, there was a long pause. Finally, Leslie said, "You're probably wondering why I asked to meet."

"I imagine it's about the Rio Hot Springs mineral discovery. Billy must have filled you in."

"He doesn't tell me everything."

A flash of doubt crossed Maria's face. The waiter arrived with two glasses of sauvignon blanc. Over a long sip Maria considered her tablemate. As a television reporter, she had done plenty of interviews, but this woman was tough to read. From a trophy wife on Billy's arm to marketing director of LaCour Financial. Something was not ringing true, especially Billy's reported lack of candor with her. He'd always been an open book.

Leslie tasted her wine, then continued. "Billy told me your father asked for his help with the Rio Hot Springs minerals. But when he and Luke Stasney got a joint venture offer from Trans-National, the chief balked. He invited some other tribes to invest and looked to Luke for help with securing additional financing."

"So Trans-National is out of the picture?" Maria asked.

"No. According to Billy, they are standing by with their checkbook open, waiting for the tribe to come crawling back. He says the joint venture would have provided a lot of front-end cash for each Chinati and there are still quite a few supporters in the tribe."

"I've heard that, too," Maria said.

"That's why I found it interesting you picked this time to launch an investigation of illegal kickbacks to Trans-National executives. You must have known it would hurt Trans-National's chances for a deal. Buck Olmeyer can't be too happy, either."

Maria dismissed the comment with a backhand wave. "I'm a journalist. Ruffled feathers go with the territory." But then, refocusing, she paused to reconsider. "Unless, of course, you're suggesting my report was intended to influence those negotiations."

"That possibility occurred to me," said Leslie. "But intentional or not, it's bound to have an impact, don't you think?"

Maria considered Leslie's line of questions.

She's probing. Trying to figure out which side I'm on. But why?

Leslie took another sip, looking at Maria over the rim of her glass.

"I have some information that might be useful to you, if you're interested."

"Reporters are always looking for new leads," Maria said, reaching into her purse for a pad and pen.

Leslie leaned forward and recounted what she knew of Buck's efforts to wrest control of the Rio Hot Springs minerals from the Chinati. She detailed what she'd heard about blackmailing the chief by resurrecting an old rape case. And, if all else failed, implementing a so-called Plan B. Finally, Buck's order to sell all his company stock and pension fund stock.

"And that," she continued, shaking her head, "is classic insider trading that could put him way at Club Fed for a good long while. Unless, of course, Trans-National can convince the Indians to take some kind of deal. That would delay the marketing of a gasoline additive and keep oil prices high for a long time. At least long enough for him to retire with his pension intact and his Trans-National stock at full value."

Maria had scribbled three pages of notes, and was now trying to process the bonanza of information without appearing overwhelmed. She put down her pen and looked up, her brow furrowed. "How did you learn all this?"

Leslie shook back her hair and adjusted an earring. "Let's just say I know Buck—professionally of course."

Both women were quiet. Maria twirled the stem of her glass between her thumb and forefinger while Leslie assessed her reaction.

"So why are you telling me all this, Leslie?"

"To save my marriage. The Trans-National proposal has put a lot of pressure on Billy and our relationship. Olmeyer thought the deal was in the bag. Now that it's not, Billy's afraid Olmeyer will blame him. He's so scared he started drinking again. That will be the end of us."

"I have no power over Olmeyer," Maria said.

"More than you think," Leslie countered. "If Trans-National loses the deal because its own dishonest conduct is made public, Billy will be out of the line of fire."

"So, you want me to expose the dirt on Buck Olmeyer to be sure Trans-National never gets hold of the minerals?" said Maria.

Leslie glanced over her shoulder, then back at Maria. "Yes."

"And if the Chinati can't develop the minerals on their own, they could end up with nothing," Maria said. She took a sip, then lowered her glass slowly. "Look, Leslie, what goes on between you and Billy is none of my business. But I know Billy. I'm sure he's doing the best he can for the two of you—and our tribe—without my help. He's nothing if not loyal. After all, isn't that why you married him?"

Her question elicited a glare. "What would you know about that? As I recall you weren't around for the glory days or the downfall. A small-town kid expected to win every game. You don't have a clue about the nightmare we went through. At least I was there for him."

Maria tabled her hands on either side of her glass.

"Come on, Leslie, I'm not judging you."

"Like hell you aren't."

"Well, believe what you like. I know Billy and I know he's a good man. For better or for worse means something to him."

"And not to me? That sounds pretty noble coming from the cheap seats."

"Like I said, I know Billy. And I know he loves you."

Leslie cocked her head and narrowed her eyes. Then her pursed lips slowly blossomed into a smile.

"Now I get it. This isn't about my relationship with him at all. He's the one that got away, isn't he?"

"That's nonsense. All that was years ago. Now I only want what's best for him, and you."

"Well, if you're so concerned about Billy, just why did you pursue a story that was sure to put him—and me—in Olmeyer's sights?" Leslie demanded.

Maria let her head drop back and eyes close. "I didn't. It pursued me."

"How so?"

She told Leslie about the anonymous caller.

"The day after the call, an email showed up. Attached was a spreadsheet showing windfall profits for oil field service companies supporting Trans-National hydraulic fracturing operations. But the big surprise was who owns these outfits. The names were listed. Several are Trans-National executives. It's an off–balance sheet way to funnel more compensation to them."

Leslie began to nod, grasping the scheme. "And Olmeyer?"

"Double his regular salary and bonuses."

"Double?" Leslie whispered, her eyes widening.

"That's right. And that's not all. The owners include a Who's Who of politicians, lobbyists, and campaign contributors who support pro-fracking legislation in Texas. When you see the money being paid to these guys, it's easy to understand why they'd never do anything to jeopardize use of that technique."

"Or the market price of oil," Leslie added.

"Correct."

"Did you independently verify the ownership of these companies?" Leslie asked. "That kind of information is not filed with the State or published anywhere else."

"Good question. It was the first thing I asked for," Maria responded. "The next day I received from the tipster copies of the operating agreements and corporate minutes for each company providing fracking products or services. Apparently, the real vendors, like suppliers of sand and labor, are required to sell to these front companies, who, in turn, mark the price up by half and resell to Trans-National. It wasn't easy ferreting out the true owners. Each company is owned by multiple layers of other entities. But eventually, I received the corporate documents for all of them."

"Who in the world would have access to all that information?" Leslie asked, cocking her head.

Maria motioned the waiter. Both ordered refills. "The tipster refused to reveal his or her source," Maria continued. "When I threatened to withhold the story unless I had verification, I received copies of transmittal letters from Boykin & Jones, P.C., Attorneys, forwarding the corporate documents to Trans-National executives along with invoices for their legal work. It appears the insider executives all used the same law firm to form their companies."

"There must be a second leak inside Boykin," Leslie said.

"Correct. A disgruntled paralegal wanting to even the score on her way out the door."

"The source told you her name?"

"Yes. I spoke to her by phone."

Leslie tried to act calm. "And?"

"Very credible. Wouldn't reveal the tipster's name. I'm sure she was paid plenty to provide the documents and keep her mouth shut."

"Who was she?"

"You know better than that," Maria laughed. "I don't reveal sources either."

The waiter arrived, and Leslie leaned forward over a fresh wine. "Buck Olmeyer must have some powerful enemies."

"My thought exactly," said Maria, taking a sip. "But they could be after any one of the other secret owners. The list is impressive."

Maria paused. She began to realize the impact her story, bolstered by Leslie's information, could have on everyone involved with the Rio Hot Springs minerals. Buck Olmeyer would be destroyed by his own hand. Any chance Trans-National had to control the dysprosium would go down the drain. It would clear the way for Billy and the tribe to develop the minerals independently. And for her it would prove that, despite the prison rape, she was not intimidated by a dangerous story, the biggest of her career. *It might all work out for the best*, she thought. Then, in the back of her mind, *Is this about my own ambition? Aiming too high, again?*

Across the table, Leslie's mind also drifted. *Is it really over with Billy? Is the high-dollar life we shared really what I want? After all, Daddy made millions but still divorced Mother when I was in grade school. Am I trying to hedge against that kind of dependency?*

After a long moment, Leslie offered, "It's odd to be viewing the same issue from such different perspectives."

"I'm not sure we're so different," said Maria with a smile.

"No, think about it. You grew up with Billy, I married him, and neither of us really know him anymore."

Maria looked perplexed. "So, you think that's what all of this is about?"

"You tell me," Leslie answered.

35

MARIA REPORTED TO THE STUDIO AS NORMAL at 3 p.m. The station manager, Leonard Cox, was waiting in her office. A weaselly man with thin, receding hair slicked back to a silver sheen, beady eyes, and a semi-chin, his roving hands were an occupational hazard for all female employees.

"Hi, Maria. Can you come down to my office for a second?"

"Sure," Maria said, and followed him down the hall. When he closed the door, she went on high alert, expecting an unwanted advance.

The walls were lined with photos of other people shaking hands with network celebrities while the Weasel looked on. Previously director of advertising, he'd been promoted to manager after three terms as the volunteer president of Vanessa Wilcox's adoption center for abandoned horses. He'd excelled at slinging horseshit in drop-off corrals behind the station, and at donor cocktail parties.

With a nervous smile, she took a seat on a chrome sofa with black leather cushions. The Weasel sat behind his desk. They made small talk about Nielsen ratings and the new fall lineup till the air hung heavy and silent.

The Weasel broke the silence.

"Vanessa Wilcox tells me the network is interested in you. That's quite a compliment."

"Thank you. I'm thinking it over. There are pros and cons."

"Chances like this don't come along often. We think you should give it serious consideration."

Maria cocked her head slightly and offered, "I'm surprised it's generated that much interest. And, by the way, Leonard, who is we?"

"Station ownership."

"I see. And if I decline?"

"As I said," he volleyed with one arched eyebrow, "we are very hopeful you will accept."

"I get the feeling there is some other reason you're not telling me."

The Weasel squirmed and began doodling on a yellow pad. "It's about the Trans-National story you've been working on. It was supposed to be about Big Oil's contribution to the energy boom."

Maria raised her chin and sat back with arms crossed. "I'm always on the lookout for good stories, Leonard. It's part of the job, right?"

Her eyes fixed on his until he gave way and returned to doodling.

"This is a story that has upset station management."

"You?"

He laughed nervously. "Not exactly. The editorial board."

"Didn't know we had one," Maria said, "unless you're referring to the station owners."

"Well, FCC regulations require us to have that oversight function here at Channel 7. Vanessa and Chet Wilcox are on the committee."

"Anything in particular about the story?" the anchorwoman intoned dryly.

He answered in a thin voice, throwing his pencil on the desk. "Buck Olmeyer of Trans-National."

"What a surprise."

"Look, Maria, I'll shoot straight with you."

"That would be a nice change."

"Either you take the New York network job or you're off the air."

Maria shivered. A connection between the Olmeyer research and the network job had never occurred to her.

"I don't suppose the New York offer was because of the investigation?"

"I'm not at liberty to talk about that, Maria."

"What a surprise," she responded.

"We'll need your answer within the week. But for now, you're officially on vacation. And you're not to continue with the Olmeyer investigation. Do you understand?"

"Too well," she answered, bolting for the door.

When the Weasel called her name, she turned and saw him reach into his desk. "I think you'd better have a look at these while you're making up your mind." He held out a manila envelope.

Maria backtracked and reached for the package. Cox pulled it away, waited, then smirked and offered it again. Inside were black and white photos of her arm in arm with Sunny Langford at the network party. The final shot showed Maria lying nude on Vanessa's bed, eyes closed, with the New York woman's head between her legs.

Maria's hands trembled. "These are a fraud," she said, her lower lip twitching.

"Look, Maria. What you do with your private life is your business, but when it reflects on the station, there is simply no room for you here."

"Who took these? Where did you get them?" she demanded, still shaking.

"I told you, Maria. I'm not at liberty to—"

"Damn it, Leonard! Don't you care about the truth? These were taken at Vanessa's apartment after the network party. They must have slipped something into my drink. I don't remember a thing."

"Think it over, Maria. Of course, we have the negatives and will deliver them to you just as soon as you're on the air in New York. It works out for everyone."

36

"**ADRIANA MCCLINTOCK,**" the mayor said into her cell phone as she wheeled her SUV into her reserved parking space behind Houston City Hall.

"Hello, Mayor McClintock? This is Maria Cloud. We met at the Cattle Baron's Ball a few months ago."

"Of course. How are you?"

"Well enough. But I have a favor to ask of you."

"I'll try," Adriana said, switching off the engine.

"You might recall my father was in a leadership role with my tribe, the Chinati Indians of Big Bend."

"You're being modest. I believe he is chief, correct?"

"Was. He passed away about a month ago."

"I'm sorry, Maria. I didn't know."

The phone went quiet. "Maria, are you there?"

"Yes. I'm sorry. This is difficult. There are some things about his death that are troubling me. I didn't know who else to turn to."

"I'm glad you called," Adriana said softly.

"Would it be possible for us to meet in person to discuss this?" Maria asked.

"Of course. Could you do it around five tomorrow afternoon? I have a meeting with the Memorial Park Conservancy Committee. I can see you after."

"It's kind of personal. How about the little coffee shop on Woodway, just west of the park?" Maria proposed.

"Perfect."

The warm smell of kolaches and black coffee engulfed Maria as she entered Bronco Joe. A red neon sign of a coffee mug ringed by a blinking yellow lariat hung in the front window. The same logo appeared on the black polo shirt and baseball cap worn by a young Latina behind the register. When the broadcaster approached, dressed for the camera in a white blouse with blue jacket, the cashier did a double take.

"Hey, aren't you that TV lady?"

"Afraid not," Maria answered, then ordered an espresso and headed for a round table in the corner. She sat facing the door in one of two hardwood chairs. At tables on either side, middle-aged women in designer sweats sat huddled behind iPads.

Ten minutes later, Adriana hurried from her SUV into the shop. With casual confidence, she unbuttoned her brown trench coat and looked across the room until her eyes met Maria's. A smile crossed her lips. Approaching the table, she extended her hand.

"Nice to see you again, Maria."

"And you as well. Thanks for coming. Would you like some coffee?"

"No," replied the mayor, sliding into the open seat. "I had more than my limit with the park people. What can I do for you?"

"Before his death, my father was faced with an unusual challenge." She told the story of the Rio Hot Springs, Trans-National's attempt to gain control of the dysprosium by a joint venture, and the tribe's decision to form an alliance with other tribes to develop the minerals on their own.

"With the help of Luke Stasney from Stasney Energy, a foundation formed by the tribes was able to borrow development money from the Plains Bank in Midland. It seems Dad had a contact there. That was three months ago."

"Fascinating," Adriana said, shaking her head in amazement.

"The development was going more slowly than planned. Some members of the tribe wanted to renegotiate a deal with Trans-National to get money sooner rather than later. When Dad died, they stepped up their pressure. There was never a conclusive autopsy. You can understand my concern."

Adriana leaned back in her chair, shaking her head. "Good Lord. I've never heard such a story."

"There's one more thing."

Maria recounted the call from the mystery tipster, his story of the kickback scheme, and the trumped-up rape charge against her father.

"He advised me to dig into both."

"Do you believe him?" Adriana asked.

"I'm not sure how he could have known so much unless he was inside Trans-National."

"And he didn't ask for anything if the tribe held onto the minerals? A cut of the profits?" Adriana asked.

"No. Nothing. He said he made the call for his own reasons. But it's clear he's warning that Trans-National, Buck Olmeyer, and no telling what other Big Oil interests, will stop at nothing to cover up the kickback and prevent the production of the dysprosium fuel additive."

Maria glanced around the room, then leaned in closer. "After the call, I began reporting on the air about the kickbacks."

"Yes," said the mayor, "I recall seeing that broadcast."

"Yes. The station fired me for it."

"No!"

"There has been some interest in the story from a public broadcasting station in San Antonio. We're currently talking about a special assignment to continue the investigation and pursue other special features."

"What do you know about the rape charge?" Adriana asked.

"Nothing yet," Maria answered. "I can't imagine it's true, but I've had no way to investigate."

"We don't know his side of it," the mayor said. "Have you spoken to Billy about this?"

"No."

"Why not?"

Maria sighed, then told Adriana about her prior relationship with Billy. "It ended badly. When my father asked for my help, I planned to look into Billy's background after he left the tribe, as my father requested, but not to interview him. In fact, my father asked me to keep my distance."

"I understand," said Adriana. "These things can get messy."

Maria pulled her chair closer. "The mystery caller also warned me to be careful who I took into my confidence about the things he told me. He said keeping the dysprosium additive off the market was so important to Trans-National that Billy and Luke were under electronic surveillance.

If I told either of them about this, it would tip off Trans-National and put everyone in danger, including me."

"And me?" asked Adriana.

Maria blushed and lowered her gaze. "I'm afraid so, which is why I'll understand if you'd like to leave now. I need access to the Houston Police Department files to check out the rape allegation. You are the only person I know who could help me."

"What do you intend to do with this information?" asked Adrianna.

"The best way I can help derail Trans-National's effort to cover up this scandal, and its plan to permanently thwart the development of dysprosium, is to keep writing and reporting about it. No holds barred. Only the truth. That's my plan."

"I'll see what I can do."

"Please be careful."

37

BILLY PARKED SAM'S PICKUP on an area of crushed grass fronting the Rio Hot Springs. Nearby stood a double-wide trailer and a large Quonset hut. The November afternoon sun glinted off a metal yard sign that read *Native Development, LLC*. Behind the buildings crouched Billy's Piper Cherokee, wings lashed down and engine wrapped against the swirling sand.

Billy stepped down and walked ten paces to the trailer's screen door. He stepped inside where two plastic chairs flanked a table made from an empty plywood reel. A rusted piston collected cigarette butts.

"Clive?" he called.

From the back came a gruff reply. "In here."

Billy peered through a second doorway where he found the professor seated at a card table poring over stacks of paper. The trash can was overflowing. He passed a row of filing cabinets and took a seat in a folding metal chair. Clive acknowledged Billy with a nod, tossing down his ballpoint in frustration. From his cage in the corner, Porter welcomed him by whistling the first line of "Dixie".

Billy swept aside a pile of old newspapers with his foot. "I like what you've done to the place," he said.

"Bite me."

"We could at least afford a proper desk."

The old man stood and walked to an open window. He dug his hands into faded overalls and exhaled audibly. "I don't need a desk, Tonto. I need to figure out why this fucking additive only works about half the time."

Billy's brow furrowed. "Last week you said we were on track."

"That was then, this is now," said Clive.

Billy closed his eyes and rubbed his neck. "Clive, we don't have time for this. If there's a hitch, I need to know now."

The professor whirled around. "Look. I've got ten Apaches who can barely read, a half dozen Cherokees who blow weed all day, and three Coushatta women who feed them. What do you expect?"

Billy grimaced. "Don't forget what came along with those people. Two hundred fifty thousand dollars to kick-start this lab."

"Lab? Ha!" Clive replied disdainfully. "If I had a decent setup like we were supposed to have with Trans-National money, we'd be in production by now."

"I suppose all that money would have made the additive actually work?" Billy retorted. When he saw the hurt look on Clive's face, he was sorry he'd said it. "Come on, Clive. We've been all through this. Trans-National would have sabotaged us. Every shred of evidence pointed to that. They'd have bought off the tribe and killed this project in a year. We went along with Chief Whitecloud's foundation because we knew it was our only chance to produce the additive—and for you to prove that your theory about dysprosium was correct."

Clive's shoulders slumped and he looked back out the window. "You still think it's only a theory?"

"I didn't mean it that way. I've spent almost every day for the past six months defending this project. If I didn't believe in it, I could never have done that."

Returning to the table, Clive sat down and began shuffling through the pile of reports. "I needed time and money to perfect this thing, Billy. Now I've got neither." He sank back into the chair.

"What's the specific problem?" Billy asked gently.

Clive sat looking at the table, mute. He was expressionless, as if he'd never seen the pages before.

"Tell me about it," Billy said.

"Ever since you flew that death trap in from New Orleans with the metric clarifier unit, I've been able to extract plenty of dysprosium from the well water. Used it to run a hundred tests trying to recreate our success of ten years ago."

"And?"

"Working out the process to produce the additive was not difficult. It works equally well on gasoline and diesel, same as before. I just can't figure why we haven't had consistent performance."

"How much of the stuff have you been able to produce?"

"About five gallons," he answered. "But that's plenty enough to verify its capabilities. Hell, back at UT a thimble full in a gallon of gas ran that old lawn mower for two days."

"I remember."

"Most tests on the diesel generator out back work like a charm. It runs for days on the original lawn mower formula. Then, tests on other equipment run dry in a few hours."

"Do you have enough fuel to keep the testing going?"

"That's a problem. It comes by truck from Midland, over two hundred miles away. To keep the electricity on, we've got to run the generator day and night. That burns through most of it."

Billy stood. "Show me where the testing is done."

The two men walked in silence from the trailer to the metal hut. Inside, a series of wood tables lined the walls and naked light bulbs dangled above. The atmosphere was dank with the pungent smell of petroleum.

"Over there," Clive pointed, "is the clarifier unit. Water from the springs is funneled in, then a clarifying agent is added. It changes the electrical charge of the dysprosium particles making them attract and drop to the bottom. The top water is boiled off, leaving about 75 percent pure dysprosium in the sludge."

They proceeded to an aluminum vat. "We pump it through this scrubber. The end product is ready to blend with gasoline or diesel. It's not rocket science."

"Where is the testing done?" asked Billy, looking around the room.

"Usually we pour the additive into the big generator out back. It's not covered, so when the weather looks bad, we tank up the portable generator and run it in the shed."

He pointed outside to the larger unit. "We started this test two days ago with one gallon of gasoline. So far only 5 percent has been consumed."

"Are the generators the same?" asked Billy.

"The only difference is size. It's a goddamn mystery."

They returned to the front room of the double-wide. "Clive, I know you're doing all you can. But in fairness, I have to tell you the window for this project is closing."

"What the hell is that supposed to mean?"

"We're running out of capital and time. If we don't prove this stuff works, and soon, we'll be out of business."

Clive's fingers spread and combed through his mop of gray hair. He stared at the floor and inhaled deeply. "When we started this adventure," he said in a low tone, "it was your job to provide the money and the opportunity to develop the additive." A long pause hung heavily.

Billy stood back with hands on his hips, girding for another blast.

Instead, when Clive looked up, his chin quivered and his eyes glistened. "You've done your part. I've let you down, Billy," he said between chokes.

"No, you haven't, you . . ."

"Shut up."

His former student fell silent.

"I've spent my life at the lip of the cup. I'm there again with the same result. Nothing. I'm a loser, Billy."

Clive's shoulders heaved as he buried his face in his hands. Billy walked to his old friend, paused long enough to touch his arm, then continued out the door. From the backyard, the hum of the generator blended with the sound of Sam's truck sputtering to life. Billy steered the vehicle along the dirt road, then turned onto the highway. Porter was silent.

Billy drove into the burnt orange sunset, thinking about his meeting with Clive. The asphalt was still hot from the afternoon sun and, through the open window, he could hear it sticking to the tires. The road smelled of hot petroleum. Suddenly an idea took hold. He pulled the truck to the shoulder and sat a moment with the engine idling. His lips curled into a smile and he did a one-eighty back toward the Rio Hot Springs.

Dust billowed as he navigated the dirt road from the highway to the trailer. He braked to a stop and jumped out. Flinging open the door, he called out for Clive.

"In here, you damn fool," Clive responded from the tiny kitchen. "I heard you from the highway."

"Sit," ordered Billy, thrusting a chair toward the professor.

Billy pulled up another chair, turned it backward, and leaned on his forearms over the top.

"Petroleum reacts to heat, correct?"

"Brilliant."

"Do you know how dysprosium reacts to heat?"

Clive's eyes narrowed. "We haven't tested for that. What are you getting at?"

"Is it possible that heat, sunlight specifically, is the catalyst for the reaction between dysprosium and hydrocarbon?"

Clive scratched his beard. "Sometimes we add additive to the diesel indoors then pour the mix into the generators. Other times we fuel the generators first and top them off with additive outdoors, in the sunshine."

"And," said Billy, "the other variable is cloudy days."

Clive stared at the quarterback in amazement. "My God. This is too simple. Even you figured it out."

"How soon can you run some tests?" said Billy.

"As soon as you get out of my hair," answered Clive, hustling toward the hut.

"Amazing, isn't it?" Billy called to him. "And I had such crappy instructors in college."

"Go away, Einstein," Clive shouted over his shoulder. "I'll call you tomorrow."

38

"YOU KNOW THIS IS HIGHLY UNUSUAL," the archive sergeant said as he walked Adriana into a cavernous room beneath City Hall. From a vent in the ceiling, a stream of tepid air set up a musty circulation through the rows of shelves, each piled high with binders.

When they had walked twenty yards through the stacks, Sergeant Rankin pointed to an old wooden desk in the corner paired with a threadbare swivel chair. When she sat, it pitched forward with a screech.

"Would you like me to help you with whatever you're looking for?"

"No thanks. I'll call if I get stymied."

"Okay," he replied, and walked into the adjoining office. She nodded to him through a glass pane embedded with wire mesh.

The archived files were arranged numerically, based upon case number. In a booklet on the top shelf, she found an index and located case number 73251 R-1960, the number provided by Maria's tipster.

The mayor retrieved the file from the stacks. Stapled to the front was a mug shot of a dark-skinned teenage boy with high cheekbones and broad nose, holding a placard saying Alpine Police Department. Inside was a transcript from the Brewster County grand jury. Charge: Rape. Location: Alpine, Texas. Victim: Miranda Sterling. Defendant: Angus Whitecloud, Chinati Flats, Texas. Adriana's pulse quickened as the name registered. *Didn't Maria say she was Chinati? Perhaps Cloud is short for Whitecloud. How many Whiteclouds could there be in that tribe?*

Adriana read on. There were no eyewitnesses and little physical evidence. The victim was seventeen and pregnant. Her parents moved her to Houston to have the child. When the Brewster County sheriff made inquiries, the family refused to cooperate. The Brewster County grand jury issued a subpoena for her testimony. It was served by the Houston Police Department. But no further action was taken when a handwritten affidavit prepared by the girl surfaced, claiming there was no rape. In the margin of the file was a note: "Suspended by Attorney General. Affidavit to C.L."

Where was the affidavit? Who or what is C.L.?

Adriana reached up and rapped on the window with her knuckle. The sergeant looked up from his paper.

"C.L.?" she mouthed, raising her eyebrows.

He bobbed his head and responded in a loud voice. "Crime Lab."

Perplexed, Adriana walked to the door and peered through. "Why would an affidavit be sent to the crime lab?"

"It wouldn't, unless there was some physical evidence involved. What kind of case?"

"Rape."

"I can't figure it, but there must be something."

"Can you help me?"

"I'll try, mayor, but the lab is a nightmare. How old's the document?"

"Nineteen sixty-three," she answered.

He gave a low whistle. "That'll be a crapshoot. Follow me."

The pair headed into a narrow hallway and followed it like a maze to a tiny elevator. The sergeant pushed the down button. When the door opened, they stepped in and descended two floors to the basement.

They exited into a dingy bullpen with low ceilings, linoleum tile, and flickering fluorescent tubes overhead. A half dozen wooden tables were bolted to the floor. Each had a waist-high platform piled high with pliers, forceps, and other forensic tools. Plastic bottles filled with a rainbow of chemicals lined the base of the walls and squeegee mops hung from hooks. It smelled like a janitor's closet.

Crumpled cardboard boxes had been haphazardly stored in rows of five-foot-high metal cases. Some brimmed with paper files, others with plastic bags filled with firearms, drug paraphernalia, and other would-be evidence.

A lone worker with a huge Afro, wearing a stained lab coat, leaned against a center table, talking on her cell phone. She didn't acknowledge the sergeant or his guest. Beneath the woman's table, Adriana saw a shopping bag marked "Prosecution Exhibits" with a rip down one side from which random pills, syringes, and bullet casings had spilled onto the floor.

The mayor had defended this place for years against criticism of sloppy science and incompetent staff. This was her first visit. Lying was the part of her job she hated most.

"See what I mean?" Rankin murmured as they worked their way toward the back. She nodded.

A gray cubicle in the far corner bore a nameplate: Special Projects. Inside sat a uniformed policeman playing video games on his computer. Adriana thought he bore a striking resemblance to the Pillsbury Dough-boy. From his desperate combover to the rolls of sweaty flesh lopping over his collar, the mayor judged him to be qualified only for projects well-short of special. *He gives a new meaning*, she thought, *to the phrase "Houston's Finest."*

"Plumb," barked Adriana's escort.

"Yes, sir," the Dough cop responded with a start, fumbling his computer mouse. Surprise morphed to panic when he turned and recognized the mayor.

"Hello, hello. What can I do for you, Mayor Whitlock?"

Adriana handed him a piece of paper with the rape case information. "I'm looking for any documents or other evidence you have on this matter. It's very old."

Officer Plumb held the paper with one meaty hand while stroking his chin with the other. His brows arched. "So now they've sent you to find the affidavit, too," he said.

"You know about the affidavit?" Adriana asked, her eyebrows knitting.

"Sure. A fella from Austin was here last week looking for it. Came in with the chief."

"Chief Dillon . . . of the HPD?" asked Rankin.

"Yup."

"And who was the other man?" Adriana queried.

"Said he was from the attorney general's office. A lawyer, I think. I told them it would be a miracle if we found something that old, but I'd try."

"And did you?" the mayor asked.

He proudly reached into the desk drawer and retrieved a manila folder. "This case had been dormant for fifty years. That is, until the AG lawyer and Chief Dillon came to see me. I was going to call them today. Found this folder in a file cabinet marked *Proprietary*. Never knew exactly what that meant."

He handed it to Adriana.

She removed a handwritten affidavit with a tiny cellophane bag stapled to the bottom containing what appeared to be a lock of dark hair.

"I'll take care of it from here on out," said Adriana.

Dough cop glanced at Rankin, then responded, "Okay. Can't argue with the boss."

Rankin gave him the kind of patronizing smile that meant the question of who was working for whom would be revisited soon.

Mayor Whitlock and Sergeant Rankin retraced their steps, then rode up to the main floor of HPD records. "I'm not going to ask why you need that affidavit," he said. "But I've got to keep the original. I'll make you a copy."

"Of course," she said, handing it to him. "What about the hair?"

"You keep it safe," he said. "Return it when you're done."

Adriana thanked him.

The duplicate came back to Adriana in a fresh envelope.

"Anything else I can do for you?" Rankin asked.

"One more thing, if you will."

"Yes?" he answered, exhaling audibly.

"Keep the original in your possession until you hear back from me personally. If Chief Dillon asks about it, refer him to me."

Rankin's eyes narrowed, and his head ticked to the right in a skeptical gesture. "Oooookay."

Adriana took the elevator to the top floor and made her way past the receptionist to her office, closing the door behind her. The chair at her mahogany desk squeaked as she leaned back, affidavit in hand. She began to read:

Before me this 15th day of May 1960, after being duly sworn, appeared the undersigned and testified to the following: My name is Miranda Sterling. I am a resident of the City of Alpine, Brewster County, Texas. On May 13, 1960, I gave birth to a baby girl at St. Joseph's Hospital, Houston, Texas. She is dark-skinned with a port-wine birthmark in the shape of a crescent moon above her left ribcage. I named her Adriana. I love my daughter, but cannot give her a good home, so with deep sadness I offer her for adoption. My sexual relationship with her father was consensual. He is a member of the Chinati tribe from Brewster County, Texas. His name is Angus Whitecloud.

It was signed, Miranda Sterling.

39

THE TRIP FROM HOUSTON TO ALPINE had been a long one, but offered Adriana the opportunity to consider the magnitude of her mission. She parked her Suburban in front of a modest stone house with a rocking chair on the porch. After taking a deep breath, she stepped down from the truck and walked slowly to the white wooden door. With a trembling hand, she tapped with the brass knocker.

The door opened, revealing a small, elderly woman, who looked her up and down. "Yes?"

"Are you Miranda Sterling?" Adriana asked.

"I am. How can I help you?"

"My name is Adriana Whitlock, from Houston. Were you acquainted with Angus Whitecloud?"

The woman raised her hand to her mouth. Her brow furrowed. "Yes, I know Angus."

Adriana could hear the concern in her voice. "I have some news about him." She watched the woman flinch and reach for the door frame.

"Please come in."

Adriana followed her through a living room, nicely furnished with a large fireplace. The mantle was crowded with framed photos, in the fashion of old people whose lives are summed up by such collections. They continued through the dining room and kitchen, then out the backdoor to a patio, where they sat beneath two pinion pines in black cast iron chairs.

The weathered hands of the old woman clutched the arms of her chair. Finally, in a voice just above a whisper she said, "Angus?"

Adriana replied softly, "Miranda, Angus is dead."

Miranda closed her eyes and let her chin drop to her chest. Tears rolled down her cheeks. "When?"

"A month ago. They're not sure of the cause yet."

She looked up and asked, "You knew Chief Whitecloud?"

"No. I only learned about him a few weeks before his death."

"But you're here now."

"I am."

"Why?"

Adriana clenched her hands together and leaned forward. "He was my father."

The woman's face paled. "So—you also know who I am?"

"Yes."

The two women sat in silence. The only sound was the distant call of a circling hawk and the sigh of the wind through tree limbs above. Adriana reached over and held her mother's hand. Miranda responded in kind.

"This has been a long time coming," said Miranda.

"Yes. I never dared hope it would happen."

"How did you find me? The affidavit?"

Adriana nodded. "The chief's other daughter, Maria, told me about a tipster who informed her Angus was being framed with a bogus rape charge. She asked me if I would check out his story in the police records."

"That's exactly why I signed the affidavit," Miranda said. "I was afraid they would trump up some charge against him. Shortly after I signed the affidavit, I was able to get word to him about our baby—you—through a mutual friend. I hoped he approved of your name."

"I can't imagine how difficult that must have been," Adriana said.

"So, you spoke to his other daughter? I believe she's a television reporter."

"Yes, in Houston."

"Small world. How did you get access to the police records?"

"Through my job."

"Secretary?"

"Mayor."

"Of Houston? Oh my."

Miranda looked down at her feet, ankles swollen with age, and said, "Adriana, I'm sorry. Your father and I loved each other very much, but it was not the kind of romance that could survive in those times. My dad was a rancher and owned the local bank. He was, as they say, a pillar of the community. There was no room in his life for a half-breed child. I hated him for what he did to Angus and me—and to you. But after his death, as I took my turn struggling with life, I became more sympathetic. He did what he thought was best for all of us."

"Do you think your father would have approved of our meeting?" asked Adriana.

"Who knows. But once he understood the success you've made of your life, despite the difficulties, I think he'd be proud. I know I am."

The next hour was spent trading stories. Miranda told of her childless marriage to a school principal, of being widowed at sixty, and of her career as an officer of the family bank. "Plains Savings became my family," she explained. "We helped a lot of folks over the years. Almost everyone did business with us. In the eighties, when S&Ls were failing throughout Texas, we held on and even expanded with branches in Midland and San Angelo."

Adriana recounted her life in the modest home of her adoptive parents. "There was never any secret about my adoption. They knew nothing of my background—except my name—which was probably a good thing. For as long as I can remember, they told me I was more special than other kids because they had chosen me. They spared nothing to help me get an education. I miss them."

Miranda listened intently and then asked the question she'd pondered for years. "Did you ever consider searching out your biological parents?"

Adriana paused and gazed past her mother to the mountains on the horizon. "Of course. I knew one day I would go looking. Did you think about it?"

"Every day of my life," answered Miranda. "I just didn't have the courage to face you. I had no idea you'd become famous. Mayor of Houston. Angus wouldn't have believed it."

Adriana leaned over and embraced her mother. They cried. Above, the hawk continued its circles.

The exchange of life stories was complete, and shadows were creeping closer. "I should be going now," Adriana said.

"Before you leave, I have something for you," said Miranda. She arose and motioned for her daughter to follow her into the house. In the living room she nodded toward a leather davenport and Adriana sat down. "I'll be right back."

She returned with a worn leather briefcase and handed it to her daughter.

Inside were stacks of small white envelopes, each addressed to Miranda at the bank. She picked one and withdrew a birthday card. On the front was a picture of a little girl blowing out five candles. Inside, under a colorful logo that said, *Happy Birthday!* was a handwritten message. It began with *Dear Adriana* and ended *Love, Daddy*.

"Are these from . . ." Adriana began, her voice catching.

"Yes. From Angus Whitecloud. All of them."

The card Adriana held in her hand told her how much he missed her and about his life on the reservation. Adriana's eyes glistened. "Every year?"

"Yes. Without fail. Except for this year. I knew something was wrong."

"Did you ever see each other again?"

"Three times. The first was by chance when he came to Alpine to attend a rodeo. It was held in the same arena where we'd first met. Maria was competing as a barrel racer. She was fearless. When the show was over, I saw him scanning the crowd. His wife was with him and I was with my husband. Our eyes met, and he smiled. We waved."

"And the second?" Adriana asked.

"About six months ago. Angus, Billy Strikeleather, the Chinati football player, and an oil man named Luke Stasney came looking for a loan to mine something called dysprosium from the Rio Hot Springs. The loan was a big one for our bank. Three million dollars. Stasney Energy agreed to pledge all its assets, which were considerable. The borrower was a foundation cobbled together by Angus with three other tribes to provide start-up capital for the Indians. A great idea. I was all for it. But I was having trouble convincing the rest of the loan committee. Angus was way ahead of us. He produced a four-million-dollar loan commitment from the United Auto Workers Pension Fund. They obviously had valued the Rio Hot Springs minerals much higher than us. Their underwriting was very thorough and enough to convince our committee. We made the loan.

"The last time I saw Angus was the day of the loan closing," Miranda continued. "We had only a little time together. He was passionate about the foundation, and saw it as the most important thing he'd ever done. But mostly we spoke about you. He asked if I'd given you his cards. I had to tell him I didn't know where you were. He was sad. He was a widower by then and my husband had died many years before. We agreed to stay in touch, but never did."

Adriana told her mother about the continuing efforts of Trans-National to get control of the Rio Hot Springs. "Dysprosium poses such a real threat to Big Oil, they'll stop at nothing to prevent its conversion into a fuel saving additive."

"Now I'm happier than ever we made the loan," Miranda said. "I hope the project goes well. Too bad Angus won't be there to see it through."

"There are problems," said Adriana. "The development has been slower than the tribe hoped. They're behind schedule. Without the chief, a lot of Chinati want to sell out to Trans-National."

Miranda frowned. "As I recall, the death of a guarantor is technically a default under the loan. But as long as there is reasonable progress, we would never call the note. Of course, the new owners might have a different view."

"New owners?"

"A few weeks ago, we received an offer from a Houston investor group to buy the bank for twice what it's worth. It was a deal we couldn't refuse. The closing is set for next week."

"Who is the buyer?"

"I don't recall the exact name. I have a copy here. Would you like to see it?"

"Please."

Miranda went to her bedroom and returned with the contract. She handed it to Adriana.

"E-4 Investments, LLC, a Texas limited liability company, by Buchanan T. Olmeyer, Manager," read Adriana aloud.

"Do you know him?" asked Miranda.

"Too well. He's the CEO of Trans-National."

"My God," said Miranda. "We didn't know who they were when the contract was signed. It looks like they are a front for Big Oil. This explains why their offer for the bank was so high. It's the note they want. With the chief's death, they will be able to declare a default at any time. A quick fore-closure will give them the Rio Hot Springs."

A second later, she looked up at Adriana disconsolately and said, "And the chief's death may not have been from natural causes?"

Her voice trailed off.

"I wouldn't put it past them," Adriana said.

"Maybe we should talk to the law," Miranda said.

"Maria warned me they're in on it, too."

"Oh darling, what have I done?" She covered her face.

"How could you have known?"

They sat in silence for several moments. Outside the window, an eve-ning dove cooed.

Miranda cocked her head slightly and fixed her gaze on Adriana. "There might be a way. If we could find a buyer for the note, we could sell it before the closing. Note sales of this kind are not unusual in a small bank. It happens all the time."

Adriana's brow creased. "What would the price be?"

"The principal balance, around three million dollars, or a fraction less."

"I have emergency discretionary spending authority of that much from the city," said the mayor. "It could be done."

As both women considered the possibility, the full picture began to emerge. "That would mean," said Miranda slowly, "the city of Houston could declare a default and foreclose on the Rio Hot Springs and its miracle mineral?"

Adriana nodded. "E-4 would be out and the city would be in control of the dysprosium."

"With oil being the cornerstone of Houston's economy, how would the voters feel about the development of a dysprosium fuel additive?" Miranda asked.

"The decision would be theirs," Adriana said. "It could hurt a lot of them badly, very badly."

"On the other hand," Miranda said, "it would put the city in control of the most revolutionary energy discovery since the splitting of the atom. What would they do?"

"I don't know. My term expires in nine months. I could hold off the decision on foreclosure for that long. If the Indians were successful first, and the world could see proof the additive worked, I'm sure other financing could be arranged to pay off the note."

"Yes, but think of it," Miranda whispered. "Cheap energy at last. It would be an economic boon to the world. And the Indians would be in control, again."

"The circle would be complete," said Adriana.

"How long would it take to arrange the funds from the city?"

"No time, really. I just have to call the city comptroller and give him wiring instructions. I could deal with any blowback after the fact. It's actually a good investment. What would be involved on your end?"

"I'm the CEO. I'd just have to verify receipt of the city's funds, endorse the note, and hand it over to you. I don't think we need any lawyers."

"That's not a problem," said her daughter. "I'm an attorney, too. I'll order the funds tonight."

40

PATRICK RED EAGLE STRODE TOWARD MID-COURT in the tiny gymnasium of the Chinati Flats School. The sound of the restaurateur's black Lucchese boots echoed off the hardwood floor. A makeshift platform had been erected from plywood placed on concrete blocks. Flanked by flags of Texas and the United States, it fronted twenty rows of folding chairs filled with murmuring Chinati Indians. On the first row sat Billy Strikeleather, along with the tribal council. Maria Whitecloud was seated in the back of the room.

"Thank you all for coming," said Red, in a loud voice. "Since it affects each one of you, the council decided to call this meeting of the tribe to consider the future of our Rio Hot Springs mineral project. For those who don't know, our late chief, Angus Whitecloud, formed an alliance, Native Exploration Foundation, with the Cherokee, Apache, and Alabama-Coushatta tribes to develop the minerals. It hasn't gone well. Since the chief's passing, many of you have said we should ask Trans-National if it's still willing to take over the project and pay us for our interest. Tonight, we will vote on it. Anyone can speak. Just raise your hand."

He continued, "Before we start, there are some things you should know. We took out a loan with Plains Savings to help cover costs. One of the covenants was that Angus Whitecloud remain chief. His death meant the bank could have called our loan and foreclosed on the Rio Hot Springs. Although they chose not to, we learned this morning the bank was purchased by a group whom we believe to be closely aligned with Trans-National and other Big Oil interests." He paused as the crowd began whispering. "If the new owners decided to foreclose on the note, we would lose the Rio Hot Springs to them in thirty days, and we would receive no money at all.

"To give you a clear choice tonight, I contacted Trans-National and asked what offer they would make us now in exchange for our conveyance of the Rio Hot Springs and dissolution of Native Exploration Foundation. The answer was enough to pay off our loan, repay the money invested by the other tribes, and put $20,000 into the pocket of each registered Chinati, Cherokee, Alabama-Coushatta, and Apache. Our partners have left the decision up to us since we are the managers of the Foundation. The floor is now open."

Billy raised his hand. Red pointed to him and he stood to address the meeting.

"I'm proud of our team at the Rio Hot Springs. It's taken longer than we anticipated to work out the process for refining dysprosium from the Rio Hot Springs water, but we've overcome those problems and we're close to producing a marketable product. All that's needed is some more time to implement our new manufacturing procedures. It would be foolish to quit now. We should look for a new lender who will give us the time we need."

From the back row, an old man shouted, "And who would that lender be, Billy? You?" A laugh rippled through the audience.

Billy winced, but inside he knew it was fair. *I've made more in the last ten years than the entire tribe combined, and what do I have to show for it? Maybe Red is right.* He sat down.

"Does anyone else have something to say before we pass out ballots?" Red boomed.

Randy Kickingbird looked around nervously for Oliver Greentree. When he couldn't find him, he rose from his first-row seat and turned to the crowd. "There are other investors who have an interest in the minerals." His voice quavered. "Before the council decided to go with Plains Bank for financing, the United Auto Workers in Detroit had expressed an interest in financing the Rio Hot Springs project."

Red laughed loudly. "When the chief convinced the council, not including me, to get this cockamamie loan from Plains Bank, the only other solid proposal on the table was from Trans-National. Where were your union friends then?"

"I'm told they were prepared to loan the tribe four million dollars and are still willing to consider it."

"You've been told that? By whom? On what terms?" barked Red. "Why aren't they here?"

"Oliver Greentree has spoken directly to them. He was supposed to be here tonight to explain. I'm sure he's just been delayed."

The attendees craned their necks, searching for Oliver. He wasn't there.

Spreading his arms wide, Red gave an exaggerated shrug and proclaimed, "Randy, I don't know what that boy is up to and I don't care. What I do know is Trans-National has made a firm offer. Unless you've got something more than a notion, there's really nothing to discuss now, is there?"

Kickingbird was sweating. "Look, I'm not a businessman. I'm a school principal. Oliver will explain when he arrives."

"Well, we don't have time to start over, especially with the unions. I'd rather deal with people who know what they're doing. Is anyone here interested in getting in bed with the labor unions?

"We've got an offer on the table from Trans-National," Red continued, sounding more and more like a tent preacher. "Foreclosures happen fast in Texas. Thirty days. Now that they control the bank, Trans-National is going to get their hands on the Rio Hot Springs either by foreclosure, in which case we get nothing, or purchasing it, in which case we get $20,000 apiece. I say we vote to accept their proposal before we end up with nothing."

No one spoke. "Okay, pass out the ballots. Let's get this done quickly," said Red.

Ten minutes later the votes were being tallied. Billy sat stoically, his eyes straight ahead.

From the back row, Maria watched the proceedings and wondered if it would all end here as it had so many times before. *Perhaps, the closing paragraph of my story will be an epitaph for the Chinati tribe. A cruel irony. My own people surrendering again with a whimper—for a string of beads.*

While bits of conversation from the crowd drifted back to her, mostly about how they would spend their windfall, Maria saw a woman enter the side door of the gym. The new arrival was tall with her hair pulled back, wearing gray pants, white blouse, and a black suede jacket. She strode toward the podium.

Red bellowed, "This meeting is open to only Chinati tribe members."

The visitor smiled at Maria and touched her on the arm as she went by. Maria did a double take.

"Are you deaf?" Red said.

Maria stood and said, "This is Adriana Whitlock. She is the mayor of Houston. If she has come this far to speak to us, I think we should listen."

Adriana mounted the platform. "I have some information I think you'll want to hear."

She recounted how she had met Maria, her resultant investigation of the Houston police files, and Trans-National's attempt to extort Chief Whitecloud into turning over the Rio Hot Springs by dredging up a thirty-year-old spurious rape charge. The crowd was riveted as Adriana told about the affidavit signed by the alleged rape victim, exonerating the chief and professing her love for their baby.

"Next you'll tell us the governor was conspiring with Trans-National to give Angus a heart attack," scoffed Red.

Edith Landrum spoke from the front row. "Why are you so interested in helping us? What's in it for you?"

Before Adriana could respond, another female voice from the crowd chimed in, "Yeah. Even if you are the mayor of Houston, that doesn't entitle you to speak at our meeting. Let's finish counting the votes. I want my $20,000!"

"She's right!" blurted Red, seeing his chance to regain the floor. He jumped to his feet and barked, "I'm going to have to ask you to leave, now."

Adriana stood her ground. "I do belong here. You'll understand when you hear this."

She reached into her leather purse and withdrew a piece of faded yellow paper. The affidavit crinkled as she unfolded it and read aloud.

When she finished, Red pounced again. "So what?"

Straightening herself, the mayor took a deep breath. "The baby in the affidavit was me."

The revelation silenced the room.

Red rolled his eyes. "Right. And I'm Will Rogers. What proof do you have?"

Before she could answer, an elderly woman in the back row stood and said, "I worked in the home of Miranda Sterling in Alpine for thirty years. There were no children. I once found a copy of this paper on Ms. Sterling's dresser. She told me the story of her baby."

The old woman paused and looked down. When she raised her head, tears were rolling down her cheeks. "She never told me who the father was. Only that her baby girl was beautiful, with dark hair and a crescent birthmark on her chest. It was the only time I saw her cry."

The woman gazed at Adriana through her tears, but with a hint of joy.

Adriana remained erect and poised, fighting back her emotions. "Thank you for telling me."

"No," said the woman. "Thank you for having the courage to come here tonight."

Red jumped to his feet. "Look, this is all very sentimental. But the chief is dead, our so-called development project hasn't produced a thing, and Trans-National may still be willing to deal. The votes are totaled. Seventy in favor of the Trans-National deal, thirty against."

Edith, her eyes now softened, rose and looked tenderly at Adriana. "If this woman is who she says, we should consider what she's saying carefully."

"There's no hard evidence," Red answered. "Only the word of an old squaw."

"If you had such evidence, would it make a difference?" Adriana asked.

The tribe nodded in unison.

She withdrew from her purse the lock of hair she'd found in the police file. "This was attached to the affidavit. I had the crime lab run a DNA test against my hair. Here it is—a perfect match."

"That could have been fabricated," Red scoffed.

The mayor of Houston removed her jacket and turned to face the room.

With a level stare at Red, she unbuttoned her white silk blouse and reached behind to unfasten her bra. His eyes followed her fingers in lurid anticipation. With a shrug she exposed her pale left breast. Below the nipple was a purple birthmark the size of a quarter—in the shape of a crescent moon.

"What do you see?" she asked.

Red turned away.

"A birthmark," Edith announced.

A buzz swept the gym. As the din grew louder, Red called out. "The vote's been taken. It's over."

"I move for a new vote," said Edith.

From all sides of the room, members of the tribe murmured their concurrence.

Billy arose and removed his coat. He walked to the podium and wrapped it around Adriana's shoulders. Turning to the crowd he announced loudly, "All in favor of taking the Trans-National deal, say aye." A smattering of affirmative votes trickled forth.

"All opposed say nay."

The response was overwhelming.

Billy smiled and shook his head. "We'll mine the dysprosium ourselves."

"It's a mistake!" wailed Red. "The bank will have our Rio Hot Springs in a month!"

Adriana held up her hand for quiet. "There's one more thing. Trans-National may own the bank. But as of 9 a.m. this morning, the city of Houston owns the note."

Red fell back into his chair.

"I authorized the city to buy it. As long as I'm mayor, there'll be no foreclosure. The tribe has nine months."

The room erupted in cheers.

41

AFTER THE TOWN HALL MEETING, Maria looked for Billy in the parking lot, but he'd gone. As she opened her truck door, she saw the taillights of Sam's truck disappear around a bend in the highway.

Billy was headed toward his motel when Maria pulled alongside him at the lone traffic light. She lowered the window and called out, "Hello. You left before I could catch you."

They pulled to the shoulder.

Billy walked to her car.

"I wanted to avoid cross-examination by the tribe," he said with a laugh.

"Billy, I have something to tell you. It's about the minerals. Can we talk?"

He paused, considering his options, then said, "Follow me."

He guided Maria to the Petrified Forest. They got out and walked to his room.

"Kind of messy," Billy said, picking up some dirty clothes. "I don't have anything to offer you."

"That's okay," she said and sat on the edge of the bed. "When I was in Houston about a month ago, I got a call from Leslie. She asked me to meet with her, so I did."

"*She* asked *you* to meet?" he said.

"That's right. She watched a broadcast of mine about excessive executive salaries at Trans-National."

"Why the meeting?"

"I had no clue. But when we met, she told me about the bogus rape charge Mayor Whitlock spoke about tonight and how Trans-National intended to use it against my father. It was as if she'd read his diary. She also told me about a backup scheme concocted by Buck Olmeyer to prevent the development of the Rio Hot Springs minerals. His so-called Plan B would blast the springs closed and disguise it as a hydraulic fracturing accident."

"So Olmeyer is willing to destroy everything before letting us develop the minerals?" Billy said.

"It appears that way. Hasn't Leslie said anything to you about all this?"

"No," Billy said.

"That's strange. I wonder where she's getting her information? She wouldn't tell me," Maria said.

"I have a pretty good idea," Billy muttered.

"Shall I go on?"

"Sure."

She repeated Leslie's comments about the poor state of her marriage and should Trans-National ever gain control of the minerals that could be the last straw. "It's for that reason she wanted to help kill the Trans-National deal."

"I find that hard to believe," Billy scoffed. "She's tight with the Big Oil crowd. Most of them are clients of LaCour. There must be an angle."

"I'm sorry, Billy."

"It's not your fault."

Maria continued, "A few days later I posted a follow-up story on my blog about kickbacks from fracking subcontractors. Channel 7 fired me. The Public Broadcasting Station in San Antonio hired me as a special features writer to continue the investigation. My first report will be a syndicated television broadcast two days from now. I'm headed there tomorrow, if I can stay ahead of the snowstorm that's predicted to hit. This time it could be more than a twelve-hour drive."

"If you broadcast what you've learned from Leslie about Trans-National's intentions, all hell could break loose. You're aware of that?" he said.

"It's something I've got to do, Billy," she said. "I've got no choice. People need to know the truth."

"That's your call. We all have to do what we think is best now."

"Be careful, Billy. Leslie warned your phone might be bugged—maybe your room, too."

"I'll watch out. Goodbye, Maria."

Within five minutes, Buck Olmeyer's phone went off, waking him from a restless sleep.

"Yeah?"

"Strikeleather's been tipped off about Plan B," said a voice, fuzzed by static.

"How?"

"A meeting with Maria Cloud. We wired his room."

"Maria Cloud?" Buck grumbled swinging his feet off the bed. "How the hell does she know?"

"We're working on that. There's more."

"Let's have it."

The caller reported to Buck what transpired at the town hall meeting.

"A lot of good it did to put Red Eagle on the payroll. The mayor, huh? That crazy bitch. This town will lynch her, but not before I've taken care of this mess for good. Keep a close watch on Strikeleather."

"Yes, sir."

Buck hung up.

42

WHEN MARIA LEFT THE MOTEL, Billy fell back on the bed with exhaustion. He checked his cell phone and found a voice mail from Sam's attending nurse at the Brewster County hospital, where he had been moved for coma care. Billy had visited him often, but worried about his prognosis. It had not been good.

"Mr. Strikeleather, this is Nurse Kennedy from Brewster General. We've met on several of your visits to your uncle. I've noticed a change in his condition. Please call when you can."

The call was a surprise. He had been thinking for months about moving Sam to a long-term care facility, but had not done it because it smacked of surrender. He pushed the callback number.

"Nurse Kennedy," came the answer.

"Ms. Kennedy, this is Billy Strikeleather."

"Yes, Mr. Strikeleather. I'm glad you called. It's about your uncle."

Billy braced himself. "Has something happened?"

"Well, yes. Although the doctors' official prognosis for him is still very guarded, I've seen a difference in his behavior."

"Behavior?" Billy asked. "There's never been a hint of consciousness in six months, except the few times he's opened his eyes. Even then
there was no sign of awareness."

"I know that," she replied. "And, as I said, the doctors don't place
much stock in my opinion. However, over the past few weeks I think his
coma has started to lift for short periods of time. Sometimes he hears my
words. His eyes seem to track me in the room. He still can't respond in a
normal way, but I think he's trying to tell me something."

Now up and pacing, Billy pressed for more information. "Why do
you think that? What has he done?"

She exhaled audibly then explained. "This is going to sound weird,
so stay with me."

"Go on, go on," Billy said impatiently, spinning his free hand around
as if cranking a fishing reel.

"A few weeks ago, we began replacing the curtains in all our rooms.
The patients had a choice of red or blue. Since I always raise the head of
his bed and talk to him as if he can hear, I asked which color he preferred
and held them up one at a time. I didn't expect him to react, which is what
happened with the blue. But when I showed him the red, he began to blink
his eyes. I didn't think much of it till the next day."

"That's it?" Billy said with an edge.

"It dawned on me that he could distinguish colors. I found a paint
chart in a magazine and pointed to each color. He had no response until I
got to red. His eyelids fluttered, faster than the day before."

"So, he may be coming out of the coma?" asked Billy.

"I can't say that," she answered. "The doctors think it's a coinci-
dence, but I wanted you to know. There's something about the color red."

"Yes, there is."

43

IT WAS SIX O'CLOCK THE EVENING following the town hall meeting. The temperature was plummeting, and gray clouds were rolling in from the west. Billy turned up his collar and the heater in his uncle's pickup. He'd promised to deliver supplies to Clive before the snowstorm hit.

On the outskirts of Chinati Flats, Billy spotted a state police car hunkered in the dark, along the shoulder of the road. He checked his speed. It was well below the limit. Nonetheless, once he passed, he saw flashing lights in his rearview mirror and heard the siren.

Billy pulled over and checked his mirror again. An officer in a brown State Trooper uniform emerged from the cruiser, donning his wide-brimmed Stetson hat. In the frigid night air, his breath streamed like white steam. As Billy watched him walk toward the driver's side of the truck, he heard a sharp thump. When the beam of his flashlight shown through the glass, Billy rolled the window down.

"Looks like you've got a busted taillight, partner. Do you mind getting out of the vehicle?"

"Would it matter?" Billy asked.

"Just do it, sir."

Billy complied.

"License and proof of insurance," commanded the officer.

While Billy dug through his wallet, the trooper leaned into the cab and dropped a plastic baggie of cocaine on the floorboard of the passenger seat. When Billy looked up the officer said, "Sir, can you tell me what that package is?"

"What package?"

The flashlight beamed down. "This one."

Billy's eyes narrowed. "That's not mine, and you know it."

The trooper reached into the truck and removed the packet. He opened it and sniffed.

"Sir, you are under arrest for possession of an illegal substance. Put your hands behind your back."

The cuffs snapped. "You have the right to remain silent . . ."

A few minutes later, the squad car pulled into downtown Chinati Flats. In a diagonal space in front of the police station, the driver cut the engine, stepped out, and opened the back door. "Let's go." He pushed Billy's head down and pulled him from the car.

Inside the station the trooper banged the counter bell. Deputy Marty Metcalf emerged from the back room with half a hamburger in his hand and the other half in his mouth.

"Some intake you've got here," the trooper said.

"Works for us," Marty flannel-mouthed, backhanding mayonnaise from his lips. "Who've you got here? Billy Strikeleather! Is this a joke?"

"Nope. Mr. Strikeleather had a little extra cargo on board tonight." He dangled the plastic bag in front of Billy's face. Marty reached into the desk and handed him a manila envelope. When the evidence was sealed, the trooper handed it back and said, "Put this in your evidence room."

"You bet," Marty replied, tossing it back into the drawer.

The trooper frowned and shook his head. He unlocked Billy's cuffs and pushed him forward through the swinging half door. "He's all yours," he said, turning to leave. "I'll file a report later."

When they were alone, Marty led Billy into the single cell in the back room. "Okay, what the hell is going on?"

"It's a frame-up, Marty. You know I'm not into drugs."

"That's not for me to decide."

The metal door clanged shut. "I wanted you to hear it from me. He planted that bag."

A half hour later, Marty brought in a paper plate of enchiladas, warmed in a microwave. "Dinner is served."

"Marty, I want to see a lawyer. I need to get out of here. It's important."

"I'm sure it is. But there's not an attorney south of Alpine, except for Harry Thistle over in Terlingua and he's always too drunk to drive by this hour. The judge will be here tomorrow afternoon. He's elk hunting on his ranch north of Marathon but is making a special trip just for you. He's not happy."

"Don't I get one phone call?" Billy pleaded.

"That's only in the movies." Marty opened the cell, placed the food on a low table, and closed the door with a metallic clink.

"Marty, will you at least make a call for me?"

"Not supposed to," he said, shaking his head.

"Give me your pen."

"I could get in trouble."

The deputy handed Billy a ballpoint.

Billy scratched a phone number on the back of a Native Exploration business card and thrust it between the bars. "Maria Whitecloud."

Three hours later, Marty reappeared. "Awake?" he asked.

"Of course."

He reached into his shirt pocket and withdrew an envelope. "When I got back from making my rounds, this was under the door. It's addressed to you. Regulations say I'm supposed to read it first."

"Go ahead," said Billy.

Marty tore open the letter and scanned it for fifteen seconds, handed it through the bars to Billy, and walked out.

Sitting on the edge of the bed, Billy began to read. It was only one line:

Billy: Plan B at daybreak. I'm sorry for everything. Burt Cole.

"Marty! Marty!" he yelled.

The deputy returned, carrying Billy's coat. "I called Maria. She's in San Antonio. Told me about Burt Cole."

Billy looked at the policeman with the kind of stunned expression you get when you've underestimated a person badly.

Marty unlocked the cell and stepped in. Handing the coat to Billy he said, "It's wrong what they're trying to do to you. You've got ten minutes. Stay off the main roads. They'll be looking for you." He picked up the plate of food and threw it against the wall. "The story will be you overpowered me. I'll need a black eye."

Billy smiled, took the jacket, and put his hand on Marty's shoulder. "Thanks. I won't forget this." Then he decked him with a right cross.

44

A BLUE NORTHER BARRELED EAST over the Chisos Mountains, catapulting down the slopes and across the plains toward the reservation like a frigid tsunami. Billy looked out the front window of the police station. Snow crystals were blowing diagonally through the beam of a street light. He slipped out the back door and ran three blocks to the far end of the alley that opened onto a stand of mesquite trees. He hid among the low branches as they danced wildly in the wind. The cold air penetrated Billy's jeans and sweater. His toes were turning numb, protected only by a pair of worn sneakers.

The sound of sirens in the distance confirmed his escape had already hit the police wire. If the message from Burt Cole was true, he had only a few hours to warn Clive of the planned destruction of the Rio Hot Springs. Even Buck Olmeyer wasn't crazy enough to attempt it in darkness.

Billy dug into his coat pocket for his cell phone. The battery was dead. "Crap," he said. He would have to deliver the message himself.

It was fifteen miles to the Rio Hot Springs by truck. With state troopers patrolling the highway, he would have to stick to the trails. While more direct, they covered rough terrain he'd not traversed since his days of roaming the desert with Maria. By Billy's reckoning, the trail distance was about three-quarters that of the truck route. His black sports watch registered 12:45 a.m. Sunup was around seven. He had six hours.

He set off following a dry creek bed, snaking through arroyos and mesquite groves. In an hour, the adrenaline waned and his bad knee began talking. First a twinge, then an ache, and finally a stab with every step. He altered his stride. Running on the inside of his right foot transferred the force from his knee to his hip. It worked for another hour until his lower back, now carrying a double load, began to cramp. He stopped, bent down, and put his hands on his knees, panting.

At the Trans-National drill site, a quarter mile across the Rio Hot Springs from the Native Exploration facility, two black panel trucks rumbled off a county road, passing rows of tankers carrying water and sand for hydraulic fracturing. They stopped at a twenty-four-inch-wide iron pipe protruding ten feet from the ground with valve wheels blossoming in all directions. It was a wellhead tapping into an underground gas deposit, six thousand feet down. Also attached to the pipe was an octopus of smaller tubes linked to more tank trucks parked nearby. The operation was run out of an aluminum double-wide trailer with a sign in front—*Trans-National Exploration.*

Buck Olmeyer and Colt Stone, each dressed in a black ski jacket and jeans, stepped out of the lead vehicle. "Anybody home?" Buck shouted.

The trailer light flickered on and the door opened. "Who the hell wants to know?" growled the gray-haired rig boss, Jake Carpenter, staring into the darkness. His steel-toed boots clanged down the metal steps toward the visitors. The earflaps of his wool hat framed cheeks furrowed like dry stream beds from years of exposure to the elements.

"Hello, Carp," Buck said. "It's been a long time since we drilled those slant holes down in Plaquemine Parish."

"Buck!" he responded, pumping the CEO's hand. "What the hell are you doing out here at this hour?"

"We've got a new formula we want to try out on the next fracking cycle. I understand it's scheduled for this morning."

"Not exactly," Jake responded. "We usually wait until early afternoon so we can double-check all the calibrations."

"Well, this one's going off at daybreak."

"Okay, boss," said Jake with a nervous smile.

"Let my men here get things ready while you and I catch up," Buck said.

"I don't know, Buck," the old hand said in a worried drawl. "This is a pretty tricky business. The wellhead pressure and blast balance have to be just right."

Forcing a laugh, Buck slipped his arm around Carp and pulled him toward the trailer. "These boys know what they're doing."

Five minutes later, with Carp sent home to an early breakfast, Buck reemerged to take charge.

"Did they get the message about the lateral drill distance?" he asked Colt.

"Yes, sir. The well's been cased for fifteen hundred feet due west," said Colt, pointing across the arroyo adjoining the drill site toward a flicker in the distance. "That son of a bitch reaches all the way under the Rio Hot Springs."

Colt gave a piercing whistle. Four men, wearing black hooded jackets and charcoal gray hard hats, stepped out of the second truck. From across the yard, they melted into the morning gloom, traceable only by their white breath. They began unloading dozens of six-foot-long cylindrical tubes packed with explosives and honeycombed with tiny apertures. The crew was experienced with the process of hydraulic fracturing, which consisted of lowering these perforation guns to the bottom of a well and firing them electronically through the holes. The force would free gas deposits trapped in solid rock. What they had not been told, Colt knew, was the uranium charges in this cache of perf-guns were fifty times more powerful than regulation. Buck's orders had been for an explosion equal to a Richter magnitude 5. He wanted it powerful enough to choke off the Rio Hot Springs with tons of volcanic rock—and obliterate the Chinati lab.

Ten miles west, Billy plodded on. In the darkness, all he could see were shadows of boulders lining the path. He glanced at his watch. It was 3:30 a.m. To make the Chinati lab by dawn, he would have to pick up the pace. His knee pain began competing with a burning tide of lactic acid in his thighs. The icy wind cut through his jeans, now damp with perspiration. He tried to block out the pain by thinking of what he would do upon his arrival. First, he would look for Clive, probably asleep. They'd gather the additive samples. *No, you idiot, first the calculations that produced them. What good are samples if you can't recreate them?* Fatigue was taking its toll. He could no longer prioritize tasks or calculate his arrival time.

Billy's mind began to play tricks. Floating between the outcroppings he saw the laughing faces of two tribal children. The girl's dark hair was pulled back in a ponytail, the boy's captured under a headband of white leather. They hovered just ahead, motioning to him. *What are they doing here?*

Soon the first signs of dawn emerged as a pink glow in the eastern sky. The snow clouds parted briefly, revealing a crescent moon rising above the tree line. Through the twilight he made out the image of an old mining shack, a familiar resting place he and Maria frequented on their way to the Rio Hot Springs decades before. *Three miles to go.*

Dawn was breaking at the Trans-National installation. Once the perforation guns were stacked next to the wellhead, Colt turned to the crew. "There's been a change of plans, men. We won't be needing you tonight. You can go on home now."

They stared back blankly. "Where is Mr. Olmeyer?" said a young roughneck, peering from under his metal hat.

"He's in the control room, but he okayed your leaving. Hit the road."

"Well," said another of the crew, "he ain't never run a fracking job on his own. We'd better at least get these guns down the hole for him."

"Look, I don't have time to explain," snapped Colt.

"But what will Buck say when—"

"NOW!" bellowed Colt.

All eyes widened as their owners hustled back into the trucks. "It's your funeral," the roughneck called out as they left.

Colt crept to the electrical box on the side of the trailer and unlatched the cover. He pulled a flashlight from his left coat pocket and scanned the circuits. The beam stopped at a red wire grounded to a twelve-volt relay. He knew from blowing bridges in Vietnam what the color signified— ignition. His eyes followed the wire out the bottom of the box and down the side of the trailer. From there it disappeared into a PVC pipe pointed toward the wellhead.

He put the flashlight under his arm, still trained on the relay, and reached into his right pocket for a screwdriver. After unfastening the connection, he withdrew a ball of conduit from his jeans, peeled off the end, and twisted it onto the red wire. He retraced his steps to the perf-guns, playing out line as he went. Working quickly, he began wiring the weapons together in sequence. One electrical charge, he calculated, would detonate them all in a lethal chain reaction.

Snow was falling harder now and the flakes blew thick across Colt's face. Finishing the final connection, he stood and walked to the front door of the trailer. After exhaling a deep breath through ballooned cheeks, he entered.

Buck was hunched over a control panel covered with a maze of buttons and switches. He turned his head and barked over his shoulder at Colt, "Well, pal, it's showtime. Come over here and give me a hand disengaging the electronic safeties on the guns. Those blanket-asses will never know what hit them."

"Buck, are you sure you want to do this?" Colt responded without moving.

"What are you talking about?" Buck answered without looking back.

"A charge big enough to do the damage you're looking for will prompt an investigation," Colt said.

Buck turned and gave Colt a steely glare. "This is my fucking deal, Colt. Do what you're told—like always."

"These people didn't ask for the minerals, Buck. It was pure luck. Besides, the odds of them producing anything worthwhile are a hundred to one."

"Colt, I don't know what you've been smoking, and I don't have time to find out. Right now, we're going to put a stop to this Rio Hot Springs crap, once and for all."

Swiveling back to the control panel, he began switching off all the safeties. "It's time," he growled.

"I'm afraid I can't let you do that," Colt said.

"Look! I told you to drop the bleeding-heart shit," Buck snarled. Wheeling around, he came face-to-face with the muzzle of a thirty-eight caliber Glock in the hand of his most trusted assistant. "What the hell do you think you're doing, Colt? Put that away before someone gets hurt."

"There's not going to be any fracking today," Colt said in a steady voice. "Your high octane perf-guns are stacked around the wellhead and wired to the trigger. If you pull it, you'll send the well and both of us up like a Roman candle."

Buck's eyes narrowed to a hostile squint.

"You've got one chance to live, Buck. Walk out of here with me. Pack up and leave this place without looking back. No Plan B. No reports to the authorities. No investigations."

Buck reached into his coat pocket and silently switched on a yellow walkie-talkie. "You're way out of your league, sport," he said, coolly coming to his feet. "You think I'd rely on just one set of guns? A man always needs a good backup, right? Like those two parallel circuits I had another crew wire yesterday morning after they down-holed uranium charges all the way to the springs. Your boys were just insurance."

"You're bluffing, Buck," said Colt.

"Am I? You gonna risk blowing up yourself and the Rio Hot Springs to find out?"

"I don't think so," said a voice from behind Colt. He spun around and saw Patrick Red Eagle standing just inside the door, pointing a 30-06 deer rifle at Colt's chest. "I might have missed Sam, but I won't miss you," he said with a smirk.

Colt hit the floor in a roll and came up firing, hitting Red in the forehead. The big Indian pulled the trigger, blowing out a rear window of the trailer before collapsing.

When Colt turned the pistol back on Buck, their eyes met in an icy stare.

"I've always liked you," said Buck, "but you're a crappy poker player." He stabbed the red ignition button.

On the far side of the river, Billy was working his way along a dry stream bed leading to the Rio Hot Springs. Snow, wet and heavier by the minute, swirled through the pine canopies on either bank and sifted down through shadowy trunks across the trail. His stride had shortened from fatigue and treacherous footing. *God, help me make it in time.*

When Billy cleared the forest, the Native Exploration office came into view. It was silhouetted against a crystal fog of snowflakes drifting up the sides. His anxiety contrasted with the pastoral scene, making it feel like a dream. *Nothing so horrendous could happen here. It must be a hoax or a cruel trick.* His brain struggled to fight through the exhaustion to a rational answer. *If I am dreaming, it's time to wake up. Wake up!*

In the Trans-National office, the electric charge took two seconds to travel from Buck's finger to the wellhead igniting the perforation guns. A fireball mushroomed twenty stories high, belching thick black smoke and turning the metal frame of the wellhead into a molten pyre. Flames hopscotched through the rows of tank trucks, melting tires and igniting fuel. The aluminum walls of the office blackened, then cracked open like an overripe banana. Both its occupants were blown into the yard, their clothes ablaze.

Clive lurched out of the Native Mineral trailer, eyes bugged. "What the hell are you doing here?" he shouted at Billy. "And what the hell was that bomb?"

"No time to explain!" Billy wheezed, giving him a bear hug. "We need to get out of here. More explosions may be coming!"

They scrambled up the quarter mile of dirt road to the parking lot, stopped, and looked back, wheezing.

"Olmeyer decided to torch our lab and the Rio Hot Springs. I couldn't reach you by phone," Billy breathed. "Looks like something went wrong."

"You ran here?"

"Right."

"You crazy redskin."

A second massive explosion rocked the Trans-National site as gas from the wellhead ignited, shooting a vapor trail of red flames into the morning sky. After several minutes, all you could hear was a roar from the burning gas.

Billy and Clive crept back down the road until the Trans-National installation came into view. Clive went to the office and returned with a pair of binoculars. He scanned the blast area. The devastation was complete.

"Oh my God!" he exclaimed. "There are two guys lying in the debris."

"We've got to go help," Billy said.

"Are you kidding? Those bastards tried to blow us off the planet."

"If they're alive, we can't just stand by while they burn to death."
Billy started toward the plume of black smoke.

"Wait, you goddamn hero. Let's take the tractor."

45

CLIVE BROUGHT THE FLATBED TRACTOR AROUND from the tool shed. Billy jumped in and held tightly to the seat with both hands. The engine revved, propelling them through the blizzard, down a dirt road, toward ground zero.

As they approached, black smoke billowing from the scene obscured the entrance to the drill site. They gauged their proximity by the intensity of the heat. When the tractor bumped onto a board road, they knew they were close. Suddenly, flames appeared overhead, licking at the dark cloud and casting an eerie orange glow over the carnage. Buckling sheet metal issued a cacophony of sickening groans, like the collapse of girders on a sinking ship. The stench of burning rubber hung heavy, and fragments of drill pipe and truck parts blanketed the yard.

"I can't see a damn thing," Clive yelled.

Billy jumped off the tractor and advanced in a crouch past the burning wellhead. He spotted the melted Trans-National sign and crept toward it. Twenty feet shy, he stumbled onto a man, his clothes burned off and skin charred, struggling to pull another free from the flaming wreckage of the trailer.

"This way!" Billy shouted, waving his arms.

When the man turned, Billy felt his stomach roll and he vomited. The victim was burned so badly his facial features had melted into a festering blister. The only hint of humankind were dog tags hanging from a leather necklace. Billy dragged him to the tractor, then went back for his companion. The second man was alive but the skin on his back and legs was charred the color of tree bark. When Billy returned to the tractor, Clive helped him hoist both victims to the flatbed, laying the first man on his back and the second on his stomach.

In the tractor, they retraced their route to the Chinati lab. There they discovered the desperate condition of their passengers.

"Jesus," Clive breathed. "I don't know what we can do for these guys."

"There's only one thing *to* do," Billy answered. "Get them to a burn unit."

"The closest one is San Antonio, 375 miles," Clive said shaking his head. "In this weather, that's an eight-hour drive. They'll never make it."

Billy looked down at the men, writhing with pain and drifting in and out of consciousness. He reached for the dog tags on the faceless one and squinted to read the name. "James Littlebow," he said in amazement. "It can't be. He was killed in Vietnam."

The man came to. He reached for Billy's hand, pulling him close to the melted cavity where his lips had been. "Billy," he rasped from the back of his throat. "I'm not Littlebow. I'm Burt Cole."

"The note—at the jail," said Billy.

"Yes. Lost my nerve in the war. Switched tags with Littlebow to cover my tracks." He nodded slightly toward the man lying next to him, "Olmeyer here kept my secret. But I couldn't let him destroy you." He lost consciousness again.

"What the hell?" Clive said softly.

Billy stared at the grotesque face. Tears welled in his eyes as he realized the only sabotage that day had been carried out by his own father—and the target was Plan B. *What makes a man do this? Guilt? Love? Desperation? Would I have had the courage?*

Clive saw Billy's eyes move past the injured men to the airplane parked in the lee of the double-wide. "By air we could make San Antonio in a few hours. They'd both have a chance," he said.

"Are you out of your mind? We're in a damn whiteout, the only gasoline we've got is diesel to run the generator, and that crate of yours hasn't been off the ground in months!"

Billy pushed his fingers through his hair, weighing the odds. "If we left now, we could get ahead of the front. Let the tailwind carry us."

"You mean instead of gasoline?" Clive fumed.

"The additive will work. It has to."

"Are you willing to bet your life on it?"

"I flew her in. With the formula, I can fly her out. But I can't pilot the plane and keep these two guys alive." He looked up at his old professor.

Clive realized where Billy was headed and shook his head. "Oh, no. No fucking way. That contraption barely made it here with you in good weather. Besides, we syphoned out most of the gas to use in the tractor."

"How much additive have you got?"

"Maybe a pint that I'm sure was produced in the sunlight."

"Gasoline?" said Billy.

"A few gallons," said Clive.

"We'd have a shot, Clive."

"What do you mean we? Besides, that plane can't haul four people."

Billy felt a squeeze from his father's hand and leaned over. "Put me in the trailer, son," he rasped. "It'll be okay. Buck's got a better chance. I challenged him. He couldn't help himself."

Clive had moved in closer to hear Burt's words. He glanced at Billy and said, "Even if you could get airborne, both of these guys are going into shock. You couldn't keep them alive for an hour."

Burt began to shake violently. "Jesus!" cried Billy. "His throat is swelling shut. Too much smoke. He's going to suffocate. Quick, bring me a length of the plastic tubing you use to refuel the generators!"

Clive stared at his student in disbelief.

"Do it!"

He bolted toward the trailer and returned, kneeling next to Billy with a coil of tubing.

"Hold him up straight," Billy said. From behind, Clive cradled Burt's head in his hands and laid him back against his chest. Billy gently opened his father's blistered lips and fed the tube down his windpipe. Burt groaned loudly and shuddered. When the tube was eight inches deep, Billy reached into his pocket for a jackknife and cut the plastic. Air whistled in through the opening.

They turned their attention to Buck. The oil man was trembling, lying on his stomach, the charred remains of his jacket and shirt fused to his back by layers of melted skin, like rayon on a hot iron. Billy took his hand. "Buck, can you hear me?" he said into his ear. Olmeyer nodded his head slightly. "We're going to take you to the hospital."

Buck's left eye quivered open and, for a second, looked into Billy's face. He tried to speak, but his face and jaw were frozen by a seizure.

"At least help me get them into the plane," Billy said, without looking at Clive. "And get some blankets."

Clive exhaled audibly, dropping his chin and stared at the frozen sod.

He stood silently for a moment, rubbing the back of his neck, then made his way into the trailer, returning with four brightly striped Indian blankets. Billy told him to lay two on the ground. Clive then helped Billy lower the victims onto the blankets and cover them with the other two. Neither injured man was moving.

Billy ran to the plane and broke away a mantle of ice from the red canvas shielding the engine. As he unfurled the tarp, an arctic gust ballooned it away into the winter maelstrom like a parachute. He untethered the wings and swept them free of snow. When he checked their undersides and ailerons, he grimaced and bellowed, "Shit! Iced!"

"What's wrong? Where the hell are you going?" Clive shouted as Billy hobbled back toward Sam's pickup. When he returned, he had removed one glove and was struggling to open a fifth of Wild Turkey.

Guess I can't blame him, Clive said to himself.

The cork finally came out in Billy's teeth and he spit it to the ground. He poured the liquor over the front edge of the wings and flaps and wiped away the ice with his gloved hand.

Snow swirled outside the cockpit as he pulled up the handle and slid inside, his bad knee screaming. A dashboard of frosted gauges and dials fronted two seats, each with a U-shaped steering yoke. He pulled his seat forward and reached behind into the passenger compartment, lowering the matching seats toward horizontal. Turning back, he stepped down gingerly to the white turf and limped to the tractor.

"Let's go," he barked, grabbing one edge of his father's blanket. Clive took the other and they walked him sling-fashion to the plane. "Watch the tube," Billy warned. They laid Burt on his back across one seat and returned for Olmeyer. When both victims were aboard, Billy wheeled toward Clive and said, "Bring me all the gasoline and fuel additive we've got."

"Billy," pleaded Clive. "This is insane."

Billy knew he was right, that his chances were paltry at best. *But the odds were long when I first left the reservation. I may have made a mess of it then, but I've come full circle. This time it's not about me. I can handle that.*

Ignoring his professor's protests, Billy climbed into the left pilot's seat. He turned on the fuel pump and threw the master switch, then primed the engine by pumping the choke three times. Without engaging the magneto, he cranked the engine repeatedly to move oil into the frozen motor. He set the fuel mixture to rich and fired the machine again. It sputtered to life, belching flumes of white exhaust that enveloped the plane before dissolving into the winter haze. He wiped the frost from the gauges and watched as they danced to life, all except one—the fuel gauge, which barely moved above the red warning line.

The sound of the propeller was deafening. It jolted both injured men to consciousness. Burt began clawing at the tube in his throat. Olmeyer tried to raise his head. Billy reached back awkwardly in an attempt to quiet them.

Clive stood outside, peering through the cockpit window. He saw Billy make a whirling motion with his finger and responded by pushing the plane around, so it headed west down the temporary runway into the teeth of the gale. With flaps down in take-off position, Billy gunned the motor, whipping up a white tempest that rocked Clive onto his heels. Then, just as suddenly, he throttled back. The professor caught a glimpse of Billy in the pilot's seat with one hand on the yoke and the other battling Burt Cole who was pulling at his arm, his eyes wide with panic. The scene repeated several times as Billy struggled to calm first one injured man, then the other.

After the third sequence, Clive turned his back on the plane, looked up into the swirl of storm clouds and bellowed, "Goddamnit. GODDAMNIT!" He took a roundhouse swipe with his boot across the frozen turf like a field goal kicker, then ran to the cockpit window and banged his fist on the frosted glass.

Billy swiveled angrily and pushed open the vent. "What now?" he screamed above the din of the engine.

"Open up!"

"What?"

"You heard me!"

Billy paused for a second, considering what was at stake. Frustration and anger melted into concern for the safety of his old friend. He threw open the opposite door and Clive jumped into the copilot seat.

"I guess I've got to do everything myself," he snarled, brushing snow from his beard.

Billy studied him with the hint of a smile, then shook his head. "You don't have to do this. I can handle it."

"Like hell you can. You just burned half our gas going nowhere." He pulled his phone and snapped a picture of the fuel gauge. "Might as well document this boondoggle," he muttered. "It might be the last chance." He turned backward on his knees over the seat and took Burt Cole by the hands. When he didn't hear the throttle open, he looked back with a frown.

"Thanks," said Billy.

"Quit screwing around and launch this egg timer!"

Billy's eyes cut to the instrument panel. He pulled the choke and gunned the engine. The plane began to inch forward through the drifts. He knew the regulation take-off distance was five hundred feet, and the maximum payload six hundred fifty pounds. The makeshift runway was close to that distance, but snow packed, and the combined weight of the four men was half again the limit. He pulled a seatbelt around Clive and tightened his own before easing the throttle lever to full forward. *Thank God we're into the wind. We need the lift.*

The plane picked up speed, bouncing over moguls as it catapulted toward a stand of pines at the end of the clearing. Billy watched the speedometer vacillate between fifty and fifty-five. "Not enough," he growled, through gritted teeth, gripping the yoke tighter. "Come on. Come on!"

Clive spun to face the windshield. The motor screamed. Clouds of ice crystals pelted the glass like buckshot, blurring the onrushing forest. The professor glanced at his student, then reached over and gripped the Indian's right bicep. "Pull her up, Billy!"

Billy's heart raced, and his breath caught as he pulled hard against the yoke. The nose lifted and the grinding sound of tires against frozen turf faded. He aimed the aircraft just above the tree line. When it hesitated, threatening to stall, he inched forward on the controls for an instant, to gain speed. Suddenly, they were in the trees. Icicles exploded off pine branches, clattering against the fuselage. The landing gear fought to cut a swath through the foliage, finally emerging on the far side of the grove with chards of bark embedded in the treads.

Turbulence buffeted the plane like a ping-pong ball. Lightning crackled. As the plane fought for altitude, Billy reached under his seat and brought up a worn notebook containing control tower radio beacon frequencies. His finger went down the list. He turned the transponder to the setting for San Antonio International Airport.

"San Antonio, this is Piper Cherokee NB29! Come in, San Antonio!"

The radio burst to life. "*This is San Antonio International. Come in, November Bravo Two Niner.*"

"We are at five five hundred, heading east out of Big Bend, carrying two critically burned passengers. Extremely low on fuel."

"*Destination?*"

"The closest runway to a burn unit."

"*Understood. That would be Brooke Army Medical, San Antonio. But all airports in the area are predicted to ice over. Snowstorm's on your heels.*"

"We've got virtually no fuel and two passengers who'll be lucky to live another few hours. We'll have to try to make it to your field."

"*Are you instrument rated?*"

"Negative."

"*Unless you can get ahead of the blizzard, suggest you land or turn south out of the storm's path.*"

"Look, you're the closest destination with a burn unit. We're coming in. I'll do the best I can."

"*Roger that. We have you on radar. On your present course, you will penetrate airspace for Lackland and Randolph Air Bases unless you climb to one eight thousand and maintain until approach.*"

"We don't have the fuel to do that and our passengers would freeze to death. Can't you alert them we're friendly?"

A bolt of lightning flashed, followed by a crash of thunder. The plane shuddered and dropped, throwing the passengers against the roof.

The radio began to buzz loudly. "*Say again, November Bravo. We're losing your signal.*"

"Can you tell them we're coming?"

"*Come in, November Bravo.*"

The control tower transmission blinked to static.

"Lightning," said Billy.

"Let's try this," said Clive, waving his cell phone. "It might work."

"Call Maria," Billy said over his shoulder.

"What's the number?"

"It's in my phone, which is dead."

"Brilliant."

"Hey, didn't she call you a few weeks back looking for me?"

Clive scrolled through his phone. "Bingo." He hit the call-back button. A faint and disoriented voice answered. "Hello?"

"Damn! It worked. Maria, it's Clive Larson."

"Clive? Sorry. How are you?"

"No damn good." He quickly told her about the explosion at the Trans-National site and the two burn victims.

"My God," she breathed. "Where are you?"

"Uh, six thousand feet now, seventy miles east of the reservation in Billy's plane, heading to the burn hospital in San Antonio. Trying to out-run the blizzard."

"You're flying?" she gasped. "In that weather?"

Clive was about to answer when Burt Cole bolted to consciousness and grabbed for the tube in his throat. The professor dropped the phone and reached back to hold him.

"Hang on, partner. You need that to breathe."

When he retrieved the phone, Maria was calling out, "Clive, Clive!"

"Sorry. One of our passengers pushed the call button."

"What?"

"Never mind. The plane was the only chance for Billy's dad and Olmeyer."

"Did you say, Billy's dad?" she exclaimed. "Burt Cole? I don't un-derstand. How is that possible?"

Clint told her about the surprise revelation by Burt Cole in the snowstorm.

"And Olmeyer . . . You took Olmeyer?" she exclaimed.

"Billy wouldn't have it any other way. We need your help. We're low on fuel. Had to trust the fuel additive to stretch the couple of gallons we had. Call San Antonio International and tell them we're still headed their way. We lost radio contact with them."

"Will do," she replied, recovering quickly, adrenaline flowing.

The line went dead.

Fifteen hundred miles to the northwest, two F-15 Eagles scrambled out of Portland International Airport and flew at supersonic speed south toward Lackland Airforce Base. Each bore a tail emblem—Western Air Defense Sector.

46

IT WAS NOW EIGHT A.M. IN SAN ANTONIO and the snowstorm was threatening. A gusty wind howled as dark clouds billowed in the west. Sand trucks were out covering overpasses, schools were closed, and utility trucks were on standby. Maria's first call was to the hospital. They agreed to send an ambulance to the airport as fast as possible.

Next, she rang the control tower and confirmed for them the plight of Piper Cherokee NB29.

"We contacted the Western Air Defense Sector to advise them of the situation," the dispatcher reported. "But without radio contact," he continued, "they'll scramble the fighters."

Oh, great, she thought.

Her attempt to reach Clive's phone failed. Her final call was to the news director at the local PBS television station.

"Jesus," he said. "Sounds like a suicide mission. Have they got a chance?"

"Sure. If they don't get caught by the blizzard, run out of gas, or get shot down."

"We'll send a camera crew in case they get through," he responded in a matter-of-fact tone.

"Where are you?"

"At the hotel," she answered. "I'm close to the airport, but they're sanding the roads. It's a mess."

"We need a phone interview in five, Maria."

"Naked?"

"Your call."

She quickly dressed and threw her laptop and a hotel blanket into her backpack. The door to her first-floor room slammed as she ran down the hall, wagging the backpack behind her while squirming into a fleece-lined coat. In the lobby, the automatic entrance swished open, unleashing a cold blast. On the far side of the parking lot, her car swayed in the wind.

"Open, damn it," she swore, stabbing the remote as she rushed toward the vehicle. When the lock finally clicked, she pulled open the door and slid in. The engine cranked and strained to produce streams of lukewarm air from heater vents.

Her cell went off. She hit the answer button. Her hands trembled.

"Are you there?" she heard the director shout.

"Yes," she replied, her voice quivering.

"Okay. We go live in ten seconds. Ready?"

Before she could respond, he counted her onto the air. "Five, four, three, two, one."

"This is Maria Cloud with a David and Goliath story for the ages." She gave a summary of the Rio Hot Springs mineral dispute, the plan to frack bomb the Indian facility, and the Trans-National explosion.

"So now a washed-up Chinati quarterback, a science teacher, and two men burned within an inch of their lives are somewhere up there, trying to find their way home. The only thing keeping them airborne is a miracle fuel additive and a prayer. Stay with PBS for continuing coverage. This is Maria Cloud, back to you."

"That was great," gushed the director. "Could you post an update on your blog before you head out?"

"I've got to get to the airport!" she snapped. "These people are friends of mine."

"Hold it together, kid," the director said. "This is a big story. The network wants to run a live report from you at the airport. A national feed."

"Okay, okay," she said, fighting for composure. She flipped open her computer and wrote three quick paragraphs on her blog about the morning's events, then dodged falling tree limbs to reach the street. The air had turned frigid.

Her car crept toward the airport. Traffic lights bounced overhead. The thought of Billy and Clive racing against the storm brought tears to her eyes.

In Piper Cherokee NB29, now above the storm clouds, the fuel gauge was off-limits. *Looking at it might cause a drop*, Billy told himself. *The reservation is an hour and forty-five minutes behind us. At this speed we should, by dead reckoning, be twenty miles or so from SAT. We could pull this off. No, no . . . don't jinx it.*

At first it sounded like a train approaching from behind. Then, on his left, an F-15 Eagle jet with a thunderbolt on its tail burst through the haze below and pulled alongside. "We've got company," Billy said.

"I heard," said Clive, who was force-feeding water to Buck Olmeyer from a plastic bottle.

Billy tuned the radio to 121.5 MHz, the international distress frequency. The speaker crackled like water on hot grease.

"This is November Bravo two niner. Come in, F-15 Eagle," Billy barked.

The jet roared ahead then fell back by turns. Pacing November Bravo was a problem.

"We're too slow," Billy said. "He can't stay airborne at our speed."

On the next pass, the military pilot, who wore a red helmet and aviator glasses, closed the distance between the two craft. When he'd made eye contact, he pointed to his radio headset. Billy acknowledged by responding in kind, then gave a thumbs down. The jet roared ahead, gaining altitude.

A second F-15 took its place on the opposite side. The blue-helmeted pilot peered through the glass at the cargo of November Bravo.

Clive climbed forward into the second pilot's seat and pointed to the two burned men in the passenger compartment. The jet accelerated past the smaller plane, then gave a salute by dipping its wings before descending into the clouds.

"Did they understand?" Clive asked.

"They want us to follow them down," answered Billy. "But we're at least ten miles out of SAT. We need the burn unit."

"Maybe he was just acknowledging our radio problems," suggested Clive.

"Or waiting for orders about what to do with us," said Billy.

Two minutes went by. Clive dug through the storage box beneath his door for pen and paper. He found a black marker and scrawled in block letters on the back of a log book: *Burn victims/No radio/Low Fuel.*

Thirty seconds later, the red helmet reappeared to Clive's right, this time closing to within ten yards. Clive held up the sign. The pilot nodded, saluted, and was gone.

"Guess we're on our own," Billy said softly.

"What else is new?" Clive said.

The parking lot at the airport control tower was deserted, but for a handful of cars scattered near the entrance. *These are the ones who have been here all night*, Maria said to herself. She idled the engine. A call to the dispatcher upstairs brought down a fortyish Hispanic man in a blue woolen sweater. When Maria spotted him, she cut the motor and made her way through a peppery cloud of ice crystals to the entry. With a push of the red security button, he opened the door and greeted her. She hurried in.

"Hell of a storm coming. Worst I've seen in my twenty years in the control tower," he said, extending his hand. "Leon Garcia, assistant air traffic controller."

"Maria Cloud. Thanks for letting me in."

"No problem. You're here about that crazy four-seater up there, right?"

"Yes. I'm a reporter with the Public Broadcasting System." Brushing ice from her hair, she asked, "What's happening?"

"We're tracking them on radar. They're about fifteen miles west of the airport, just ahead of the blizzard. About fifty miles out, they entered restricted airspace around Lackland Airbase. That scrambled two F-15s from Portland to intercept. Got here in twenty minutes going supersonic. We gave them the information you reported to us and they verified. Radio is out. Two burn victims aboard. Not much else they could do."

A black PBS van pulled up with a television broadcasting antenna fastened to the roof. Wilson Johnston, a fat man with a florid face and black horn-rims, leapt out and ran to the tower entrance, his overcoat flapping. Garcia let him in.

"Maria Cloud?" he asked breathlessly.

"Yes," she answered.

"We've got to get you on the air—fast! The network ran your phone report and posted your blog to their national website. The phones went crazy—so many calls it had to shut down for a while. Over ten thousand in twenty minutes!"

Maria closed her eyes and exhaled, more anxious about Garcia's report than the station director's news. "Okay, okay. First I've got to go upstairs and find out what's happening to my friends in that plane."

Johnston hooked her arm as she brushed by. "Look, Maria. This story has exploded. People all over the country are following it. Even the big three commercial networks are running with it. We've got the exclusive and PBS wants to air it now, live! It's the break you've been waiting for!"

She turned away and began to cry, her face buried in her hands. "You don't understand," she wept. "Billy Strikeleather is . . . is a friend." She sobbed silently now, her shoulders rolling.

The two men stood motionless. The director, realizing he'd misunderstood the origin of Maria's passion for the story, put his cell phone away and gave her a moment. When she recovered, she looked up at him.

He waited.

"Thanks . . ." she stammered, forgetting his name.

"Wilson," he said with a smile. "Wilson Johnston."

Maria opened her bag, dabbed at her cheeks with a makeup brush, and reapplied her lipstick. "Okay, Wilson Johnston," she said. "I'm ready."

"Outside?" he asked her with a hopeful tone.

She nodded and headed for the exit. Looking back, she asked the assistant controller, "Will you give us a quick interview?"

Garcia straightened his collar and smiled proudly. "Of course."

Johnston framed a shot with a backdrop of swaying light standards silhouetted against the black cloud bank. The telescoping antenna, buffeted by the wind, fought the efforts of the cameraman to lock into broadcast position. When it finally clicked in, he called out, "Better hurry while we've still got a pole."

Wilson Johnston handed her an earpiece, connecting to the network anchorman.

"Maria, this is Bill Strong at PBS in New York. Great story. I don't want to step on your toes, so I'll just ask you a few preliminaries and let you take it from there. Okay?"

"Fine," Maria said into the mike. She pulled the controller in closer and, in her ear, heard Strong say, "On Maria in five, four, three, two, one." The camera's red light flickered. The operator pointed at the reporter.

The PBS anchor switched into his radio voice— "We have with us now PBS reporter Maria Cloud in San Antonio, Texas, with the latest on the story that has gone viral on the PBS website. A small plane with critically burned passengers is attempting to land just ahead of an arctic storm. What can you tell us, Maria?"

"That's right, Bill. I'm in the shadow of the control tower with Leon Garcia who works there.

"Mr. Garcia. I understand you've been tracking the private plane from West Texas trying to make it to Brooke Army Medical Center. Can you tell us the latest?"

Before he could respond, a ferocious gust of snow and ice pellets blasted the trio like a scattergun. "Whoa!" Garcia bellowed, steadying himself against Maria. "The plane is now about six miles west of here. No radio, and from what we can tell, very little fuel."

"Do you know how much fuel?" she asked.

"We're not sure."

"PBS has learned they had less than two gallons when they took off," Maria said. "However, they have a new fuel additive that could stretch the miles per gallon by tenfold."

"Well," said Garcia, rubbing his forehead, "they've got a big tail-wind. But a hundred and fifty miles to the gallon is off the charts."

"They're still airborne, right?" she asked.

"Yes. As of a few minutes ago we had them on radar. If you're right on the fuel, it's a miracle they've made it this far. Give me a minute—I'll call upstairs for an update."

"Please do." She turned to face the camera. "If you've just tuned in, here is the backstory." She repeated a summary of her earlier report about the Rio Hot Springs minerals. "PBS has also learned that aboard the plane is the CEO of Texas Trans-National Energy, Inc., Buck Olmeyer, apparently one of two victims badly burned in a fracking accident this morning. The pilot is Billy Strikeleather, ex-NFL quarterback and a member of the Chinati Indian tribe." Her voice began to quaver.

Garcia walked back into the shot and she thrust the mike under his chin. "I'm told by the tower they have the plane—NB29—on radar about eight miles due west, still at around ten thousand feet—that's above the storm. They appear to be looking for a hole in the clouds. Unless Mr. Strikeleather is an experienced pilot with an instrument rating—"

"Explain please," Maria interrupted.

"Trained to land by instruments alone," he continued. "This could be a disaster in the making. Once you drop down into those clouds, and without a radio, you could become disoriented. There would simply be no point of reference to guide you in."

In the distance, the sounds of sirens wafted across the field. Two ambulances and a fire truck swung into the parking lot, red lights flashing. At the same time, from out of the tower elevator, a stocky man emerged wearing a toboggan over his gray hair and a leather jacket marked 'Security.' He bounded across the sidewalk and into the lead pumper as it roared off toward the runways.

Maria kept the interview going. "Can you tell us what's happening now?" she screamed over the sirens.

Garcia shouted back, "That was Ed York, head of airport security. They've activated emergency landing procedures."

More sirens interrupted him from a hanger across the field.

"Tankers to foam the runway," Garcia said. "They're expecting a dead-stick landing, which usually means tire blowouts and fire."

Johnston pulled his pointer finger across his throat.

"Maria Cloud, reporting from the tarmac at San Antonio International Airport. Back to you, Bill."

"Thank you, Maria," said Strong, on the air from New York. "Stay with the story."

"We'll be right back to you."

When the camera light went black, Johnston turned toward his reporter and her subject. "Great stuff!"

At ten thousand feet, it was clear and sunny. A stiff tailwind catapulted the Piper Cherokee along. There was no hint of the whiteout below. For a second, Billy lapsed into mock confidence, the kind he felt from a belt of whisky.

There was a time, he thought, fingering the feather on his necklace, *when I didn't need good luck charms. I made my own luck. And I didn't need booze to solve problems. Freedom from doubt was a given. I was bigger, faster, and stronger than opponents. I was a winner. Then one day, I can't remember when, my confidence turned to arrogance. Like a disease you catch that doesn't present till it's too late. You spend a lifetime trying to recover, but the mistakes are always with you. Thinking about them only brings back the pain. If only I could have made it right. Now, there's no time, unless . . . No, don't kid yourself. Just do your best. They'll remember you tried.*

In the passenger compartment, Clive was worried about Burt Cole. The low humidity at this altitude was drying out his windpipe. His breath through the homemade tracheotomy tube was labored. He needed hydration to survive.

"Billy, we're losing your dad," he said. "He's burning up inside. I'm going to have to pull the tube and try to get some water in him."

"Do your best," Billy said. "We're close to San Antonio. I just can't tell how close from this altitude. We're going to have to start our descent."

Clive gently pulled the plastic tube and examined Burt's throat. For the moment it remained open. He drizzled some water from the plastic bottle past the charred remains of Burt's lips. The victim gagged and clutched at his throat.

"Try to swallow. You need the water."

From the corner of his eye, Clive caught sight of something trailing beneath the left wing of the plane. He looked again and saw nothing. *Maybe a tree branch from take-off*, he thought. *There it is again.*

"I'll be damned," he said.

"What?" Billy asked.

"Look out to your left."

A rust-colored bird with a four-foot wing span, a fan of red tail feathers, and a bright yellow beak glided in the slipstream of the plane.

"It's a red-tailed hawk," Billy responded in amazement. "Only females get that big. She probably got caught in a thermal updraft when the storm cleared the mountains. What the hell is she still doing here?"

"What do you think, Junior Birdman? Just like us. Trying to find a hole in these clouds," said Clive.

The engine coughed, then caught again. Billy pumped the choke furiously. The hawk eased ahead of the plane, alternating between flapping and gliding. Now she dipped slightly, heading toward the cloud bank below. Billy turned back and locked eyes with Clive. "Are you thinking what I am?" he said.

Clive nodded. "If she's found a crease, we need to follow. She can be our eyes."

"Auto pilot says we should be within five miles of SAT," Billy said. "They can see us on radar, but without a radio, can't guide us in."

"Well, if she can find a way down, and we can keep up with her, we might make it down through the blizzard," Clive responded.

The engine sputtered again. Billy rocked the wings to milk every drop of fuel from the tanks, then nosed into the cloud bank behind the hawk.

At the airport, security vehicles of every type began closing on the main east-west runway fronting the tower. Foam trucks coated the landing strip, and red pumpers with yellow trim squatted along the service road next to the tarmac.

The PBS van had followed close behind the emergency vehicles onto the gate area. York jumped from the lead fire truck and was trying to block traffic at the entry to the runway. Maria leapt from the van and ran up to him, waving her microphone for an interview. While she prepped him for his television debut, Wilson Johnston attached the cameraman's cord to the antenna—now fully extended.

"Okay, Maria," he shouted over the howling wind. "On you in thirty seconds."

She reached up and brushed back her hair. When she lowered her glove, it was speckled with snowflakes. Looking at the sky, she cocked her head and said to York loudly, "Well, the blizzard—it's here. Where's the plane?"

"That's what *they* want to know," York bellowed, nodding to his left toward a line of cars miles long creeping off the freeway service road into the parking lot. With headlights piercing the blowing snow, they looked like a ghostly centipede inching ever closer to the terminal. Some were out of their cars. "They heard your broadcasts."

York looked past her right shoulder and pointed. She turned. Riding the west wind was a red speck bouncing just below the clouds. The sporadic hacking of a dry engine grew louder as it approached. "My God," she said. "It's them. I've got to get closer. You see, Billy Strikeleather is . . . is . . ."

"I know. I heard," York said. "Go on. But remember, it wasn't me that let you through."

Maria ran for the van as it began pulling forward toward the runway. The line of cars followed, leaving York alone by the road, mesmerized by the drama unfolding above.

Inside the van, Wilson Johnston thrust a pair of headphones into her hands. She put them on.

"Maria!" she heard Bill Strong scream. "What's happening? We need video, now!"

The van stopped just short of the landing strip. Johnston and the cameraman clambered out and the camera rolled.

Suddenly the coughing engine stopped. The plane glided over the crowd as silent as a ghost. She could see Billy grappling with the steering yoke and Clive turned backward, holding their passengers.

"Now, Maria, now!" screamed Johnston, pointing at her wildly.

"This . . . this is Maria Cloud," she stammered, "at San Antonio International Airport."

The sound of metal rasping against concrete ripped through the crowd, drowning out the reporter. Maria spun around and watched in horror as the plane, pummeled by the wind, careened diagonally across the tarmac. Both tires blew, and the cabin pitched forward, driving the propeller blades into the ground. They sheared off like machete knives, crashing through the cockpit with an explosion of shattering glass. The momentum flipped the plane forward onto its back where it skidded tail first through the safety foam another fifty yards into a drainage ditch. Black smoke poured from the wreckage and blew back across the throng of onlookers.

"Okay!" yelled Johnston. "Keep it going. Back live in five, four—"

Before he could count farther, Maria threw down her headset and sprinted toward the crash site. Emergency vehicles struggled to cross the infield grass between runways. She was the first one to arrive. Clive had freed himself from his seat and dropped to the inverted ceiling of the plane. The burn victims, still wrapped in blankets, were suspended in midair by their seatbelts. Billy hung motionless from his harness, his neck slashed open.

Maria clawed at the cabin door, but it was wedged shut. Clive crawled over to Billy and struggled to unfasten his seat belt. Pulled by gravity, blood now flowed freely from Billy's wounds. He was bleeding to death.

At that moment, Maria was brushed aside by two firefighters who wrenched the door free and cut Billy down with metal shears. They laid him in the frozen grass and applied a compression bandage to his wound.

"Hold this," they shouted to Maria over the howling wind, placing her hand on the cloth, then went back for Buck and Colt.

Maria held him in her arms and repeated his name. "Billy . . . Billy!" There was no response. Clive knelt next to her. A minute passed. Paramedics arrived and applied maximum pressure to the bandage, stemming the blood flow.

Maria heard a familiar call. On the top branch of an oak tree near the runway's end, the red-tailed hawk that had led them home stood guard.

Billy squeezed her hand. He opened his eyes and smiled. She bent down and whispered in his ear. "Welcome home, Billy. Welcome home."

ACKNOWLEDGMENTS

I AM MOST GRATEFUL to Thomas Taschinger, editorial page editor of the Beaumont (Texas) Enterprise, for taking a chance on a fledgling columnist like me; Rusty Graham, my dear friend and former editor with the Examiner Newspaper Group (Houston) for running my columns and for buying my coffee on Friday mornings; and Angela Wilson, community news editor of *The Galveston Daily News* for helping me reach a new group of readers along the Texas Gulf Coast. Through them I honed my craft as a writer.

Ally (Peltier) Machate and her cat suffered through my early efforts to move to a longer literary form, then dragged me across the finish line with the aid of her editors at The Writer's Ally, Lauren Moore and Harrison Demchick.

My publisher, Storehouse Media Group, including Sherrie Clark and Emily Hitchcock, provided invaluable help with all the details of getting the book to market.

Others to whom I owe a debt of gratitude are Patricia Curtis, who has been faithfully at my side from the beginning and convinced me that my manuscript might actually have some merit; Michael Griffin, who refused to accept my excuses for not finishing the book; Greg Smith, who educated me on the strategic air command; my high school English teacher, the late Mattie Bell, who is no doubt rolling in her grave; and last but not least, my band of loyal readers who for years have been overly generous with their praise for my little columns.

To all the above, thank you. I hope this book will in some small measure validate your faith in me.

Malcolm Gibson

ABOUT THE AUTHOR

Photo by Kim Christensen

MALCOLM GIBSON is a Texas attorney and journalist who grew up working as a roustabout in southern oil fields. He spent his legal career representing oil producers, land owners, real estate promoters, and the banks that back them in the high-stakes world of international hydrocarbons. He knows the territory. First place winner of the 2018 National Society of Newspaper Columnists writing contest, his writing style hits quick and hard–just like Big Oil.